DEFENDERS OF TIME
GOING BACK

John

Enjoy
the Sequel,
Kidnappers from the
future will be out
Oct 8, 2021

DEFENDERS OF TIME

GOING BACK

GENE P. ABEL

Indigo River Publishing

3 West Garden Street, Ste. 718

Pensacola, FL 32502

www.indigoriverpublishing.com

First edition, 2020

Printed in the United States of America

Going Back | Gene P. Abel, author

ISBN 978-1-950906-74-1 (paperback) | 978-1-950906-75-8 (ebook)

LCCN 2020938444

Edited by Earl Tillinghast

Cover design by Robin Vuchnich

Interior design by Nikkita Kent

Special discounts are available on quantity purchases by corporations, associations, and others. For details, contact the publisher at the address above.

Orders by US trade bookstores and wholesalers: Please contact the publisher at the address above.

With Indigo River Publishing, you can always expect great books,
strong voices, and meaningful messages.
Most importantly, you'll always find . . . words worth reading.

My sincere thanks to my beautiful wife, Susan Anne, her sister, Cindy Akin, and my friend Al Rittenhouse for their help and encouragement to write this book.

1

SYMPOSIUM

At the International Symposium on Time Travel, Professor Gregson's little talk, and the peace of the room, were abruptly interrupted when the central double doors at the back burst open, accompanied by a man in a military uniform, his manner as abrupt as his entry. He was flanked by a pair of soldiers bearing sidearms, while a flow of local security mixed with police and military soldiers hurried across the hall behind them. If his entry failed to get everyone's attention, what he called out in his commanding voice would not.

"This entire place is hereby under lockdown, by order of the secretary general." He marched down the central aisle as if he owned it. Wide-eyed audience members shuffled around or stood on tiptoe to see who was creating the stir. Behind the podium, Professor Gregson was also shocked at the intrusion.

"Now see here," the professor objected. "You cannot barge in here and take control of our conference! We have all the proper paperwork and clearances with the various agencies and—"

"None of which matters anymore," the military man stated flatly.

The men flowing in behind him spread across the room, taking positions at any possible exit and dark corner, searching behind curtains and folded room dividers, as well as among those seated, and receiving a flood of annoyed remarks in the process. The man in the center of it ignored the professor's protests and hopped up onto the stage, while two more men from each wing of the stage rushed up to surround him, pulling Professor Gregson away from the podium as their commander now took the microphone.

"I am Colonel Matheson, and this entire conference is hereby under military command."

"This is outrageous," the professor began. "You have no reason to—"

"When a murder has been committed, I have *all* the reason!"

* * *

"Time travel is a thing of the past."

The man with the trim white beard at the podium delivering this statement got a few scattered chuckles from among those in the crowded assembly hall, along with one or two eye rolls. He waited a couple of seconds before replying with a smile, "I see that joke is starting to get a little bit old . . . Well, I guess it's about time."

The speaker got fewer chuckles this time and took an even shorter pause. "Okay, enough with the bad jokes. Welcome to the International Symposium on Time Travel, a platform whereby we can exchange current theories and technological developments in the science of time travel. I am Professor Gregson, the symposium host and head speaker, and my job is to keep things flowing while making sure none of you violate whatever your nation's secrecy act happens to be."

A few more chuckles came in response this time, the mood of the assembly settling down to something a bit more comfortable. The speaker noted this change before continuing. "Now, seeing as how this is our first little get-together, before I leave you in the hands of our other speakers, I thought a quick recap was in order."

He shuffled his notes, bringing one pair of the small index cards he held in his hands to the forefront, cleared his throat once, and began. "As you all no doubt know, temporal waves were discovered in a lab in

San Jose. The scientists there were actually looking for gravity waves, and for a while that's what they thought they had. But time and space are interlinked, and once the source kept tracing back to a location here on Earth—well, they arrived at the obvious conclusion that they were looking at a TW. Since then, government labs around the world have been hard at work developing new and better ways of detecting and using these temporal waves.

"The lab discovered that because of the way time and space are so interwoven, the origin of these TWs could be traced back not only to a given period in time but to a physical location as well. The precision of such measurements has been getting better over the years, but of course there is a limit to the resolution dictated by the uncertainty principle; one cannot know with absolute precision both the exact time and place at the same time."

Several in the audience nodded; others looked bored. This part was already quite well known to everyone attending. Professor Gregson shuffled the next index card to the top of his small stack and resumed.

"Such waves carry with them invaluable information about the past, allowing someone with the proper technology to use them as a window into the past and to see for ourselves the flow of history as it *actually* occurred. That is the impetus that drives us all in our research and the reason why we are here today to exchange information. We have many hurdles to overcome yet, and also many dangers to be aware of; but I'll get to those in a minute."

Somewhere in the back of the hall he could see a man in a white suit approaching another white-suited security guard who stood his position by a set of closed double doors. The one guard spoke in furtive whispers to get the other's attention. The professor, though, paid the side conversation little heed and continued with his narration.

"Normally such waves are smooth, acting as carrier waves for the information they allow us access to. But with the genie of time travel set loose, we have to now consider other possibilities as well, and so it has been theorized when the smooth flow of these TWs may be disrupted. In essence, time-space is like an ocean, smooth and calm. But what if some agency from outside its own time were to go back in time and create some change in history? That disruption would cause a ripple in the smooth flow of the temporal waves, manifesting as what we would call a temporal disruption wave, or TDW. The cause of such a TDW would, naturally, be a temporal disruption event, or TDE. Such a TDW would be like a sudden surge on our smooth ocean, with the bigger the change in history resulting in larger-amplitude TDWs. These changes would then ripple forward through time until any changes they carry have caught up with our present. After that, the possible results are all quite debatable. Would we even remember the former past? Or, as some would argue, do cause and effect have to be preserved over the four-dimensional realm, meaning that at least a few people somewhere would have to remember *both* versions of history? And what about the possible paradoxes that might result; how do we resolve those?"

He let these statements linger for a moment, watching the quiet discussions build through his audience before grinning. "Of course, such TDWs have not yet been detected, and some would argue that, by their very nature, since we have yet to detect one, we never will." He heard a few chuckles in response, to which he gave a nod and continued.

At the back of the room, a third security guard had briefly joined the other two before all three hurried out the back door.

"To continue with more current events in our field, efforts have been focused the past decade on using these TWs as a window through which to see our past without running the risk of physically traveling back—at least not yet. It is fairly common knowledge among our rarefied group that three main teams are working on developing equipment to actually travel back in time: the Americans, the Germans, and the Japanese. But don't worry, no one's actually turned their machine on and used it yet; we're all too afraid of what could happen if one of us accidentally killed our own grandfather."

After the smattering of uncomfortable laughter had quieted, the professor continued, "That brings us to the current state of time travel itself. All three teams are rumored to be working on their own variation of the same technology, but as some of you already know, it does not look like your classic science-fiction approach, where you simply walk into a machine and come out the other end in a different time. In fact, if space-time is like that calm ocean, then time traveling is like a bottle afloat on that ocean, and the message inside that bottle is the time traveler. Because, you see, we do not send a traveler back per se, but rather the traveler's *information*."

He shuffled to the next index card while his audience absorbed the explanation. Some knew of this already, but others were hearing this for the first time. After all, the purpose of this conference was to get everyone up to speed on current developments.

"Traveling through time involves the creation and use of an Einstein-Rosen bridge through space-time. Many of us would know that by its more common name: a wormhole. For bulk matter to go straight through a wormhole, however, could be quite hazardous, at least with our current understanding. But that does not mean we cannot make an appearance back in the past. Dr. Hamilton will be going over this in more detail in his lecture at two, but in essence, we send our *information* back through time. Trying to send matter back through a wormhole still poses almost as much risk as diving into a black hole, but data is another story. The data in this case would be of the traveler plus everything on him: clothes, equipment, and whatnot. Our traveler would manifest, in essence, as a ghost. He would still be connected back to the present through the wormhole by a sort of energy umbilical, and through this umbilical his ghostly form would be given solid mass."

A quiet sea of voices rose as people discussed among themselves the possibilities this raised and all that it implied. Not all of the voices, however, were discussing the subject at hand. A small huddle of security personnel had gathered at the rear of the room, intent on their own conversation spoken in hushed whispers.

"The original body of our traveler would remain here in the present, sealed away in a pod, but his information would be sent back through the wormhole, *as well as* his consciousness. One mind, two bodies, as it were, one of them an avatar in the past. Then to get back, you either turn off the energy stream or kill your avatar—and *hope* that doesn't kill your consciousness along with it. Those would be some of the problems still yet to be solved, but Dr. Sam Weiss of the American team will be going over that in a lot more detail in his lecture later on."

At the far end of the chamber, a couple of the security men appeared to be quietly securing the doors, while others in blue uniforms crept in for a quick discussion with them.

"Also on the schedule will be a talk by Dr. Graystein, an American doing excellent work on fine-tuning the resolution of tracing temporal waves; he says within a year or two it may be possible to narrow our resolution down to within half a day and a couple of miles. Then this evening, British Professor Miles will be discussing his work in using TWs to create a temporal map that would allow one to see the regular flow of history. By examining the amplitudes and phases of time waves, we would be able to see if someone tries to change history. Then of course there's Dr. Hamilton, as I've mentioned, and a guest from the Japanese team, who will—"

* * *

"I am Colonel Matheson, and this entire conference is hereby under military command."

"This is outrageous," the professor began. "You have no reason to—"

"When a murder has been committed, I have *all* the reason!"

Colonel Matheson's statement immediately got the attention it was designed to, as all in the room now fell into stunned silence.

"*Two* murders, in fact," the colonel continued. "Dr. Graystein and Professor Miles have both been found dead in their rooms, each one killed by a knife wound to the back. Now, if you'll all just cooperate, I'm sure we can have you on your way before the weekend is up."

Professor Gregson was not the only one left in open-mouthed shock.

2

PROJECT ENLIGHTENMENT

Monday in the vast emptiness of New Mexico is particularly empty where the Chihuahuan Desert crosses into Texas. Nothing would catch a passerby's attention save for a small cluster of dusty buildings surrounded by wire fencing and aged trespassing signs.

Of course, appearances are often deceiving, and in this case very much so. For the cluster of buildings was the entry into the world of wonder that lay below, where scientific and military facilities spread through the cavernous lairs of one of the most highly secured facilities America had to offer. This setting was the hidden home of, among other things, Project Enlightenment, the code name for the American effort in time travel.

Lt. General Karlson was in his late fifties with a touch of gray in his hair. His military bearing left no doubt he was in command of this operation. When he walked into the command room with a nod to the one standing guard by the security door, the room was a small hive of activity, though most of the talk centered on the murders at the symposium.

The perimeter of the roughly circular chamber was lined with technicians and scientists at their stations, examining readouts from their monitors, entering new data, and performing various functions while discussing the news with each other. To the far left of where the general entered, the main display took up most of the wall; it looked like a very large monitor screen, but everyone knew it was a bit more. Currently it displayed glowing lines overlaying a map of the world.

To the right of the general was his current destination: a short flight of metal stairs up to a balcony running the length of the wall opposite the large screen, where two more technicians sat before another smaller bank of controls at an open alcove that stretched out from the center. Front and center was the general's chair. He walked up the steps to take his place, a couple of soldiers a step behind him, while keeping an ear open for the conversations circulating in the room.

"Killers got away clean, and they examined everyone at that conference," one man said.

"Just a bunch of eggheads," a second man responded. "Who'd want to kill either one of them?"

"Isn't it obvious? Graystein was working on bettering our resolution, and Miles was midway through that temporal map of his. Someone's laying the way for some time travel without getting caught."

"That's pure paranoia."

"In the kind of research *we're* in? We should have expected this to happen at some point."

"The data they brought with them was gone, and their laptops were missing," a third man remarked. "I'd say that spells motive enough right there."

The general let the cross chatter waft around the room as he examined his surroundings. Research scientists were hard at work taking readings and analyzing the various TWs as they came in, trying hard to keep their focus on their jobs and not let news of the murders distract them overly much. The task was a difficult one, though; many there had known Dr. Graystein personally.

"General Karlson, sir."

He had barely sat down in his chair when the technician at the station behind and to his left called to him. He swiveled his chair around, and the technician sitting before one circle of monitors continued. "Security in and about the chamber has been tightened per your orders. We have also increased the alert status for all TW monitoring."

"And the board?" General Karlson turned back around for a glance at the large screen as the technician gave reply.

"The board is clean, sir. Not a single blip in the way of—"

"Then what," General Karlson said, his eyes narrowing as a large glowing red dot appeared, covering a good third of the screen, "is *that*?"

"By all the—"

"We have one," came from the pit of the chamber below as one of the technicians cried out from his station. "An actual TDW!"

"Double-check that," the general ordered. "I've been half expecting something like this ever since those murders. I want amplitudes and a trace immediately."

Suddenly the pit below was a hive of scurrying activity. Equipment was double-checked, readings confirmed, as somewhere else buried in the facility the small mountain of sensor equipment was ramped up to the highest degree of sensitivity that the team could safely manage. Voices called back and forth across the pit as the general sat above it all, awaiting the results.

"Coolant temperature remaining optimal."

"Speeding-sensor drum rotation up twenty percent."

"Data coming in."

One of the men below at his station paused for a moment, the rest of the room falling into an anticipatory hush, as he focused on his own private display before spinning around in his chair to call up to the balcony. "Confirmed, sir. We have an actual TDW. It looks to be a small one, but there's no telling how big it could get in time."

"Resolve time and location as much as you can," the general snapped back. "I want to know when and where that came from as precisely as you can manage."

"Yes, sir!" The technician on the floor spun back to his display, fast at work, while the rest of the room was for a moment stuck in shocked silence at the implications. But only for a moment before General Karlson snapped them out of it.

"I should be hearing people *working*."

The quiet was broken, replaced by a buzz of activity the likes of which this facility had not seen since the detection of the first temporal wave.

"Looks like someone jumped the gun and turned their machine on," the general muttered to himself. "But who? The Germans have that neo-Nazi movement building that may have a few over there wanting to 'fix' the Second World War so the Germans come out on top. But the Japanese have that Shinto thing going that might also have them wanting to recover their honor from the same time period. Hmm . . ."

He thought for a moment more and swiveled in his chair to once more face the technician behind him. "Lieutenant Marx, give me your assessment."

The other man turned in his seat to face the general and give him his full attention.

"The German and Japanese teams: What do we know of their capabilities? Do either one of them have the capability yet to travel back and make changes? Does either team know enough of time travel theory to *risk* such a trip?"

"To be blunt, sir, that's what we would have found out at the symposium," Lieutenant Marx replied. "It was supposed to be an across-the-board exchange of information on current theory and technology."

"Which the murders neatly put an end to," General Karlson mused. "Which makes that the third victim in addition to the two scientists."

He turned back around for a glance at the board. Currently the display was zoomed in on the northeastern part of the country, with various dates shown here and there, ranging from 1850 to 1960. The display was in constant change, the view zooming in a bit more from time to time, dates on either end of the range dropping away as the temporal resolution narrowed. A disturbing possibility was starting to go through his mind when a senior officer to his right rear spoke up.

"General, sir."

"Colonel Matheson," the general acknowledged.

"Even if we locate the place and time," Colonel Matheson continued, "how can we ever track down what was changed? For that matter, how can we know if the changes even happened? We may already be caught up in the result of what someone else did and have no way to tell the difference."

The other man seated in the alcove behind General Karlson replied, the general leaving them to their debate but listening carefully. He always listened to any and all cross chatter that came up from the pit; it was usually quite educational.

"There would be two possibilities, Kurt," Lieutenant Marx stated. "One, if the change is already done, then we're stuck with the results and have no way to tell the difference. Second"—here he turned in his seat to look at the glowing area of red on the board's map as others homed in on the signal—"since we *can* still pick up that TDW, that means the changes to history haven't caught up with us yet and there's still time to go back and undo them."

"Granted," Colonel Matheson admitted. "But that brings up a host of other disturbing problems. I got a kid that just got into Stanford; if we send anyone back, how can we be sure that what they do won't change something so my kid instead misses out on his opportunity? Maybe some changes have *already* been felt and that's why he made it into Stanford."

"Or, on the other hand," Lieutenant Marx countered, "there might be some poor kid somewhere who could end up a lot better off. It works both ways, you know."

Much the same talk was filtering up from the pit below as the map narrowed down to upper New England, the dates ranging now from 1890 to 1945.

"Even if we can get back there in time to stop whoever it is, we might make things worse," someone called across the pit.

"Or maybe someone went back to make things better for all," another countered.

"You're dreaming," said a third. "The only reason why someone would dare something this big is for purely selfish motives."

"Then there's the butterfly effect," Colonel Matheson supplied. "Everything could go absolutely perfect as far as mission parameters go, but some small element of history that no one knew about gets changed. Some kid gets saved from drowning, and that looks good, but what if he would have grown up to become a dictator that makes Hitler look like a nice guy?"

"Or," Lieutenant Marx countered, "time could be a lot more resilient than that. Some things may not be *possible* to change."

"You don't *know* that, and that's the problem!"

The debate grew more heated in pace with the narrowing of the image of the TDW on the board. But General Karlson had been listening to every word, carefully weighing what was said against his single overriding consideration. "Enough," he said, standing up abruptly.

All there knew that attitude; the general had made a decision, and now nothing on this planet would change his mind. The room fell once again into silence. A couple of the scientists continued to work on pinning down the TDW, while all other eyes focused on General Karlson.

"There's only one question that counts in my view. What is the goal of that time traveler? What do they want, and how does it affect the security of this great nation? And if they did it once, what's to prevent them from doing it again and again, continuing to wreak untold damage in our present time, and this country specifically? Can anyone answer me that?"

None could. Meanwhile the view on the board continued to narrow. It now displayed lower-state New York with a date range of 1905 to 1925.

"The possibility now stands," General Karlson continued, "that one of the other teams out there may know something more about traveling through and manipulating time than we do. *That* is the only issue worth considering at this point. All else is peripheral."

He turned to face Colonel Matheson on his right, snapping out an order. "For the last couple of years we've had a hot team on twenty-four hours' notice for just such an occurrence as this. Notify the team that they have their notice and are to assemble immediately."

"Yes, General," Colonel Matheson replied.

General Karlson faced back to those in the chamber before him, his words precisely clear as well as the historic consequences they implied.

"Get that wormhole revved up. The mission is a go."

3

BRIEFING

B y Tuesday morning the team was assembled, all six of them seated at the front of the small conference room, waiting for their briefing. They were dressed in whatever clothes they had been wearing or could grab when the MPs had come for them, and were already generally familiar with one another per protocol. Long ago the team had established relationships with each other, as for a mission such as this, there would be no time to get to know one another in the field.

"I seriously never thought we'd *really* be called in for something like this," one man remarked. "To get a chance to see history for myself, to *be* history, is very exciting!"

The man was in his midthirties, an inch below six feet, and in good enough physical shape for an obvious academic, and had short black hair, dark eyes, a slight tan, and what he called his big Jewish nose. The clothes he wore were baggy enough for the many pockets filled with various notes, and in one case a small pocket computer.

The man seated next to him was a little shorter, about the same age, and a bit on the skinny side, and had tousled brown hair down to his ears, and hazel eyes. He looked as though he was in desperate need of a bit more sunlight in his life. "I'll admit to some intellectual curiosity myself, Professor Stein," the second man said.

"Oh please, it's just Ben."

Seated with them were the others: a lean young black woman with short-cropped hair whose gaze constantly assessed any possible threat in her environment and those around her; a man who had "career military" stamped all over him—fortyish, muscular, with crew-cut hair and a no-nonsense demeanor; and a younger man, six foot and all muscle, his uniform neatly pressed.

Finally, a man sat in the third row behind them all, carefully observing the other members of the team as if with a look he could assess their worth. Also in his midthirties, everything about him screamed average save that look in his eyes of careful deduction and a high degree of reasoning. Behind it was a mind that broke everything down into cause and effect, data and deduction.

General Karlson entered the room with an aide by his side. The facing wall had a six-foot monitor built into it. The aide approached it, sticking a small data stick into a slot while the general addressed his team.

The general got straight to the point. "We've just gotten word that both the German and Japanese teams are either assembling their own teams or have already done so. At the least they have both picked up the same TDW we did; at worst, one of them is the *cause* of that TDW. The goals of those teams are unknown but assumed to be nationalistic in nature."

The screen behind him now lit up, displaying a schematic map of New York with various lines of data streaming by beneath it.

"Analysis of the TDW indicates that while it appears small in amplitude, it could still build like a tidal wave by the time it catches up to our present. Your mission is to make sure that tidal wave never happens. Now, as you can see by the display behind me, we've traced it to New York City around the year 1919."

"No closer?" Professor Stein interjected. "That's a pretty big city, even back at the turn of the last century. Close to six million people, as I recall."

"We're lucky we got it down *that* far," the general stated. "We believe that this time and place is a temporal hinge point, which Dr. Weiss here can briefly explain."

All heads turned to the one seated beside Professor Stein, who cleared his throat and proceeded to explain.

"A temporal hinge point is when a lot of key events are happening that will ripple around the globe and on through history. Picture it as something like a lit match—by itself nothing of any real consequence, but if said match happens to be lying within an inch of several loose trails of gunpowder and some highly unstable explosives, the result of lighting that match could be catastrophic. Or like a game of pool: a simple shot of the Q-ball into a cluster of other balls could scatter them all over the place. A temporal hinge point is like that: make a change at such a point and there's no telling how many different cause-and-effect ripples it will send through history.

"We've been mapping a few of them," he continued, "but the problem is that not all such hinge events involve actions known to our history books. Such a hinge point can range anywhere from a day up to a week."

"Then that's how long you people will have," the general stated. "New York City of the year 1919 is one such point, and whoever went back before us has changed that hinge point. Your mission orders are to discover who's gone back to that period, discover whatever it is they changed, and undo or prevent that change from happening, if in the judgment of your team leader such a change is inimical to the better interests of the United States."

"A week," Professor Stein said in a breath. "That's not much time to track through a city of six million."

"It'll have to be," the general stated. "Now I know you are all generally familiar with one another, but just to make things clear, allow me the introductions. Professor Ben Stein here is your historian. Besides being specifically versed in this period of history, his little data computer you see sticking out of his pocket is programmed with everything we know from the year 1850 to 1980."

"Which I would caution," the professor broke in, "is not everything that *has* happened in history. Prohibition was just ratified; President Wilson returns to New York from the Versailles Peace Conference about early July with his League of Nations proposal. There's post-war recovery problems, an influenza outbreak. The Bolshevik Revolution just happened in Russia only a couple of years prior, and that has everyone on the lookout for anarchists leading to the Red Scare, and of course the Fascist movement in Italy. But those are only the major points. We need to be on the lookout for seemingly innocent events."

"Which is why you're on this mission," the general continued. "Sitting next to him we have Dr. Sam Weiss, your physicist specializing in temporal mechanics. He'll be on hand to handle any technical problems."

Dr. Weiss gave a nod, and the general moved on to the lean black lady behind Dr. Weiss.

"Agent Sue Harris, special ops and combat specialist. Her job is to make sure that the rest of you survive long enough to complete your mission. Beside her is Captain Robert Beck."

The fortyish man with the crew cut gave a terse nod.

"He's the military observer to make sure this mission comes off at all costs."

"*All* costs?" Professor Stein asked uncertainly. "What does that mean, exactly?"

"It means that we're expendable." Agent Harris put it matter-of-factly. "But the mission is not."

"Our very history is at stake here, people!" General Karlson snapped. "And to make sure that nothing gets in the way of that mission, we come to Lieutenant David Phelps, combat and infiltration specialist. He's your muscle."

The younger man in uniform beside the captain responded with a slight nod but nothing more. That left the man in the back, in the third row, whom the general now indicated with eye contact.

"Your team leader is Special Agent Lou Hessman. It's his job to play detective and figure out what's going on in 1919 and what caused that

TDW. Professor Stein, you'll be working closely with him to make sure he has everything he needs in the way of known events of that period."

"Of course." Professor Stein nodded.

"He also has his own little pocket computer with dossiers of the possible candidates that may have been chosen from the German and Japanese teams, complete with pictures to identify them when you encounter them. Remember, you have to complete your mission before they complete theirs."

"So, in a city of six million, we have to track down whatever got changed and whoever did it, without even knowing the nature of the event we're trying to track down," Professor Stein summed up. "That's a pretty tall order."

"The resolution of the temporal scanner has been getting better," Dr. Weiss stated, "but it still has its limits. If we'd had Dr. Graystein and his notes, we no doubt could have pinpointed things a lot more precisely. Or even Professor Miles's temporal map."

Special Agent Hessman finally spoke up in his quiet tone. "Murders that I don't doubt were to pave the way for this TDW. General, as Professor Stein has noted, this task could take weeks or months, but I'm guessing we have significantly less time than that."

"And you would be right," General Karlson grimly replied. He indicated Dr. Weiss, who replied with the details.

"Analysis of the TDW leads us to believe that this particular temporal hinge point covers approximately one week local time. If our mission is not accomplished within that time period, then whatever changes that have been created by the other unknown team will most likely be permanent, or at least well beyond our capacity to repair."

"A week," Professor Stein quietly remarked, "to search for a needle in the haystack of New York City."

"You will be dropped off as close to the origin day of the TDW as possible," the general told them. "Now, if there are no other questions, you'll be taken to outfitting and given some period clothing and equipment to wear, as well as some cash from that period to use as needed.

Professor Stein's and Agent Hessman's pocket computers are a couple of the few non-period items that'll be allowed. Am I understood?"

"Perfectly," Captain Beck replied.

"Good. Then this briefing is at an end."

With that, the general turned on his heel and headed for the door. His aide pulled the data stick out of the wall before following along behind him, while the others got to their feet as a soldier came forward to lead them away to be outfitted.

4

THE CHAMBER

Officially the space was known as the temporal projection chamber, unofficially "the Bubble" due to its general shape. The team members walked in dressed in their period clothing and for a moment gawked at what lay before them, while Dr. Weiss beamed with pride at what he'd had a part in creating.

The whole large chamber was circular and stretched a hundred yards from one side to the other. The expected banks of computers, control equipment, and status monitors lay ringed around the outer walls, while on one far wall twenty feet above floor level was a stretch of armored glass behind which was the control booth. The main center of attention, though, was at the middle of the room, comprising a good chunk of its width.

A circle of man-sized pods ringed a raised central platform, the pods lying horizontally and covered with clear lids, currently hinged open. The pods were festooned with control and read-out panels and bathed in a soft inner light. At the back of each pod was an arm-thick braided cable stretching into the air to the apparatus fixed into the ceiling forty feet above. The circular platform on which the pods were arranged was elevated a step above the ground and was currently a hub of activity with a pair of technicians doing their last-minute checks.

The ceiling resembled a large alternator or generator of some sort, with each of the pod cables connecting to its edge at a different point along its circumference. From there a tangle of thick cables wound their way around the hundred-foot circle of tightly wrapped wiring to meet in the center at what looked like a large metal ball, polished to a mirrored sheen. From the back of the ball projected two long metal arms attached end to end behind the ball in a straight line, growing wider toward their ends. The arms stretched along the arc of the curved cable-covered portion of the ceiling before slanting down a couple of feet past that portion of the apparatus, their wider ends bearing a resemblance to propeller blades.

That the twin arms were made to spin, using the ball as their axis, was obvious from their appearance. The inner edges of the arms seemed like they would barely touch the tightly packed mass of cabling above them, lending even more of a resemblance to a generator.

For a moment all the team could do was stare as the double doors hissed closed behind them, marveling at what they were about to climb into.

Agent Sue Harris made the first remark. "Do I *have* to wear these heels? The dress I can understand, but I've managed to stay away from high heels for most of my adult life."

The incongruous remark snapped the men out of their daze and earned a flicker of a grin from Professor Stein before he gave his reply. "Period clothing usually precluded women wearing anything you might term as comfortable. It was all about elegance, at least in the circles we must engage with. You should be more concerned about being a black woman in New York in the year 1919. Not as bad as down in the southern states of the time; more like 'sophisticated discrimination.' Interestingly, when it came to blacks, the women's suffrage movement—"

Agent Hessman cut him off. "Ben, I think we can worry about that later."

"What? Oh, right. Sorry, I can get carried away sometimes. In fact, there was this one party when I—"

"Ben?"

To Agent Hessman's more focused glare, Professor Stein dropped into immediate silence.

The clothing Agent Harris was complaining about consisted of a calf-length velvet dress colored different shades of maroon, with some patterning sewn in down its length, and wrapped at the waist by a velvet belt. On her head she wore a wide-brimmed, floppy hat topped by a flowered decoration that might have accented her features if she could have done anything but scowl. Then, of course, she had donned the aforementioned footwear, which was less like modern-day high heels and more like high-heeled women's boots.

For the men, the attire was pretty uniform: slim-fitting business suits with high-, white-collared dress shirts and matching vests—navy worsted for Professor Stein, dark brown pinstripe for Lieutenant Phelps, and gray worsted for Dr. Weiss, all with matching bowler hats—while Captain Beck had a striped double-breasted suit and a fedora. A pocket watch and bob on a gold chain hung between his breast pockets. The lace-up boots the men all wore were ubiquitous for the period.

Agent Hessman stood out a little from the rest, his suit being more of a light green summer color, with a straw boater hat atop his head. He was also less overwhelmed by the apparatus before them than the rest. His mind was already totally on the mission.

"Welcome to the Bubble, as we like to call it." Dr. Weiss beamed. "It should be quite the show to see this thing finally fired up."

Ben, for one, immediately went from awe and wonder into a concerned glare, while Lieutenant Phelps's eyes narrowed considerably.

"You mean it's untested?" Professor Stein asked.

"We have yet to send back so much as a squirrel," Dr. Weiss stated with a grin as he gazed nearly lovingly at what lay before them. "This will be the first time, and we the first-time travelers—well, besides whoever beat us back there, of course. But you get my point."

"Okay, enough of the gawking," Agent Hessman said, taking charge. "We've all been outfitted with period clothing and enough period money for anything we might need."

"Reasonable facsimile of period money," Ben said, taking out a couple of bills from his pocket to briefly wave around, "but I don't think they have anything back in that period to detect our little forgeries. Just keep spending to a minimum. For that matter, *any* sort of interaction."

"Agreed," Dr. Weiss stated. "The less of a temporal impact we make, the better."

"Ben's pocket computer is one of the few concessions to modern technology we're allowed," Agent Hessman continued. "As are *these*." He took out of his pocket what looked like a metal golf ball with two red buttons on either side of it.

Dr. Weiss then continued with the explanation. "Our beacons. Pressing both buttons at the same time will send out a weak artificial TDW that the equipment here in the present will then pick up. When it does, the apparatus here will immediately yank your consciousness back into your body."

Captain Beck now spoke up as they proceeded to step onto the central platform. "Just so we're clear, Doctor, a quick refresher on what's about to happen, if you don't mind."

"Of course," the doctor said as he stepped up. "The apparatus above us will create a wormhole through space and time to the destination we have set. Our consciousnesses will then be pulled through and projected back into the past, where exact replicas of our bodies and everything on us will be created from the energy umbilical connecting us back to the present through the wormhole. Once our beacons are activated, the projections of our bodies in the past will be uncreated and drawn back as energy through the wormhole, with our consciousnesses going immediately back into our original bodies here in these pods. It should be perfectly painless."

"So is death by lethal injection," Agent Harris deadpanned.

"Don't worry, we have run plenty of simulations and tests. Also, one caveat about these beacons: While we are *pretty* sure they should work as designed, this *will* be the first time they'll have been used. And by their very nature, these beacons are a one-shot use."

"Getting back would be nice," Captain Beck stated, "but as long as this mission comes off, the rest doesn't matter."

"This umbilical," Ben asked after a moment of uncomfortable silence, "and the wormhole, for that matter. If anyone from back in 1919 sees it—"

"Invisible to all concerned," Dr. Weiss assured him. "The wormhole can only be seen or entered by way of certain energies the technology back then simply does not possess. We'll also be able to go anywhere in the world and still be connected through the wormhole, though the farther away from our drop area we go, the more energy our bubble chamber here will draw. But that's a concern for our technicians here."

He beamed a quick grin at the nearest lab-coated worker, who replied with a brief nod, then returned to prepping and double-checking the chamber.

"Question." It was Lieutenant Phelps, speaking up for the first time that anyone could remember. "What happens if this energy umbilical is somehow broken or the wormhole and power flow disrupted?"

"A very good question," Dr. Weiss replied with a slight nod, "and one we aren't entirely sure of the answer to. You could be stuck back in time in your fabricated body while your original back here in the present immediately dies, or your consciousness could simply snap back into your present-time body here in these pods. It's about an even chance of either possibility."

"Second question," the lieutenant replied. "How will our bodies be maintained while we're gone?"

"After our bodies are scanned and our minds sent back, tethers within the pods will hook up to us to handle such needs as food, water, and waste," Dr. Weiss explained.

"But this is time travel," Ben said. "Wouldn't it just be a matter of returning the same moment we left, or something like that?"

"Logically, yes," Dr. Weiss agreed. "But remember that we'll have a wormhole kept open with a live real-time connection to us the entire time. So for every day you experience back in 1919, your bodies back here will also experience that same length of time. Which brings up another matter limiting our time." He paced over to one of the pods, his back to it as he slowly sat down while explaining.

"Besides having no longer than the length of the temporal displacement event to fix things, the wormhole imposes its own limits in the amount of power required to hold it open. If we have not yet returned before the power requirements become too severe, then the energy umbilical could snap, trapping us back in 1919."

"How long?" Agent Harris asked flatly as she went over to her own pod to sit down.

"There has been some debate about that. It could be as much as ninety-six hours or as little as forty-eight. We really aren't sure, this being the first time and all."

"Let's assume forty-eight," Agent Hessman stated. "Two full days to find out what's happened and stop it before we risk mission failure. Everyone clear?"

No one said a thing.

"Good. Then strap us into these things."

They each picked a pod and lay down within it, the technicians quickly hooking up various wires and sensor pads around their bodies before closing the lids on the pods. They resembled a circle of elongated eggs. The technicians then cleared out of the chamber through a door that led into the main control booth. Then came the wait, as even Dr. Weiss wondered what their journey would be like.

The wait would not be long. Power surged suddenly through the mass of wiring, spitting down through the thick cables to each of the pods and surrounding them in a brightening glow. But as Professor Stein wondered what was to happen next, he and the others were quick to discover this was but the start. High overhead, the large twin metal propeller blades that curved beneath the wire-covered dome began to turn, slowly at first before spinning up to speed. Electrical sparks leaped from the backs of the blades to the cabling above.

Faster and faster the blades spun, the sparks more intense until the whole ceiling began to glow. The spinning blades became a blur, the electrical activity they generated filling the entire ceiling with a bright white light, until nothing of wires or spinning blades was visible.

Through their transparent pod lids, the team members could see the entire dome above them now like a small star as the chamber filled with the resonating echo of power. The roar of creation itself unleashed until the very mouth of that beast fully opened above them. In the center of that circle of blinding brilliance an eye opened, a dark pupil a dozen feet across, while a crack of thunder shook the chamber.

In the moment the eye lashed out, pulses of energy shot down the cables to the pods; then all within the pods filled with white light.

Up in the main control booth, General Karlson silently wished the travelers well.

5

THEY ARRIVE

The white flash that blinded the travelers seemed to clear, revealing before them a vista unseen by any living eyes for a full century.

They appeared mostly on a sidewalk, except for Agent Harris, who stood out in the street enough to nearly get hit by a passing car—specifically something in the Model T category. She quickly jumped out of the way, then joined the others in assessing their surroundings, though hers was more of a tactical survey.

The buildings lined the streets like tall, blocky sentinels. The landscape was a strange sight to those who knew the New York of the future and were seeing many of the older buildings as new again, back in the day when they were modern tributes to mankind's reach for the sky. Missing were the truly towering behemoths that would come much later; in their places were structures seen only in old photographs. Skyscrapers had turn-of-the-century architectural styles. One building looked like a tall wedge where two streets crossed at a forty-five-degree angle; miniature towers and minarets on another gave it the appearance of a baroque castle, while most simply formed a tall wall to cast a shadow across the narrow streets below. Here and there, large billboards advertised some ancient brand of cigarettes or household goods.

The streets were filled with a scattering of old-styled cars, though they looked anything but old. Model Ts and other variations of the design tooled along, with one double-decker bus plying its way down the street, the top deck open to the air. The car about to hit Agent Harris squawked a honk from a horn the driver had to physically squeeze at the side of the door. Along the sidewalks, people were coming and going, dressed in similarly styled apparel as the team, with more variation perhaps in the styles of women's dresses, though nothing shorter than calf length. Suits seemed the order of the day for the men, the exception being the occasional small cluster of uniformed soldiers back from a terrible war, and a young paperboy calling out the day's headlines as he waved about a copy of the local newspaper. Other uniforms they could recognize as police, their hats like small domes atop their heads as they directed the scant traffic with their batons or chased the occasional young lad trying to escape with his stolen prize from a small drugstore.

"It's like . . . history just exploded all around me," Captain Beck observed.

"Somehow," Dr. Weiss remarked, "I rather expected to see it all in black and white, but I suppose that's just because of all the vintage pictures I've viewed."

As the team historian, Professor Stein was marveling like a kid gazing through a bakery window, jaw hanging open as one sight or another would catch his eye. "That's a Jordan Model F Touring car—and it's *brand-new*! A Model A, an Essex town sedan, what looks like a precursor to the old Woody . . . and the architecture!"

"Most of these buildings still exist in our time," Dr. Weiss reminded him.

"But looking this *new*? Why, some of the buildings we consider really old are just being built! This is such an unparalleled opportunity to—"

He was interrupted by Agent Hessman smacking him across the chest with a rolled-up newspaper, reminding him of why they were there in the first place.

"Start on our mission," the team leader finished for him, dropping the paper in the professor's hands.

"Right," the historian said, pulling himself back from his burst of wonder. "But you can understand how I would—yes, enough of that. To business."

He unrolled the newspaper and scanned it for information. Meanwhile, after a quick look around, Agent Harris guided them off to the side of the walkway and started the group into a brisk walk down an alleyway she'd spotted.

"Looks like we have five days before the TDE plays out, according to this date," Ben narrated as he read. "Big headline of the day is President Wilson coming back from the Versailles Peace Conference, which makes this the beginning of July."

"Summer," Dr. Weiss said. "I could have told you that from the heat and humidity. This material doesn't exactly breathe, you know."

"First order of business," Agent Hessman told them, "no titles. No doctors, professors, or agents. I'm just Lou or Mr. Hessman, the captain is Robert or Mr. Beck, Agent Harris is simply Sue, Lieutenant Phelps is David, you're Ben, and, Dr. Weiss, you're just Sam. Got it? Any military-sounding titles would be too easy for someone to verify, and I don't want to worry about anyone's reaction to titles like 'special agent.' Just keep things as generic as possible so we don't stand out."

"I know," Sue Harris spoke up. "There wouldn't be a woman agent in this period to begin with, much less a black one. But I ain't faking no Aunt Jemima accent."

"That would be down in the Deep South," Ben replied absently as he continued to read.

In the alley, a small group of young teenage boys looked ready to defend their claimed hangout. At least until Lieutenant Phelps stepped forward and flexed a muscle or two. The alley was quickly theirs alone.

"Concerns of influenza outbreak," Ben stated as he continued with his nose in the newspaper. "That checks out . . . Recent bombing by some anarchists just a few days ago . . . What looks like a rise in crime caused by Prohibition. There'll be a lot of local crime gangs in the city making money off of illegal liquor sales, not to mention all their usual activities."

"How big a threat?" Sue asked.

"The gangs can get violent, but they're still pretty small. They won't have unified into the sort of organized crime we know of quite yet. We're just on the cusp of that era. Those Prohibition-era environments we've all seen in the movies won't be kicking into high gear for about another year or two."

"I rather expected to see more girls dressed in those risqué dresses," Dr. Weiss interjected with an embarrassed grin. "Flappers, I think they were called?"

Ben brought down the paper as he replied to his companion's remark. "I'm afraid that doesn't happen for about another five years at this point, Sam. They're still pretty conservative at this point, though some historians question if—"

"Back to more immediate matters," Agent Hessman reminded him. "We need a place to start. We're in a city of millions with no traffic cams, no internet, and not so much as a stoplight, from what I can see. All we know is what's recorded in Ben's record book."

"My—oh, you mean my pocket comp—"

Sue immediately had a hand clamped over the historian's mouth, while Dr. Weiss gave him a quick reminder. "No anachronisms, not even verbal ones. We don't know what unseen person might be listening."

"Exactly," Agent Hessman said. "Your portable little history bank is a *record book*. Okay?"

Ben nodded as Sue removed her hand from his mouth, then resumed her watch of the crowd passing by outside the alley.

"With that in mind," Agent Hessman continued, "Ben, what can you suggest of where we should start?"

"Well, I should caution that, while my . . . record book is quite complete, there may be events left unrecorded."

"Like what?" Dr. Weiss asked.

As an answer, Agent Hessman took the paper from Ben's hands and turned it around to show the headline reading, "President Comes to New York City!"

"Something like that could generate all sorts of unrecorded activity," he stated. "Security precautions, high-level diplomats coming in for secret meetings that by necessity would definitely not be recorded, all manner of things of a nature that we *need* to know about."

"So we have a problem," Captain Beck summed up. "Too much is going on in this city that we don't have on record, and we have a very limited time to find out."

Dr. Weiss glanced out at the busy streets, the rows of buildings marching away to the horizon, and grunted. "A needle in a haystack would be far easier to find. When you add in that it could even be some seemingly inconsequential event, such as some kid getting hit by a car or not, the possibilities are astronomical."

Lieutenant Phelps had taken up position opposite Agent Harris at the mouth of the alley, Sue earning an occasional odd look from passersby, to which David simply glared to send them on their way. A group of people talking in quiet tones in an alley might be suspicious to some, but even in the year 1919, too much of interest was happening in the streets around them to long draw attention to their small alley.

Agent Hessman thought for a moment at Sam's remark, paced a few steps, and shook his head before speaking again. "No, I don't think we have to worry about anything on that small a level. Remember, whoever came back here before us has the same level of historical knowledge as we do. They might have a few more details here and there, or might have missed a few things, but basically we're working on the same playing field. They'll be limited to whatever has been recorded in history books or government records."

"My . . . record book," Ben began, "was loaded with everything that General Karlson could get, including sealed military and government records of any sort. It's still a lot to go through, though."

"Agreed, though it may not include all the secret files of some *foreign* governments, which in a strange way gives us a place to start. Ben, I assume that record book of yours includes maps?"

"Down to the very alley we're standing in," he answered. "Here, give me a minute."

Out of the corner of her eye, Sue caught Ben pulling something the size of a bulky cell phone out of his breast pocket and acted immediately. Stepping back to stand between Ben and any accidental street-side view, she grabbed hold of his shoulders and gently spun him around so his back was to the street, hiding any view of the device he was pulling out. Ben barely seemed to notice the act as he passed a finger down the length of the little screen.

Agent Hessman took another glance down at the headline in his hands before rolling the paper back up. "Let's assume that things start from the big headline of the day: President Wilson's pending arrival. Wasn't he about to promote the League of Nations or something? That's got to have every foreign diplomat around scurrying."

Ben replied with a slight nod as he looked at the display now on his small device. "Area maps for the year 1919. And yes, the League of Nations. With World War I finally over with and the treaty all signed and delivered, Wilson was trying to push the country into joining it. I don't recall any particular diplomatic visitation, though."

"Don't bother looking," Hessman replied. "Half the stuff those types do is all off the books."

"A question for those of us uninitiated in the way of spycraft," Dr. Weiss interjected. "You implied that our lacking any of the secret files from foreign governments gives us a place to start. May I ask how?"

"Simple." Agent Hessman paced a few steps down the alley, then turned on his heel and explained to his team. "Either the Japanese or Germans sent a team back in time to change something. A team that *would* have some information that we lack but only as it relates to their own country's activities of the day. With Wilson as a suspected trigger point, they would begin with whatever secret activity that their government of 1919 was up to that we may not know about."

"Which leaves us where?" Captain Beck asked.

"At one of the consulates," Hessman answered. "Ben, we need the location of the Japanese embassy."

"Coming up," Ben replied as he tapped a finger to his screen.

"Why not the Germans?" Captain Beck asked. "Their country would have been very unhappy with how the war came out."

"Which is why I'm putting them farther down my list," Hessman stated. "I doubt if the Germany of 1919 had anyone left to spare to send over here on any sort of mission, secret or not. They were too occupied with being wrapped up by that treaty. Even if some modern-day neo-Nazi wanted to get something going back here, their German ancestors wouldn't be up for it quite yet. The Japanese, though, would also have a gripe but with more resources readily available."

Ben paused from his work on his device to look up curiously at Agent Hessman. "Actually, that period was quite prosperous for them, Agen—Lou. They were on the winning side of that war and barely suffered any losses in it to begin with. Are you privy to some piece of historical knowledge I have overlooked?"

"Not at all," Lou replied. "It just stands to reason, since we know that Japan enters in on the aggressive side of the next world war, that they must have had something to gripe about, and looking into what that something is, is as good a place to start as any. Ben, how do we get to the Japanese embassy?"

"Coming up now . . . Quite a walk from here. I might be able to find us a subway route in that direction."

Sue Harris had been keeping an eye out for possible threats, with an ear on the conversation, and now put forth her own opinion. "Too many trap points taking the subway."

"Do you have a better way, Miss Harris?" Captain Beck asked.

She gestured with a nod in the direction of what was now passing down the middle of the street: another of the double-decker buses they had seen earlier. "We ride top level so we have a clear view of all approaches."

"Agreed," Agent Hessman said after taking a brief moment to consider. "Phelps, you lead point. Ben, you've get to tell us which bus we'll be taking."

The team then left the alleyway in relative silence, saying as little as they could as they approached a stopped bus to board and be off for the Japanese embassy.

6

GOING FOR A STROLL

o, where's the Japanese consulate?" Captain Beck asked as they
stood on the sidewalk looking around at the towering buildings.
They could see a building down the street with an attached sign
that read, "English Consulate," before them a "Horn and Hardart" dis-
pensing quick food to impatient customers, but no sign of a Japanese
consulate.

"It was here in 2018," Dr. Weiss casually remarked.

"Well?" Agent Hessman asked, eyeing Ben.

"Twenty . . . oh, of course," Ben replied, quickly reaching into
his jacket.

Agent Harris saw the motion and immediately stepped over to block
any errant spectator from seeing what the professor was pulling out.
Ben brought out his pocket computer and quickly tapped on the screen
a few times.

"Ah," he then continued, "Japanese consulate didn't exist yet."

"Then why—" Captain Beck began.

"But the Japanese Society building *does*," Ben amended. "A few
blocks down. Whoever programmed this thing must have forgotten to
crosslink the two or something."

Dr. Weiss casually leaned over to Captain Beck for a quickly whispered comment on the matter. "That would be *your* people, Bob."

"Enough," Agent Hessman stated. "Let's just get there. Ben, lead the way; Harris and Phelps, flanking."

They spread out into their little formation, Captain Beck walking beside Agent Hessman at the rear while Dr. Weiss joined Professor Stein, with Agent Harris and Lieutenant Phelps to either side.

"I must say," Dr. Weiss remarked as they walked, "these sidewalks are a lot more spacious than I remember them. And the streets so narrow in comparison."

"Not as many cars back in this period as in ours," Professor Stein told him. "Once cars started getting popular, they had to widen the streets, which meant cutting the sidewalks down to about half their width."

Dr. Weiss sighed. "Pity. These walkways are made for more leisurely strolling."

They set a slightly more than leisurely pace, eager to be about their investigations while trying not to stick out overly much. As a historian and mission specialist, Ben Stein was caught between marveling at the sights of a bygone age and knowing the need of maintaining a good pace.

"I must say, though," he remarked as they walked, "I could never ask for a better opportunity to study something like this. Grainy old black-and-white pictures pale in comparison to being here in full living color. Anyone think to bring a camera?"

"No unnecessary technology," Dr. Weiss reminded him in a whisper.

Ben sighed. "More's the pity."

"Say, do you think this Japanese Society will have any of those geishas or those bathhouses where the girls—"

"Yes, and, Sam, I'm surprised at you. You're starting to sound as bad with the young women as I am with the historical aspects."

"Hey, I may be a physicist, but I'm a thirty-five-year-old man whose last date was with a female physicist with a harelip—or was that a hairy lip? Either way, it was most unpleasant."

Before Ben could remark or smirk at his companion's statements, two things happened nearly simultaneously. First came a shout and the sound of a police whistle, and then came the hand of Agent Harris grabbing Professor Stein to pull him back, while Lieutenant Phelps did the same for Dr. Weiss. An instant later, the disruption to the day's peace came running across their path from an adjoining cross street.

The first man to rush by had a haggard and desperate look, but also something unsavory hid behind his eyes. He held a gun in one hand that he used to fire off a couple of shots behind him before continuing on.

"Don't get involved," Agent Hessman warned as the event played out before them.

Next to come were a group of four local policemen, three of them waving their batons while the fourth fumbled with his own pistol. "Don't shoot if you don't have to," the lead policeman called back to his fellows. "Too many people around."

"All I'd need is a single shot, crowd or not," Lieutenant Phelps quietly remarked.

"David, mind on the mission," Captain Beck warned. "We are not here to prove your own . . . What the . . . ?"

"Excuse me; reporter coming through!"

Abruptly pushing through the group was a young woman in her midtwenties, about five and a half feet tall, and of a slender, if pleasant, frame. With a pearly-white complexion to contrast the mop of black hair trailing down the middle of her back, she was clothed in a series of layered white dresses of the era, white boots, and a floppy, wide-brimmed white hat. A purse dangled at the end of a long strap from her left shoulder, while with her right hand she was busy pushing Captain Beck out of her way.

For a brief moment, Ben's eyes happened to meet those of the young woman. The encounter was long enough, however, for him to see the small card jammed into the brim of her hat that read, "Press," before she flashed a quick smile and pushed on through.

That's when the next shot rang out from the fleeing man. He called out a challenge in a tongue that most there could not understand. The woman ducked behind the men, while they in turn hid behind Harris and Phelps.

"That sounded like Italian," Professor Stein stated.

"Italian?" the woman asked. "Great, that gives me a definite angle. Say, you don't think your two bodyguards could get me closer to the guy with the gun?"

"Bodyguards?" Ben replied hesitantly." Wh-what makes you think—"

She nodded in the direction of Harris and Phelps, who had their backs to the action while shielding the two intellects in what amounted to a group hug.

"Though I must say," the young lady continued, "I've never heard of a negress trained as a bodyguard before. Hmm, suppose that would make her perfect for the job. Well, on with *my* job."

Out in the middle of the street, the man being chased had run afoul of another group of police coming at him from the other side of the street. He now stood in the middle, spinning back and forth with his gun, aiming at one group and then the other, while traffic came to a standstill and pedestrians tucked themselves fearfully behind any available cover. Many of the women screamed at the sight, while the men held them secure.

The young woman who had barged in between Ben and Sam, however, was definitely not screaming. "I've got to get over there to see what's really going on. He can't just be a random criminal."

"He certainly looks like one to me," Ben remarked.

The young woman fixed him with an annoyed glare. "Criminals rob places for money; *anarchists* bomb places for other reasons. Or didn't you see it go off a couple blocks down?"

"*Bomb?*" Professor Stein exclaimed. "There's a bomb around here?"

Just then a sharp cry came from the man who was the center of attention. One of the police had caught him from behind with a flying tackle.

"Great, they got him." The young woman beamed. "Now's my chance. Thanks for the cover, guys."

She bolted back to her feet, pushing past Ben and Sam, then stopped for a brief look of appraisal at Agent Harris. "A black suffragette. I may want to interview you for a different story later on. Not sure about the short haircut, though, but the hat does a good job of hiding it."

Before Agent Harris could decide whether to scowl or frown at that remark, the other woman had bolted away, running straight for the growing pile of police now bearing down on the man with the gun.

"Hey, reporter Claire Hill here," the young woman called out to the assembly in the middle of the street. "What can you tell me about the suspect? Is he really a member of one of the Italian gangs? Does his gang have any connection with Benito Mussolini of Italy and his new Fascist Party? Any connection with anarchist activity?"

No one cowering along the sides of the streets had dared to get back to their feet yet, save the woman reporter now assaulting the police with rapid-fire questions. In response, one of the policemen broke away to try to hold her back from the group currently disarming and binding their new prisoner. She even shouted questions to the criminal himself, though the only response she got seemed to be an angry curse in Italian.

Agent Harris made a quick visual survey of events before releasing her charges with a wordless nod and standing back up along with Lieutenant Phelps. As the rest got to their feet, however, Agent Hessman looked thoughtful.

"Well, that was rather . . . disconcerting," Dr. Weiss remarked.

"The gunplay or the eager young woman?" Ben asked.

"Both, I would say."

Meanwhile Captain Beck, as he straightened himself out, caught the look on Agent Hessman's face and stepped over next to him. "What are you thinking?"

"That we may have just bumped into a convenient little tool," Hessman replied. "Ben."

Professor Stein looked back to Agent Hessman, though he still had half an eye out on the reporter. She was still hounding the police even as they dragged their suspect off the street.

"You never replied about the Mussolini connection. Can I count that as a confirmation? Can I have a quick word with the criminal?"

"Ben," Agent Hessman said, taking a step closer to the historian, "how much of an issue was Mussolini in this period?"

"Well," Professor Stein replied, "he would have just established the Fascist Party around April or May of this year, I think. In only a couple of months."

"And yet that female reporter out there's already on top of it. That must make her pretty good at her job."

"Lou," Captain Beck said from behind him, "what are you thinking? We can't involve any locals."

"Ben here has everything we need to know right on his record book," Agent Hessman told them all, "but only in relatively general terms. That woman out there is a fountain of information who knows a lot more about local events than we *ever* will. It's a resource I think we should bring in."

"But we can't risk contaminating the timeline," Dr. Weiss warned in a hushed whisper.

"We won't," Agent Hessman assured him. "We'll just say we're federal agents on a mission and need her help. Ben, when was the FBI established?"

"About ten years ago," he answered. "You want us to impersonate federal agents?"

"We *are* federal agents," Agent Hessman countered. "Just not from around here. I won't say anything too specific. Just follow my lead and let her reporter's mind fill in the blanks. Ben, by my side to make sure I don't make any historical missteps."

With Agent Harris falling in at his other side, Agent Hessman led the way across the street to where the reporter was still trying her best to get a few words from the police.

7

ENTER MISS HILL

Come on, just a single statement, something I can send to my editor."

"Sorry, Miss Hill, but he's a dangerous criminal. Now please be on your way. We're trying to clear the street to get traffic flowing again."

The young reporter exhibited a brief look of indignant frustration before calling back to the departing policeman, "It's just because I'm a woman, *isn't* it?" Another glance showed that she was now the only one left still standing on the street, while a couple of waiting cars gave her some impatient honks.

"Okay, I'm leaving," she shouted out to the streets in general. "But I'll get my story."

She turned to storm away from the direction the police were taking the criminal, only to bump into a group of several others coming right for her.

"Miss Hill, was it? I'd like to speak with you, if I could."

Standing before her was Agent Hessman, Professor Stein a step behind him, while Agent Harris came up to stand on her left and Lieutenant Phelps on her right. The captain and Dr. Weiss stayed at the rear. Claire took one look at the setup and immediately switched from indignant to cautious. "You aren't with one of those Italian gangs, are you? Because I'm just trying to get a story."

"No, Miss Hill," came the quiet response. "We're with the federal government. I'm Agent Hessman."

"FBI!" she gasped. "Well, that changes everything."

If anyone there had expected Claire to cower in the presence of the federal government, they would have been greatly disappointed. Instead, she grabbed Agent Hessman by one arm and guided him on a swift walk over to the nearest curb and away from the protesting cars. Her manner was brisk and insistent.

"Well then, Agent Hessman, I have a few questions for you. *Was* that an anarchist, and is he associated with one of the gangs that I hear Mussolini's backing? Well, it *must* be, or why else would the federal government be involved?"

They made it to the sidewalk, behind them traffic and the flow of pedestrians resuming their normal course, the incident already forgotten.

"And how did the FBI know about this? I mean, you were already on this street corner when he came by. Somehow you had to have known he was headed this way and were lying in wait. Observers, is that it? Hoping to spot his companions in the crowd? I need something to tell my editor."

Lieutenant Phelps took one look at the babbling reporter, then glanced to Agent Harris with a quick suggestion. "I could drop her."

"Naw," Agent Harris replied. "I think I like her. She just needs to tone it down a bit."

"Miss Hill," Agent Hessman said, "if you will permit me, we need your assistance."

The woman paused long enough for a cough to escape her throat, before continuing in a quieter tone, "What would the FBI need my help for? I'm just a reporter trying to break into the big time."

Here Agent Hessman glanced over to Ben. Professor Stein took the hint and control of the conversation. "Miss Hill, my name is Ben. We're here on a very important mission, but the one thing we lack is what you might call local knowledge. As a reporter, you seem to be—"

"I'm hooked into everything that's happening in this town, and that's what you need," she bluntly summed up. "A reporter who knows the gangs by name and what's happening in every seedy little section, is that it?"

"In essence, yes," Ben admitted. "If you could just come along and help us out a bit. We won't be asking you to get into any dangerous situations, just—"

"And why not?" she asked. "That'd be where the story is. Nellie Bly was on the battlefronts getting the news of what our boys were going through. If I'm to make it with some of the big papers, I can't be afraid of getting into the thick of it."

Agent Hessman stepped over and whispered a question into Ben's ear. "Nellie Bly?"

"Famous female reporter from World—the Great War and before," Ben whispered back.

Claire briefly narrowed her eyes at the almost-slip Professor Stein had made, but immediately got back to the subject. "Okay, I'll help you out, but under one condition. If the FBI is involved, that means you're hooked up to some *really* big news. I'll come with you if you give me an exclusive to what's going on. No other reporters, just me alone. Agreed?"

Agent Hessman glanced around at the others, receiving a slight nod from Dr. Weiss and another from Captain Beck. Professor Stein was still looking at Claire, a little intrigued by something about her.

"Agreed," Agent Hessman told her. "You get an exclusive on everything the FBI finds out about this matter."

"Perfect." She grinned. "Now, what's the caper?"

Agent Hessman glanced once around, then pulled her into a walk down the sidewalk, Ben falling into step at her other side, the rest in their usual positions, with Harris and Phelps keeping a watch on their perimeter.

"We'll start with some introductions," Agent Harris began. "I'm Lou, and this is Ben."

"Nice to meet you, Ben. So what's your bit? You aren't a regular agent, I can tell that. Consultant of some sort?"

"Something like that," he admitted.

"This is Sam," Agent Hessman continued. "The older gentleman is Robert."

"And the walking muscle?" Claire asked, glancing over to Lieutenant Phelps.

"Call him David," Agent Hessman continued. "And finally, the black suffragette here is Sue."

"I'd love to do a story on you. I've never heard of a negro working for the federal government before, and a *woman*? It'd really help the movement, I'm sure."

"What would really help," Agent Harris replied, "is if you stopped using the word 'Negro.' I'm a proud black lady."

"What she means is," Ben quickly interjected, "we look upon Sue as just another member of our group. An equal."

"Well," Claire smiled, "how progressive of the federal government. *Definitely* a story in there."

"Miss Hill," Agent Hessman began.

"Call me Claire, Lou."

"Claire. Perhaps we can start with if you've heard of any unusual or odd out-of-towners."

While Lou questioned the reporter, Ben drew Agent Harris aside for a few quiet words. "Sue, she did not mean any disrespect using that word. It's just the way they referred to black people at the time. You've got to watch things like that."

"I'd rather wrestle a lion. Which I did once, by the way."

"Sue."

"I get your point. Things were different back then, and we've got to blend in. I'll stay quiet. But I will *not* be subservient."

"Good enough. Just try not to kill any historical figures." Ben then stepped back to where Agent Hessman and Claire were talking.

"I would have heard of anyone that unusual," Claire was saying. "A few anarchists, rumors that Mussolini is using some of the local Italian gangs to stir up trouble, but beyond that—"

"Ben, what do you know of . . . current events? Could our target be trying to hook up with organized crime?"

"So, crime is organized now?" Claire said. "Not from what *I've* heard. There's about a dozen major gangs fighting it out."

Realizing his slip, Agent Hessman let Professor Stein take over the conversation while observing the reporter's reaction.

"Just an internal designation some people are starting to use in our department," Ben told her. "Since crime is coming increasingly from these gangs instead of lone individuals—"

"Got it. So you're asking if your target might be hooking up with one of these gangs like Mussolini's doing. I suppose it's possible, but it would help if I knew more about who or what your target is. Do you have a name?"

"Not exactly," Ben admitted.

"That would be our problem," Agent Hessman explained. "We aren't really sure who our target is."

"That's a *real* problem," she agreed. "So what *do* you know?"

Agent Hessman hesitated for a moment, thinking how best to put it while not blowing their cover.

"It could be one of two nationalities."

"Visiting dignitaries. Well, that's something, I guess. So, you had a report of some foreign diplomat about to be assassinated, is that it? Or maybe one of them's a spy, waiting here for President Wilson to come into town. *That's* it, isn't it? Some foreign power has it out for Wilson, and you're not exactly sure which."

"Miss Hill," Agent Hessman began, "Claire, you do an awful lot of supposing for a reporter. Aren't you just supposed to follow the facts?"

"I follow my instincts," she corrected, "and I'm not afraid to go where they take me. Just like Nellie Bly."

"A trait I'll admit I've found useful myself in the past," Agent Hessman said. "Okay, we'll stick with the original plan and go poking around at the Japanese Society building."

"Nice place," Claire remarked. "But were you planning on *walking* there?"

"It's only a couple of blocks away," Ben said, "according to our maps."

"A couple of blocks." Claire smiled. "That's cute. Ben, a New York block can be a whole lot longer than a regular city block. We'll hop a BRT; that'll take us there in no time."

"BRT?" Dr. Weiss asked.

"Boy, you *are* new to New York, Sam. Come on, I'll show you."

She led the way in a brisk walk down the street, everyone following after a nod from Agent Hessman. They seemed to have found their guide.

8

TRAIN TRIP

The BRT turned out to be an elevated electric train, sometimes running along at street level, other times crossing above them on elevated tracks from one station to the next. For a coin each, they secured a place in the back of one of the cars. They sat in pairs, Agent Hessman with Claire to further question her, Ben with Sam, Agent Harris with Lieutenant Phelps, and Captain Beck across the aisle from Agent Hessman and the reporter, while the city whisked by beneath them.

Sam leaned in to catch Ben's ear with a whispered remark as their journey began. "I thought all trains were underground in this city?"

"They're working on it," Ben whispered back. "A few are already, but what we'll know as the modern subway system is still only partially complete. The bulk of ridership is still above ground on things like the BRT here. At least until it goes bankrupt in about . . . hmm, later this year, I think."

"Then we may be among the last people to ride this thing. Sounds like an honor."

"The fact that we're riding this train at *all* in the year—when we are, is thrill enough for me."

"I'd rather think that reporter would be enough of a thrill." Sam grinned. "Quite the spunky type for this day and age."

"An unusually tenacious woman even for our own age," Ben admitted. "To find someone like this back now, it's remarkable."

Ben glanced over and tried to catch some of what Claire and Agent Hessman were talking about, which was mostly small details of their environment. What he found more interesting was the woman herself. A young woman from a century in the past, living and breathing before him. Everything about her, down to her dress and large hat, spoke of the period, except her personality seemed to stand out more than their team did in this day and age.

"I've been around there a time or two," she was saying. "Small building, one back door, though they manage to pack quite a few things in what space they have."

"I'm sure that will be of help, Miss Hill. Just remember not to get in our way when we get there. These people might be dangerous."

"People that you don't even know specifically who they are. Got it."

That's when she looked up and happened to catch Ben's eye. She flashed a quick grin in his direction, which got Ben immediately glancing away.

"Excuse me for a second, Lou."

Agent Hessman moved his legs out of the way while Claire carefully got up, steadying herself against the motion of the train as she stepped across the aisle to where Sam and Ben sat.

"Switching seats," she told them. "Sam, you're with Lou."

Ben hesitated a moment, glancing uncertainly from one to the other, and Sam just shrugged.

"Or are you going to refuse a lady?"

To Claire's remark, Dr. Weiss stood up, and Claire sat down next to Ben while Dr. Weiss joined Agent Hessman.

"So, what's *your* story?" she asked.

"My what? I'm sure I don't—"

"Everyone has a story, and I'm pretty good at sniffing them out. Lou says he's a government agent, but the way he looks at things, like he's examining them with a microscope or he read too much Arthur Conan Doyle, he's definitely more the detective type. David—he's military if I ever saw one; must have seen a lot of action in the Great War. Your buddy Sam over there, some sort of intellect. He has the look of a scientist, I'd think. Beck . . . he looks like he could have been an officer in the war; too old for anything else. Then Sue . . . she's a puzzle. If she were a man, I'd say something like for David. I just can't quite get a line on her."

"And me? What do you think *my* story is?"

"You . . . ," she said, thinking for a moment. "You're a tricky one. The way I see you looking at everything, like it's the first time you've seen any of it. Even now, as I was talking to Lou, you had half an eye on the scenery passing by outside like you're some kid seeing the big city for the first time. But it's just the city, and I don't think you're a country boy. For one thing, you don't talk like one. Too educated."

"So I'm educated. Lots of people are educated."

"No, you're more like . . . a professor. Someone who would be perfectly at home teaching at some stuffy English university. But the rest of it . . . I'm just not sure. But I'll get it; I always do."

"You just might at that, if anyone would . . . Claire."

The train made a stop to exchange passengers, but the team took their lead from Claire and showed no sign of moving.

"Our stop's the next one," she stated as they waited.

A moment later the train was starting up again, and now it was Ben's turn for questions.

"You certainly seem to be a great admirer of Nellie Bly."

"And what's not to admire? Reported straight from the warfront, worked undercover to expose those horrible insane asylums, actually *made* Jules Verne's fabled trip around the world in less time than the book gave. She's more of a reporter than most *men*, and I have no problem admitting that she's my idol."

Before Claire could look any more defensive than she already did, Ben quickly interjected, "I see nothing wrong with that, nor with any female reporter. But I have to ask: you don't look dressed like any reporter

I've seen. You look more like . . . well, like you're getting ready for some social event."

Claire's defensive stature eased down into a soft smile and slight gleam in her eye as she bent in a little closer to respond. "But that's the trick. Sure, I can wrap my hair up into a bun and put on my checkered coat if I ever want to look professional, but Nellie herself said that a dress is a great weapon in the hands of a woman if rightly applied. A weapon that men lack. If this dress gets me into places that will keep others out, then why not use it?"

"Then it is a weapon you use quite well, Miss Hill."

She flashed him a smile. Before anything else might happen, the train once again began to slow. She coughed once and then stood up.

"This is our stop," she said. "A lot shorter walk from here than you guys were in for before."

The train came to its stop, the team following Claire out to the station. As they descended the steps to street level, Agent Hessman pulled Ben back for a quick word. "What'd you two talk about?"

"Not much," Ben replied, "except it appears that Claire is a *very* perceptive young lady."

"Then that could make her a possible threat."

"Nonsense. There's no way she could really guess. She still puts everything within her worldview of this time."

"Just be careful."

Once down on street level, Claire led the way.

"This way, as I remember," she indicated. "Entrance is shaped like a pagoda. Can't miss it."

Agent Hessman marched in front to lead the pack. Agent Harris kept a wary eye on their surroundings as always, while Professor Stein could not stop marveling at the exciting new details of his surroundings, then caught himself as he remembered what Claire had observed about him.

Their walk was a short one, bringing them to an entry whose covering arch was indeed shaped like a pagoda. Agent Hessman immediately took charge.

"Everyone just follow my lead."

He walked directly to the front and stopped. Beneath the pagoda arch, a trail of red carpeting led inside, to either side a row of waist-high vases holding tall stalks of white flowers. At the end, before the final entrance, stood a pair of stout-looking Japanese gentlemen dressed in samurai robes with swords sheathed at their belts.

"They don't look too friendly," Captain Beck remarked quietly. "What's our cover story?"

"That's what I'm trying to decide," Agent Hessman agreed. "Ben, how friendly was—is the Japanese Society on drop-in tourists?"

Claire saw their predicament and let out a sigh as she stepped forward. "Getting into this place is important to your investigation?"

"Yes," Agent Hessman replied, a little uncertainly.

"Then *you* follow *my* lead, and remember about my exclusive."

Without another word, Claire adjusted her hat so the press card was facing directly forward, then walked straight up to the two guards.

"Claire Hill, reporter. I'm doing a story on local Japanese culture. Do you mind if I come in for a tour? Oh, and this is my crew."

All it took was one smile, and one of the two men standing guard stepped inside for a word with his superior. A minute later they were being led inside.

Claire flashed a quick grin back at the group, to which Agent Hessman shrugged and led the way in behind her.

9

THE JAPANESE SOCIETY

Their guide was a short Japanese man who appeared to be in his fifties. He wore traditional robes and a pleasant smile for the reporter and her crew as he led them through the velvet-lined anteroom. From the outside the building appeared small, with only three floors, but once inside, the dimensions were deceptive. Between small hallways and walls lined in either velvet drapes or rice-paper murals and partitions, it seemed to weave about for a much longer distance than expected.

The front room had a display of colorful vases and a couple of smaller traditional murals. Their guide seemed only too eager to show them around. "Our purpose here is to spread knowledge of Japanese culture," the man was saying. "A chance to appear in your local newspapers would be most welcome indeed. Will you be taking some pictures?"

"Not today," Claire replied. "We'll bring in the camera equipment on our next visit. This is more in the way of a scouting trip to see what we may want to focus on." She then lowered her voice for her guide alone as they stepped out into an adjoining hallway. "One of my crew is actually my editor. He gets to decide how much coverage this story gets in the paper, so I really need to impress him."

The man replied with a smile and a slight bow of his head. "I shall do what I can to please your people. Walk this way."

He led them down a corridor lined with an assortment of Japanese portraits—landscapes mostly, with a few pictures of some men dressed in samurai armor. Their guide was saying something about them being famous leaders in Japanese history, to which Claire responded with appropriate comments and questions. All the while, Professor Stein was still marveling at every aspect of what he saw, like an eager boy in a toy store. When the hall widened into another room, however, was when the historian could truly marvel.

A full suit of Japanese armor was on display, along with a set of curved swords pinned up against one wall, some more vases, and other ancient bric-a-brac. And there to lend a smile and a helpful assist with the guided tour was a young lady in a kimono, her face painted in white makeup and her long black hair done up in a decorative pile atop her head.

"I just can't believe it," Ben said, almost to himself. "Those portraits are painted on actual rice paper. Do you know how hard it is to find preserved specimens of that sort of thing? And a genuine suit of samurai armor! Classic in every detail. And just look at these vases." He scurried over to the nearest one, thinking to pick it up, then stopped short of touching it. "I might break it. But oh, the opportunity!"

Claire kept their guide busy with questions and comments, leaving the others to their work. Agent Hessman, though, was less interested in the artifacts around them than of what else he might see. He wanted to hurry them through but had learned long ago how much of a virtue patience could be. So he let their guide take it at his own pace, though he finally had to step over to retrieve Ben.

"May I remind you what we're *actually* here for, Ben?"

"What? Oh, I'm so sorry. It's just that this is a priceless opportunity to see history in such detail."

"It'll still be in a museum a hundred years from now. Your job is to tell me when something *doesn't* belong around here."

"Oh, right. Sorry."

They rejoined the others as they were entering another hall. Rice-paper walls lined either side; a few backlit, creating suggestive shadows of the people beyond them.

"The tea ceremony is a key part of Japanese culture," their guide was saying, indicating one of the backlit walls. "Here, visitors from my country may enjoy a small piece of our culture in a foreign land."

"Oh, I've heard of the Japanese tea ceremony," Claire said with honest excitement. "When my cameraman comes with me next time, do you mind if I get a few pictures of a tea ceremony? I just know my readers will really enjoy it."

"I shall see what I can arrange, Miss Hill. Now, if you follow me this way, perhaps we can find one of our geishas for you to interview."

They turned left down another narrow paper-lined hall in time to see a much younger Japanese gentleman emerge from behind a sliding rice-paper door, behind him the silhouette of two more people in the room. The man, in his twenties, wore a suspicious look on his face for the unexpected tourists. He gave a brief start before schooling his features, but Agent Harris hadn't missed the expression. She discreetly elbowed Agent Hessman, who in turn reached slyly into his coat for something quite similar to Ben's futuristic reference device. Agent Harris casually positioned herself to block any direct view of his activity as he consulted his miniature screen.

The young man walked quickly down the corridor, turning right at the end. The team's guide, meanwhile, was completely absorbed with pleasing Claire and feeding her as much information about Japanese society as he could. When he came to the end of the hall, though, he started to take them to the left.

"And over here we have some museum pieces on loan from our homeland. If I may be permitted to—"

"Miss Hill." Agent Hessman pushed his way to the front, making a straight line for the right-hand hallway. "I'm thinking we might find something more interesting in *this* direction."

"Only the geisha chambers and the bathhouse are over there," their guide stated. "I am quite sure you will find something far more interesting over here."

But Agent Hessman was already midway down the other hall, Agent Harris hot on his heels. Professor Stein had paused to look uncertainly down both directions. Lieutenant Phelps grabbed him by the collar and shoved him to the right. Captain Beck and Dr. Weiss were quick to follow along, while Claire was quick to adapt.

"You'll have to excuse me," she said quickly to her guide, "but that's my editor, you see. Gotta go where he goes, I'm afraid." She ran off to join the rest, leaving a confused guide behind to puzzle over this change in plans for a moment or two before he decided to go after them.

"Wait! You really can't go there. Like I said, the bathhouse is in that direction."

Ahead of them, Agent Hessman could see the younger Japanese man ducking through another sliding rice-paper door on the left and quickened his pace. He was trying to keep it to a fast walk so as not to attract any attention, but he couldn't risk losing their quarry.

"What's going on?" Ben said in a sharp whisper as he caught up to them.

"Just ID'd one of the Japanese team members," Agent Hessman replied tersely. "We need to catch him." He then quickened his pace and headed for the same door as the suspect.

Behind them, Claire had broken into a near jog to catch up, all the while calling out observations to cover up the reason behind their detour.

"Oh yes, Mister Anda," she called out to Agent Hessman in a tone meant to be heard by their guide, "I see what you mean. We must certainly get some contrast to the story. A look at the behind-the-scenes life."

Once she reached Captain Beck and Dr. Weiss, she switched immediately from pleasant journalist to matter-of-fact investigator. "Okay, guys, what's going on?"

"You'll have to ask farther up the line, I'm afraid," Dr. Weiss replied.

"I think Lou spotted one of our suspects," Captain Beck supplied.

"Which means my story just ducked through that partition. Thanks."

A second later, she caught up to Professor Stein and Lieutenant Phelps just as they were following Agents Hessman and Harris through the partition. "Leaving without your favorite reporter?"

"N-not at all," Ben stammered. "It's just that Lou—I mean, there wasn't any time to—"

"Don't stammer!" she snapped. "*My* story and *your* suspect are getting away."

"Right."

They entered what appeared to be the outer chamber for the bathhouse, where a couple of Japanese men, wearing only towels around their waists, were just folding up their clothes before entering through the next partition to the chamber beyond. A smiling young Japanese lady in a slender kimono came over from a side chamber and spoke a few words in Japanese.

"No thanks," Agent Hessman said as he brushed past her. "I'm not staying."

She then aimed her smile at the next person in line, who happened to be Agent Harris. The young Japanese woman's smile fell into an uncertain, wavering line, to which Agent Harris replied with a hard scowl as she stormed past.

The others were not much better, though Claire paused briefly for a kinder word. "Newspaper reporter Clyde Hill. You know what it's like once you have the scent of a good story, right? Sorry about the intrusion." Before the young Japanese lady could ponder what was going on, the American reporter had left with all the other strangers.

The bathhouse was a large and spacious room with a single big tub of hot water in the floor at the center. Two men were already soaking in it, washcloths draped over their privates, while a pair of young women tended them with soap and hot towels for their shoulders and upper backs. Seeing the group of fully clothed people walk in earned a few gasps from the ladies and angry looks from the men. Agent Hessman ignored them, though, eyes darting quickly around as the others filed in behind him.

Across the room, on the other side of the pool, another bare-chested man in a towel was casually making his way to a sliding door at the far end. He was just sliding the partition aside, revealing what looked like an area to shower and rinse off, when Agent Hessman's eyes narrowed sharply on the one part of his body *not* bare. "Street shoes in a bathhouse? I don't think so. Get him!"

Agent Hessman broke into a jog, going around the outer circle of the pool, being careful not to slip, while Agent Harris used a more direct approach. Taking a couple of steps back, she ran and jumped, clearing the pool and the screaming people beneath, to land in a tuck and roll back up to her feet. Meanwhile their quarry heard the words "Get him" and ripped off his towel to toss in Agent Harris's way while bolting through the shower room.

Beneath his towel, his pant legs had been rolled up nearly to his knees, while his shirt was wrapped around his waist. The towel landed at Agent Harris's feet just as she stood up, and did little more than cause her to misstep once. The chase, however, was on.

10

CHASE

Their target ran through the rinse room, turning on a shower in his wake, ripping his shirt off from around his waist to don along the way. The other side ended at another rice-paper wall but with no exit this time.

So he made one.

Agent Harris ran for the exit, leaped across the small rinse room, ignoring the wet floor, while Agent Hessman came in behind her, much more careful of the slippery floor. Behind him, Lieutenant Phelps was the first to catch up, Professor Stein and the others a couple of paces behind. The rest of the bathhouse, meanwhile, was in an uproar, with women screaming and men angrily scowling. Somewhere in the corridor they had traversed, their guide was still calling out for them and wondering what the fresh commotion was all about.

"Get him," Agent Hessman said to Lieutenant Phelps. "He's our first lead."

A quick nod and the younger man was off, pounding his way through the shower room, not caring what got wet. Agent Hessman reached in to turn off the shower, giving the others time to reach him.

"If I may ask?" inquired Dr. Weiss.

"A member of the Japanese team," Agent Hessman shot back. "He's a match for one of their mug shots. Plus, *he* spotted *us*. I'm guessing he came here to meet with or find someone. Robert, make sure these two brains don't trip and break their heads open or something."

"Right," the captain replied.

Agent Harris broke out into an adjoining hall, her side of it paneled in more rice-paper, while the other side of the corridor sported mahogany paneling. To her left, the room opened up into what appeared to be a small shrine centered on a smiling Buddha statue being tended to by a robed priest with his container of burning incense. To her right, a pair of running feet disappeared up a set of stairs.

She took off right. Up the stairs she ran, the heavier tread of Lieutenant Phelps fast behind her, until she came to a landing on the second floor. This level appeared to be some sort of ballroom, with long curtains over the windows. A couple of workers swept the floor in preparation for some pending event. The man she was chasing now had his shirt fully on and was headed across the room toward one of the windows.

She let out a primal cry and took off like a bullet. She had nearly caught up to him when he saw her and spun around, dropping into a martial arts stance. He emitted a sharp cry, accompanied by a couple of quick jabs into the air, his face fixed in a glare of deadly menace. Agent Harris paused to survey his form, an arm out to pause the lieutenant as he caught up to her.

Following another cry, the Japanese man kicked, then lunged forward with a fist, jabbing for her face. Agent Harris merely leaned her head back to dodge.

"Standard karate," she remarked blandly. "Cute." She dropped down, left foot out in a cat stance, hands pointed up like knives to the sky, one in front of the other. "Black belts in hapkido and Tiger Crane. And you?" The slender black lady with a short haircut posed next to the mountain of muscle in front of the suspect, trapping him with only ten feet to a curtained window and little else. Except the door to his left, through which a man now came rolling out a wheeled cart full of silver

68

serving trays, small porcelain cups, and a full tea service. The suspect wasted no time and ran to his left, grabbing one of the silver trays to fling out on his way to the door.

Agent Hessman ran up the stairs, leading the others in time to see Lieutenant Phelps bat the flying tray out of the way as Agent Harris went running after the man. The tray flew to one side, close enough for Agent Harris to catch as she passed the cart and drop it back onto the stack of other tea trays before the mystified server. "Gotta leave everything the way we found it," she muttered under her breath.

"We need to go help them," Professor Stein said.

"Are you sure?" Dr. Weiss asked. "They look like they're doing pretty well."

"We only have two combative personnel on this team," Agent Hessman reminded them. "The rest are too essential to risk in a firefight. We follow but keep our distance."

"Okay, where do we stand?"

A breathless Claire came running up the stairs behind the rest, pushing her way past Captain Beck to confront Professor Stein.

"We appear to have found our target," Ben replied. "Or at least one of them."

"*One* of them? How many people are you guys after?"

"Just don't get involved in the fight," Agent Hessman stated, then added after seeing the reporter in particular, "especially *her*."

Before she could ask exactly what the man implied, Agent Hessman was running for the exit through which Lieutenant Phelps was now following Agent Harris. Ben was the first in pursuit behind him, followed by the reporter.

"I still wish I knew what you guys were after," she called out.

"So do I," Professor Stein quipped.

Agent Harris burst through the door to see before her a large kitchen and their target weaving through cooks and servers to the other side. She also saw something else: walls of cooking utensils, including several styles of knives, one of which the man they were after was grabbing off its hook as he dodged another surprised cook.

"Oh, this just looks lovely," she remarked. "A room full of designer cutlery. We know how *this* is going to end."

She charged into the room, dodging, ducking, and spinning, and then saw the one she was after raise the knife he'd grabbed as he readied to toss it. "A *bread* knife? You couldn't have grabbed anything more challenging?"

She reached for the nearest object beside her as he hurled the long bread knife. She had picked up a large ladle, and she used it to parry the tumbling knife. Behind her, Lieutenant Phelps was running around to the right of the line of culinary worktables down the center of the room, thinking to cut the man off.

After she deflected the knife, she charged, her cry warning innocents out of the way. Ahead of her the man started running again, until he came to the end of the room with nothing near him but a counter and some drawers. Agent Harris wasted no time on a speech to warn him or talk him down, but simply steamrollered her way through the few cooks who hadn't gotten the hint and already ducked out of her way. On the other side of the kitchen paralleling her was Lieutenant Phelps, who didn't seem to care much for intervening obstacles, ambulatory or otherwise. He simply batted them aside.

In a last desperate chance, the man flung open one of the drawers and reached in. There he found more knives. With a grin he threw the first one at Agent Harris, followed by another and a third. Agent Harris responded with a wave of her ladle, deftly batting each aside. The rain of knives, however, did slow her charge.

Lieutenant Phelps was still coming at the guy from the right; Agent Harris from straight ahead. To the left was nothing but a window, currently open to help vent the kitchen. The guy threw a last knife and dashed for the window. He practically leaped through it, landing with a crash against a metal railing outside. When the two caught up to him, they could see what had caught the man on the other side.

"Fire escape," she stated. "His friends might be below. Stay up here and cover me until I get down."

"With what? We didn't bring guns," the lieutenant pointed out.

Agent Harris glanced once at the drawer full of knives and leaped through the window after the other.

He was already nearly to the ground when she emerged on the second level of the fire escape, and as she had predicted, others were down below waiting for him. Lieutenant Phelps had a fist full of knives ready to hurl when Agent Hessman came running up to his side, behind him in line Professor Stein, Claire, then Captain Beck urging Dr. Weiss along in front of him.

"Situation," Agent Hessman stated.

"The rest of his team is out there below," Lieutenant Phelps reported. "Looks like six of them, including the one we've been chasing. He's running down a fire escape. Sue told me to cover her."

Then came the sharp sound of gunfire. A single shot deflected off the edge of the fire escape railing just to one side of Agent Harris's head.

"They brought guns?" Agent Hessman stated. "Ben, tell me something."

Professor Stein peered carefully through the window as another shot rang out. She ducked that one, then slid her way down the last metal ladder, while her quarry ran over to join his team in what looked like a rear courtyard adjoining an alley leading out into the streets. The Japanese team was huddled behind a large dumpster, keeping Agent Harris pinned with another shot from one of their pistols.

"Looks like World War—I mean military service pistols," he said, correcting himself for the benefit of Miss Hill's presence. "Very good repro—uh, very good shape. Browning or a Colt, I would say."

"Then they got us pinned unless Sue can distract them well enough," Agent Hessman remarked.

"Then shoot back!" Claire snapped. "You're federal agents; you must have *some* sort of firearms on you."

"It was not . . . mission parameters," Agent Hessman stated. "David, we need to get down there."

"Right."

The big man looked around, saw a convenient wok, and pointed to it. At their rear, Captain Beck scrambled for the large metal skillet and handed it off to the lieutenant.

"This should be heavy enough for those old pistols," he remarked.

"What's the fool talking about?" Claire hissed into Ben's ear. "Those look like top-of-the-line military revolvers they got out there. And what are Japanese agents doing with American guns, anyway?"

"Later," Ben whispered back. "Firefight, remember?"

"What are you people doing in my kitchen? Get out of here before I roast you!"

As Lieutenant Phelps climbed out the window, he held the large metal wok in front of himself like a shield. Angrily stomping toward them came what appeared to be the head cook, a long white chef's smock on his body and a large and intimidating meat cleaver raised in his right hand. Claire immediately leaped to the occasion, dashing over to meet the angry cook in a war of confusing words.

"Hi, Claire Hill, reporter. I'm also doing another piece on kitchen cleanliness, and did you know you have *rats* around here?"

"No rats. Just group of people ruining my kitchen. Out!"

"Oh, but we saw the largest rat, and I'm afraid that things just got out of hand. We thought we'd find and catch it before anyone in your event might spot him. Now, do you know if this could be a whole infestation or just a single intruder?"

"Get *out* of my *kitchen*!"

Out on the balcony, a shot rang off of Lieutenant Phelps's wok as he stood on the upper landing trying to make his way down the steps, while Agent Harris had found a five-foot Buddha statue fixed against the center of the back wall of the courtyard to take cover behind.

"Ben, how many shots do those things carry?" Agent Hessman asked.

"About six each, I think," he replied. "Of course if they have a gun each, then it'll be a while before reloading. And that's assuming that while they look like excellent replicas on the *outside*—"

"Right, they might have a few mods. Okay, no time to wait until they run out; start tossing out whatever those two can use."

Behind them, Claire decided to hold out against the angry head cook with a last-resort tactic that women have used for centuries. With a firm stance, her chin thrust up, she called out boldly, "You wouldn't hit a *lady*, would you?"

In reply, the chef stabbed his large knife into the wooden table next to him, reached out with both hands to grip her by both shoulders, and, to her dismay, bodily picked her up, moved her to one side, put her down, and retrieved his knife. "Now *out* of my kitchen!"

Meanwhile Agent Harris was trying to think of a way to get across to the Japanese team that would involve her actually making it over there alive. They had the bin for cover, and while she and Lieutenant Phelps could outflank them once he made it to the ground, they still had no weapons. "There's got to be another way," she said to herself.

Just as the lieutenant made it to the ground, a crash sounded, followed by two more. Both Harris and Phelps looked to see another wok come hurling out from the window to join the first two on the ground; then came a series of large kitchen knives.

"Take your pick!" came Agent Hessman's shout.

"Nothing like service with a smile," she quipped to herself.

She waited until the rain of kitchen implements stopped, and looked to where the nearest large wok had landed, but Lieutenant Phelps was ahead of her. The large man ran out, weaving from side to side, a bullet bouncing off his wok shield, hit the ground while grabbing up one of the other fallen woks, and threw it over to her. She caught it in a tuck and roll out into the open, then, with that as a shield, ran for one of the larger knives.

Back up in the window, Agent Hessman watched as Agent Harris grabbed one of the knives as she ran to one side, while Lieutenant Phelps snaked a hand out to grab one near where he lay and waited for another shot to dent his wok before leaping to his feet with a cry that sounded much like an angry bull elephant.

"Two against six," Dr. Weiss observed. "They'll never make it."

"Don't count Miss Harris out yet," Agent Hessman corrected as he watched. "She's special ops through and through."

"Out of my kitchen!"

Dr. Weiss was the first to stand up and turn around to face off against the angry man, only to discover the other guy was about an inch taller than he was.

"I thought all you Japanese guys were short?"

"*Out!*"

Faced with an angry cook with a large meat cleaver, the physicist could think of only one thing to do. "Uh, Lou? I think the man wants to talk to you." He stepped aside.

Clang!

To the sound of heavy metal meeting brain, the cook went limp and crashed to the ground like a rag doll. Standing behind him was Claire holding on to a large Japanese skillet with both hands and looking a little guilty. "There was one more wok left." She winced. "I hope I didn't hurt him too bad, but he *manhandled* me."

"Things'll get worse than that unless we can get down to that court-yard without getting shot," Agent Hessman stated. "Beck, you bring anything?"

"Officially?" the captain replied. "No."

"Unofficially?"

The captain reached into a pocket and pulled out a small gun no bigger than the palm of his hand.

"Derringer, 1875, mint condition, good for a single shot. Figured it would make for a good holdout weapon without standing out."

"That's a *girl's* weapon," Claire remarked. "It'll never hit them from way up here."

"True," Agent Hessman admitted, "but *they* don't know that. We just need it for the noise. Here."

Captain Beck handed the small pistol over; then Agent Hessman carefully leaned out the window . . .

The shot nearly caught Harris and Phelps by surprise, and certainly the Japanese team. In the confines of the small courtyard, it echoed until it sounded like a much bigger gun than it actually was. That was all the other team needed to hear. After a quick discussion among themselves and a last shot to keep the two pinned down, they made a break for it, running straight for the alley exit and the freedom of the Japanese section of the city.

Freedom for five of them, at least. The minute they broke, Lieutenant Phelps bolted to his feet, dented wok in one hand and large knife in the other, and charged straight at the nearest team member. Covering him, Agent Harris broke into a run herself, electing to give her own wok a toss like a Frisbee, followed by a thrown knife as she neared.

At the top of the fire escape, the others saw their chance, and Agent Hessman led the way as he nearly ran down the metal steps, followed in turn by each of the others. He hit the ground just in time to see the rearmost Japanese team member raising his pistol as a hurled knife from Agent Harris cut into his hand. A scream and the pistol went flying, followed quickly by the man himself as the lieutenant slammed into him.

The man hit the ground, the lieutenant's knife in his chest. The rest didn't stick around but ran off down the alley as fast as they could.

Agent Harris was the first to the body after Lieutenant Phelps, and quickly checked it.

"Dead," she announced as Agent Hessman came running up to join them.

"We need a prisoner to question next time," Agent Hessman snapped. "Okay, the two of you go after the Japanese team. The rest of us will be here looking for clues."

"Got it," Agent Harris said with a nod.

By the time Ben and Sam came jogging up behind Agent Hessman, the other two were already running down the alley after the Japanese team. Claire approached, saw the bleeding body, and swallowed a lump in her throat, while Captain Beck reached an arm around to turn her away.

"Perhaps the lady should not see this."

"No," Claire said after a moment. "Nellie Bly saw much worse in her career. I can do this."

"Well, I'm not sure if *I* can," Ben stated. "I didn't think there'd be bodies on this trip."

"A man admitting he's afraid of a little blood?" Claire teased. "Didn't you see any in the war?"

Professor Stein stammered for a moment, then changed the subject by shifting his full attention to Agent Hessman, who took the hint.

"We won't have much time before they come back here to see what all the fuss is about," the team leader stated. "Assume we have no more than five minutes. I'll check out the body. Ben, you see if they dropped anything of interest over where they were hiding behind that garbage bin."

Grateful to have both the subject changed and an excuse to avoid picking around a freshly dead body, Professor Stein hurried over to the bin while Agent Hessman bent down for his examination.

11

TIMES SQUARE CHASE

Agent Harris and Lieutenant Phelps ran down the narrow alley, sight of the Japanese team all but lost to them. In fact, all they could see ahead of them as their alley intersected with a small street was an overturned garbage bin, followed by a man who sounded like he was cussing in Japanese next to a recently knocked-over crate of ice-packed fish. Then another garbage bin farther down the alley on the other side of the small street was dislodged.

"Nice of them to leave us a trail trying to slow us down," Agent Harris said as they ran.

She leaped atop the first bin and down to the other side, barely breaking stride, while Lieutenant Phelps shoved hard with both hands to push the thing out of his way. Then Agent Harris spun her way around the fallen crate and jumped over the second bin, with Lieutenant Phelps hot on her heels as he crashed his way more forcefully through.

"Too bad the slowing-down part of that's not working out too well for them," she said, once past the obstacle course. Ahead of them she could see only a pair of running legs and what looked like the back of the head of one of the men who had shot at them. They were bolting straight for a much bigger street than the last one. "We've got to get them before they lose themselves in the crowd."

A loading ramp appeared ahead, with steps leading up for pedestrians on the near side, the other side ending abruptly where a truck would back up. She took the steps two at a time, and at the other end of the ramp, leaped through the air, aiming true for one of the trailing members of the Japanese team. Lieutenant Phelps, meanwhile, continued straight on down the alley.

Agent Harris flew as her target glanced back over his shoulder. A quick glimpse of the descending angel of death was all he needed to spin himself quickly aside and jog backward to let Agent Harris land on the sidewalk instead of on top of his back. She did a tuck and roll back up to her feet, launching herself straight at the man.

Her opponent went from jogging backward to facing her, then winding up into a roundhouse kick that caught her in the side, though even then she nearly caught his foot in the process. He resumed running away, having delayed Agent Harris just enough to gain a couple of precious seconds. By that time the lieutenant had caught up to her, and the pair found themselves racing side by side after the Japanese team.

"Okay, so he knows a little martial arts," she remarked as they ran. "I'll still stuff his karate chop straight down his gullet with a couple of spin kicks once I catch up to him."

"Looks like they ran out of room to run," Lieutenant Phelps stated. "Look."

Ahead of them the alley came to an end at one of the more major streets, complete with a mixture of both horse-drawn and gas-driven vehicles, including turn-of-the-century taxis that resembled four-door yellow Model Ts and a double-decker bus, as well as plenty of foot traffic down the sides of the wide avenues. They could see the five members of the Japanese team coming to an abrupt slowdown as they pushed their way through the crowd.

When out of the corner of her eye Agent Harris saw the lieutenant reaching for something in his pants pocket, she stopped him with a hand to his arm and a word. "No. Not here in the middle of all of these people, and especially not with that gun you're not supposed to have. We have to get them without attracting any attention, *especially* from the local cops."

"Can I at least break their legs or something?"

"*That* you can do." She shrugged.

They, too, dropped down to a rapid walk once they hit the crowd, shoving their way through the throng of humanity. Their act was greeted by many displeased looks and one remark from a well-dressed white man with his lady friend. "Know your betters, young negress! Lay hands on me or my wife again and I shall have you arrested and tossed into the dark hole in which you belong."

Agent Harris looked ready to take out her frustrations from the chase on the couple before her, but this time it was Lieutenant Phelps's turn to lend a restraining hand to hold her back while muttering his apologies, giving the first story that came to mind. "I'm sorry, but . . . my maid and I here were in a hurry and she got a bit overenthusiastic. Come on . . . Jemima, we don't want to be late for that . . . prayer meeting you have with Tom and Huck."

He pulled her away before the couple could do much more than glower at them. Once out of sight of the couple, Agent Harris shook off the lieutenant's grip with a sour look. "Okay, so I forgot that a black person shoving her way through whites in 1919 is not a good thing to do, but do you know how many levels of *wrong* that line of yours had?"

"Sorry, but I'm not good at lying or making up stories. Now let's hurry up before we lose the targets."

After a last glare, Agent Harris was back on the job and quickly spotted one familiar head making its way around the other side of a passing taxi. "There," she indicated with a nod. "Before we lose them."

Their pace quickened, though Agent Harris was careful now to be far more polite in making her way through the crowd. She led the way across the street and down the walkway, around a final clump of people loitering in conversation, before emerging into a break in the surging sea of humanity. Several yards ahead of them, at the other end of the clearing, the Japanese team members were likewise race walking through the crowd.

"Quicker," she whispered to Lieutenant Phelps. "Just no running."

"Agreed. I imagine seeing a black person running down the street is not going to be taken any better by the cops in this year than back in ours."

She shot him another harsh glare.

"Hey, I'm just sayin'. I mean, if we're to blend in, then . . . that is, all I meant was . . . I'll shut up now."

"You're actually right about what you mean," she told him, "but absolutely *wrong* in the way you tried to say it. Stick with just being the muscle from now on. Now hurry up."

Their chase became a walking war, their longer strides versus the shorter but quicker ones of the Japanese team, as each tried their best to keep from getting noticed by the general public. After a brisk walk down a street and around a corner, the five from the Japanese team were forced to wait while a double-decker bus passed by, the pair behind them nearly catching up before the five resumed once again. The Japanese men ducked into a crowd entering a theater for a play and nearly lost their two pursuers, but Agent Harris's sharp eyes spotted them on the other side of the street.

Of course, five Japanese gentlemen moving through the herd as if they were intent on a criminal mission was almost as suspicious in the eye of the people of 1919 as a large white man and a slender young black woman dressed more as though they were going out together than as man and servant. Keeping track of the Japanese men's movements was turning out not to be too difficult a task for Agent Harris, though catching up to them was problematic.

"Those guys certainly walk fast," she remarked as the street turned onto a much larger avenue.

"We've got another problem," Lieutenant Phelps remarked. "How do we take them down once we catch up with them?"

"I think between the two of us we can take them."

"Without looking like we're criminals assaulting some Japanese tourists?" the lieutenant finished.

She considered that for a moment before giving a quick shake of her head. "Let's just catch them first and worry about the rest later."

The street they turned onto had more car and bus traffic than the other, and also a more X-shaped intersection topped at one end by a familiar-looking narrow building that had become iconic even in the year 1919.

"Times Square," she said, realizing where they were. "We need to catch them *now*."

"Too late. Look."

Ahead of them the five had come to a stop in the middle of the walkway. Then one of them turned to face the crowd in the direction of their pursuers. He smiled briefly, while behind him his team dispersed— in four different directions. He gave a short bow at the waist, turned away, and made his way quickly through the crowd in a fifth direction.

Agent Harris stopped cold, an angry sigh escaping her lips as she watched their quarry drift apart like a dandelion to the winds.

"Which one do we follow?" Lieutenant Phelps asked.

"We don't," she replied. "We'd lose both them and each other in this crowd. Best we can do is report back to Lou and take it from there."

She spared a moment to let her gaze follow the one who had smiled, until all view was cut off by an intervening taxi, and turned away feeling displeased with herself. Their walk back to the alley from which they had started would not be quite as fast, as Agent Harris silently berated herself.

12

EXAMINATION

Professor Stein made a point of searching around the bin, perhaps more thoroughly than he needed to, more to minimize contact with the dead body than anything else, leaving that job to Agent Hessman. Meanwhile Captain Beck and Dr. Weiss cleaned up any sign that might even suggest the presence of someone from another time.

Claire, however, was only too eager to be observing Agent Hessman's examination. "An *actual* dead body to examine," she remarked with obvious enthusiasm. "That's *always* great for the story. I mean, I'm sorry that a man was killed and all, but the *story*—which has me wondering exactly what sort of story this all is leading to. What could be so important that this man was willing to die for it?"

"We'll know in a minute," Agent Hessman muttered.

Captain Beck glanced over and saw the reporter bending in closer as Agent Hessman searched the body, and knew his cue. He hurried over and gently pulled Claire away with a quiet word. "Why don't you leave Lou to his work and help out Ben, will you? There's a lot of area around that bin to search."

"What? Think a woman is too delicate to be around a dead body? I'm here for my story, and that body is the story. Now I will not—"

"Miss Hill, I do not think you are too delicate in the least; far from it, in fact. And you will have your story as soon as we figure out what's going on."

"Then why—"

In a rush to appease Miss Hill's curiosity but keep her away from anything she shouldn't see, Captain Beck used the first story that came to mind.

"Because our companion *Ben* is too delicate to be around dead bodies."

"What? How is that possible? The war—"

"Ben wasn't in the war," Captain Beck answered truthfully. "He was . . . teaching at a university the entire time."

"A man of letters? I figured him as a consultant of some sort, but . . . so he's never been outside the university before?"

"This would be his first . . . mission in the field, yes. Now, if you wouldn't mind . . ."

"Oh, sure," she said, with a brief cough. "But if you find anything—"

"We'll let you know, Miss Hill."

Captain Beck watched as Claire walked over to where Professor Stein was searching; then he gave a brief sigh of relief and squatted down beside Agent Hessman. "I got our reporter occupied with something else," the captain whispered to him, "in case this guy has some items on him that no one in this time should see."

"Good," the agent answered, "because I've already found one suspiciously modern-looking device that could be their equivalent of one of our beacons. As for what else I've found . . ."

While the pair conversed in low tones, Professor Stein emerged from the backside of the bin to nearly bump straight into Claire's knees as he was bent over searching the ground. Looking up, he saw what might be described as a stern beauty; her pretty facial features were twisted into the sort of look a school matron might give a disobedient student caught in the act. Seeing her with her hands on her hips and elbows akimbo, he wasn't sure whether to admire her or swallow that lump he felt suddenly form in his throat.

"You're a strange one, Ben. Robert just told me how you'd never been in the war."

"Well, yes, that's true, but it's not because I was—"

"You could have just said you were an academic. I'd have understood."

"Well, I guess I couldn't be sure if—I mean . . ."

He had straightened up to face her, unsure which way to take this story, when Claire gave her opinion. "As much as some might have wanted to pitch in, academics and intellectuals have no place on the battlefield. Just get themselves killed."

"That was . . . much what I was thinking, yes," he admitted hesitantly.

"Which is why it's so puzzling. Why then are you out here now on what could be a very dangerous mission? One man's already been killed."

"I . . . that is . . . this mission is simply too important."

"More important than the Great War?"

"You have no idea. Listen, I can't talk about it—that would be up to Lou—but just know that I'm not a coward. At least I don't think so. It's just that the circumstances of my life never led me into war. Beyond that, I'm afraid I can't say anything more."

She looked at him for a moment longer, studying him as if perhaps he might be the story she sought more so than the dead body. "You're not lying," she said. "I'd know it if you were. But you're not telling the full truth either. There's something more."

Her ruminations were interrupted by two things—a cough escaping her lips and a call from Agent Hessman. "Ben, I need you to look at this."

Only too grateful for the interruption, he hurried over to where Agent Hessman was standing up holding something, Captain Beck beside him, and now Dr. Weiss coming over to join them as well.

"What'd you find?" Professor Stein asked quietly once he had joined the group.

Agent Hessman held up a picture, but one out of step with the current time. The old picture was printed on paper far more modern than anything the year 1919 had. It was a picture of a Japanese gentleman in uniform, and on the back were printed the words "General Hideki Tojo."

"Their mission would seem to involve this man," Agent Hessman stated while Professor Stein examined the photo. "What do you know of such a person?"

"Wow," was all Professor Stein said at first. "Tojo himself. They certainly aim big."

"You know of him?" Dr. Weiss asked.

"Any hist—anyone in my field would. He's the one who ordered the bombing of Pearl Harbor and was responsible for the campaign of horrors the Japanese instigated on their prisoners of war. Or at least he will be in a few years. You think he's their target?"

"Got to be," Agent Hessman stated. "But the problem is, what would they want with him?"

"Wait, *what* bombing of Pearl Harbor? I would have heard of something like that. What do you guys know?"

That's when they all remembered that not only was Miss Claire Hill still present but she apparently now stood within hearing range and was not afraid to remind them of that fact. Professor Stein looked over to discover that she had followed along behind him and was not much farther than an arm's length away. For a moment he was flustered, trying to think of what to say. Then Agent Hessman spoke up and flashed the picture in her direction. "Tell me what *you* know, Miss Hill. What have you heard about a Japanese man named Tojo? This is important."

She took the photo, studying it for a moment before replying. "I'd *love* to know what photographic paper you guys used for this. Tojo, hmm . . . some sort of dignitary from Japan. Not a general, but—"

"So he's here? In America?" Agent Hessman asked.

"Yes, but I couldn't say why. Something all hush-hush." She handed the photo back and continued thinking aloud. "But it's something to do with a meeting of some sort, not a Japanese cultural house."

"That may be something the Japanese team didn't know," Dr. Weiss suggested.

"Agreed," Agent Hessman said. "This was their first best guess as to where to find him. Well done, Claire."

"Thanks, but this brings up a few questions," she shot back. "Like, why would a team from Japan not know where their own dignitary is staying? Are they assassins or something? What is it that you guys aren't telling me?"

"Easy there, Claire," Professor Stein said, interposing himself between her and the others. "You know about as much of this as we do right now. We said before that we don't really know what their mission is, only that it's not good."

"Again, while you're not lying, you're still leaving something out. What is it you aren't telling me?"

For a moment their gazes met, hers a look of determination rare for anyone of this century or even his own, his a curious mix of emotions he wasn't sure of himself. Their moment, however, was interrupted by Harris and Phelps jogging back into the courtyard from the alley.

"We lost them at Times Square," Agent Harris announced as they rejoined the others. "They split up, so we thought it best to just come back. You find anything on the body?"

"A clue." Agent Hessman held up the photo. "They're after this man. He'll be at a meeting somewhere."

"That doesn't narrow it down much," Agent Harris noted.

"Doesn't it?" Agent Hessman pocketed the photo as he explained. "We know that meeting's in New York City, or the Japanese team wouldn't be here. And if he's an important dignitary, the meeting he'll be at will be one with *other* important dignitaries. Something with quite a bit of security around it."

"Then what do we do next?" Dr. Weiss asked.

"Next?" Claire put in. "There's a *body* here. We're going to have to call in the police."

"Sue," Agent Hessman said, ignoring Claire's small outburst, "you lost them at Times Square, so that's where we go next."

Agent Harris nodded in acknowledgement. Then, as Claire was saying, "But the body—" Agent Hessman shot a glance to Professor Stein, who made a point of drawing her away by the shoulders to talk to her a few feet away, maneuvering her so that her back was to the body.

"Claire, we'll need your help on this. You're a native of New York City, we aren't, and Times Square can be a very confusing and crowded place . . ."

Meanwhile Agent Hessman bent down and ran a hand inside the dead man's coat, producing what he had found earlier, the device he had determined to be their beacon, fashioned to look like some decorative medallion with a large red stone in the center. Working quickly while Professor Stein talked to Claire, he placed it directly on the body's chest, slapped a hand to the red stone, and jumped back.

A dim glow rose up from within the body, quickly eating away from within it, the body falling away into glowing embers that were sucked into the red stone until all that was left was the beacon itself, hovering for a moment inches above the ground. Then a final flash and the beacon folded in on itself, gone into a point of light, then nothing.

"As much as I know a meeting with the police will slow things down," Claire was saying as she turned around to face the others, "we can't just leave—where'd it go?"

"Where'd what go, Claire?" Dr. Weiss asked.

"The body, of course."

"Gone," was all Agent Hessman would say. "Now let's get moving."

"But to where?" she asked. "And will anyone find it? And how'd you move it so quickly? My back was turned for just a moment."

But no matter how determined her questions or how much she glared at Professor Stein, no answer would be forthcoming. They left with Agent Harris in the lead to guide them along the route to Times Square, none of them speaking another word about the body.

13

TRACKING

They surveyed the situation from one end of Times Square, Agent Hessman's penetrating gaze absorbing every detail, while Agent Harris indicated the directions she had seen the Japanese team split up into. Even now, a century in their past, Times Square was a surging sea of bodies and vehicles, although gas-powered mixed with horse-drawn in 1919, while a thousand pairs of feet negotiated the walkways along and across streets.

Agent Hessman stated the obvious conclusion: "This is a tracker's nightmare. They picked the perfect place to split up."

"You ought to catch this place when everyone gets off from work," Claire remarked. "If you were hoping for any clues, you'll never find them in this place."

"I think I quite agree with the young reporter," Agent Hessman remarked absently, still searching the area. "Which is why we need some— ah, perfect." He broke into a jog, weaving through the moving crowd, with the others behind him wondering what he had spotted. When they emerged from the crowd, beaming a straight line for a sidewalk newsstand, Agent Hessman's intent became clear.

"Excuse me," he said to the man in the newsstand, "but have you seen any Japanese men running or hurrying away from this area in the last few minutes?"

"That depends," the man stated flatly. "Were you going to buy something? I make my living selling papers, not answering questions."

Captain Beck reached into a pocket and pulled out a coin from his supply of period money to slap down on the wooden counter. He then took a copy of the nearest newspaper.

"Group of them," the newsstand man then replied. "Looked like they was running from someone, then split up."

"Could you tell us where they went?" Agent Hessman asked.

"Another question, another paper," the man stated.

This time it was Agent Hessman who produced the coin, but he kept his hand on it as he looked the man in the eye. "A paper a question, okay; then here's my *one* question. What are each of the directions those Japanese men ran to?"

The man grinned in reply, actually chuckling as he pulled out one of the papers himself to hand to Agent Hessman. "You got me there. Guess it's only the one additional paper at that. Okay, the first one headed over that way, and . . ." He pointed to each of the directions he had seen the Japanese men depart, Agent Hessman noting each carefully in turn before releasing his coin into the man's care, taking the offered paper, and leading the group away to some relative privacy.

"Miss Hill," Agent Hessman asked, "what can you tell us about what's in each of those directions?"

"Hmm . . ." Claire looked out across Times Square, trying to picture the five different courses. "There's a couple of theaters in that direction . . . some manufacturing over there . . . I think the wharf is in that direction if you go far enough . . . Central Park would be over in that direction . . ."

"That's got to be it," Agent Hessman said. "What better place for a team to reassemble than Central Park? Easy to locate and get to, yet big enough they could easily lose themselves in there. Good job, Claire. How far is it?"

"There's a streetcar we could hop that would have us there in no time," she said. "This way."

She led them in a brisk walk a little way down the street, Professor Stein coming up to walk alongside her, the rest staying close. "The one advantage of Times Square," she was saying, "is that you can catch a trolley here to just about anywhere in town. Horse-drawn, electric, whatever's your preference."

"Quickest one, I would think," Professor Stein told her.

"Then this one should do it," Claire said.

She led them to a trolley stop where a nearly empty horse-drawn streetcar was coming to a pause. Agent Hessman produced a bill of 1919 currency to cover them all and led the way on board. Agent Harris was last on board, keeping a sharp eye out for any threats to her team. Then she spotted it.

A man in the crowd pulled out a pistol that caught her eye, both for the type of gun it was and the direction it was aimed.

"Down!" To her cry, everyone flattened themselves to the floor of the trolley car, Agent Harris diving in just as the shot rang out. A second shot also missed but spooked the horse into a premature run while passengers and pedestrians screamed and dove for cover. Agent Harris barely pulled her feet in as the trolley got off to a sudden start. She took Lieutenant Phelps's offered hand to get to her feet.

"Sue?" Agent Hessman questioned.

"Man with a pistol," she said as she stepped over beside him. "Only, while the gun *looks* period to the untrained eye, it didn't come out until 1930."

"Looks like one of their team found *us*," Captain Beck stated.

"Yeah, except that the man's not Japanese. I'll need to look through your record book to identify him, but I'd say we have another player in this game."

The shooter hopped onto another streetcar heading out ahead of them, a gun that should not yet exist held tightly in his hand.

14

TROLLEY CHASE

The horse-drawn trolley held the seven of them, plus a young couple at the back, as well as the driver. The shooter had hopped onto an electric streetcar headed in the same direction but ahead of them and crowded with bystanders gasping at the man with the gun. The driver of their trolley had pulled the gun-spooked horses down to a more sedate pace when Lieutenant Phelps leaped into the seat next to him and glared at him.

"Follow that trolley, and *hurry*."

Something about the large man's tone and the amount of muscle he was flexing spurred the driver into instant agreement. With a flick of the reigns and a sharp cry, he sped up the trolley.

"Robert," Agent Hessman snapped, "that derringer of yours—"

"Not enough range," the captain answered.

"Just get me close enough and I'll break the hand holding that gun," Agent Harris vowed.

A jingle signaled the trolley's approach to its next stop, but much to the surprise of those waiting there, the trolley did not even pause. Not under the constant urging of Lieutenant Phelps. It raced on by, closing in on the streetcar as another shot spat out, this time aimed at Phelps.

The bullet glanced off the frame of the speeding trolley, and nearly everyone ducked. The driver had nowhere to duck *to*, and the couple in the back were too occupied with one another to notice anything but each other's lips.

"Get us closer to that thing," Lieutenant Phelps urged the driver.

"That's an electric streetcar," the man began. "I can't—"

"And you have a pair of horses that can go *faster*, so do it!"

Another cry to the pair of horses, and Manhattan saw a trolley giving chase to a streetcar and actually catching up to it. At least until they came to the next intersection, where the man with the gun jumped off the streetcar and onto another moving behind it on a perpendicular course.

"I can only follow the track," their driver said before the lieutenant could ask. "I can't make a turn like that."

Agent Hessman called out, "Stop the trolley!"

The trolley was pulled to an abrupt halt, an act that apparently did nothing to disturb the kissing couple at the back. Before it was barely to a complete stop, Agent Harris led the charge down the opposing street, racing for another trolley going in that direction.

The next gunshot didn't happen, as the gun jammed in the shooter's hand, affording the American team time enough to board another trolley, on which the lieutenant once again commandeered the driver's services. This trolley was nearly full, so Agent Harris hung on by one arm and a leg while the others crowded in as best they could.

Dr. Weiss looked nervous, Professor Stein worried, and Claire excited.

"A trolley chase!" She beamed. "This will make for an exciting segment of the story for sure."

The horses were in as close to a gallop as their burden and attached equipment would allow, speeding down the street, barely avoiding cross traffic, the driver frantically ringing the trolley bell and shouting out apologies as he passed people. The streetcar had a decent lead on them, but then electric streetcars couldn't be made to gallop if in a rush.

They approached the streetcar, where the shooter had apparently failed to unjam his gun and looked increasingly frustrated. Agent Hessman squeezed his way into the front of the trolley, while from behind came the dismayed cries of other passengers wondering why it was going faster and passing up their stops.

"Just a bit closer," Agent Harris called out. "I'll try a flying tackle before he can unjam his gun."

This time the shooter didn't wait for an intersection. Pocketing his useless weapon, he glanced around for a good target, then leapt off the moving streetcar, rolled up to his feet, and ran. Agent Harris was after him in an instant with the same tuck and roll, while Lieutenant Phelps had the driver bring the trolley to an unscheduled stop.

Agent Hessman's team were not the only ones to exit; many of the passengers had had enough of speeding trolleys and missed stops. The rest of the team piled out while Agent Harris ran to catch up with the shooter. She leaped, hands outstretched to grab at the first body part she made contact with. She came down, wrapping an arm around one of the man's legs, and rolled her body into him to trip him up.

Her plan nearly worked, until the base of the man's pistol came out, swinging into her shoulder. With a cry, she released her grip, and the man continued running to the nearest vehicle. By the time the others caught up with Agent Harris, the man was leaping into a taxi and shoving the driver out of his own vehicle.

"Sue, are you okay?" Agent Hessman asked, running up.

He was the first to offer an arm to help her up, Professor Stein bringing up the rear with Claire, who was gaping in shock that someone had just clubbed a woman.

Agent Harris came up wincing with pain, but she *did* get up. "I'll be okay," she said, shaking her arm out, "but he's getting away."

Even now, the taxi the man had stolen was racing down the street at a bracing forty miles an hour. Captain Beck quickly raised a hand to flag down the next taxi, but by the time one had stopped, the other was already nearly a block away.

"Quickly," Captain Beck told the driver as they all piled in. "You see that yellow cab up ahead? Catch it and there's a good tip in it for you."

"Yes, *sir.*"

Captain Beck sat up front by the driver, the rest in the two rows behind them, with Dr. Weiss examining Agent Harris's injury.

"How's it look?" she asked.

"I'm not that type of doctor," he replied. "How's it feel?"

"I'm not that type of patient," she answered. "If it's still attached, I keep on moving."

Their driver was flooring it, their speed creeping closer to forty-five before they came to an intersection where a traffic cop was signaling them to stop. But when the one they were chasing refused to stop, Captain Beck reached out with one foot and slammed it down on top of the driver's foot before it could lift off the gas pedal.

"Don't stop for anything," the captain told the man.

They raced on through the intersection, horns honking as the oncoming traffic formed cloverleaves around them, trying not to hit anything. Somewhere a police whistle blew and several people shouted, all of which the team ignored. When the taxi up ahead made a sharp turn, so did they; when it sped up, they sped up even more. Slowly the gap narrowed; then came a sharp crack of thunder as a piece of the cab chipped off.

"My cab!"

"Looks like he's got his gun working again," Captain Beck called back.

"Just keep on him," Agent Hessman called. "Sue—"

"Well enough," she replied.

"I wonder if this is what it was like for Nellie Bly in the war," Claire said. "The perspective of being the one shot *at* instead of merely observing others being shot. I must say it's . . ."

"Thrilling?" Professor Stein suggested.

"Terrifying! I don't know how she did it."

The taxi ahead of them made another sharp turn, but this time when they followed it, they came to a dismaying sight. The cab had pulled up alongside a hotel in front of which were several other taxis parked two and three abreast. It parked beside one group of them. As the Americans neared, they could see the man crawl quickly from his vehicle into the passenger portion of the first taxi in that group, where they lost direct sight of him. When that taxi took off, though, Captain Beck was already urging their driver into pursuit.

Then they saw the second cab start up and drive away, followed by the third one abreast. By the time their taxi had finished turning to follow the first one, the other two were also driving away in different directions.

"Follow the first one," Captain Beck told the driver.

This chase was not nearly as long; in fact, the one they were chasing was only moving at the sedate pace of thirty-five miles an hour. They raced on down the street and got ahead of the other taxi by a car length to cut it off, the result of which was a near pileup. With drivers shouting and cussing all around, Lieutenant Phelps leaped out and ran over to the other cab, ripping the door wide open as the others joined him in surrounding the vehicle with their bodies.

"Empty," Lieutenant Phelps announced.

"Driver," Agent Hessman called up, "where'd your passenger go?"

"What's the big emergency, cutting me off like that? You could have wrecked my taxi!"

"I'll pay you for your troubles," Agent Hessman said. "Now where did he go? Please, it's important."

The man shrugged, then, as Lieutenant Phelps took out a small wad of bills, shrugged out a reply. "He paid me to just drive until the fare ran out, then got out the other side for the next taxi in line and told me to go. I didn't see after that."

Agent Hessman silently cussed under his breath and then nodded to Lieutenant Phelps. While Phelps took care of paying both taxi drivers, Hessman stepped away with a word for his other teammates. "We saw two other taxis leaving at the same time," Captain Beck stated. "He could be in either one of them."

"Or neither," Agent Hessman stated. "Make us think we had a one-in-three chance when in reality we had none at all."

"Still back at that hotel," Dr. Weiss said with a snap of his fingers.

"Not anymore," Agent Hessman stated. "We just gave him enough time to get away. Everyone, status."

"I'll manage," Agent Harris replied. "Just a little bruise."

"I don't think we left any signs in our wake," Dr. Weiss reported.

"At least nothing that time won't soon forget," Professor Stein added.

"Both taxi drivers paid up in full," Lieutenant Phelps reported.

"So who was that?" Captain Beck asked.

"We're about to find out." The team formed a circle of flesh around Agent Hessman, shielding him from view while he discreetly brought out his own little handheld data device. A couple of swipes of his finger and he motioned Agent Harris over for a quick look at the pictures scrolling by on the small screen.

"That one," she said, pointing to one.

"Are you sure?" Agent Hessman asked.

"Completely."

Agent Hessman sighed. "Then we have a new wrinkle. Because that's one of the people from the German team."

"The *Germans*?" Dr. Weiss exclaimed. "I thought it was the Japanese that created the TDW."

"I don't know what to say," Agent Hessman began, quickly putting his small device away within his coat. "At first it looked like—"

A slight cough cut him off, as all members of the team turned to see who had made the sound. Claire Hill stood there, hands akimbo as she addressed the team members with a fixed glare.

"If I might ask . . . what is a TDW?"

Answers would not be forthcoming to that question either.

15

REGROUPING

The taxi they had given chase in would be getting one more fare from them, though not for chasing another taxi this time. Agent Hessman kept it simple as he paid the man in advance. "Get us to Central Park."

Claire tried to position herself directly in the middle of the group, the better to catch what everyone was saying, until Harris and Phelps pulled her into the rearmost row to sit wedged between them while putting a hand each over one of her ears. That left the others to talk, while the driver made a point of not listening to anything anyone said as he drove them through the city.

"The Japanese *and* now the Germans," Agent Hessman pondered aloud. "Are they here for the same thing or completely different motives? Or did they come in response to the Japanese team?"

"It could be more complicated than that," Dr. Weiss stated. "While both teams arrived back here the same as we did, the Germans might not have left until as much as, say, ten or fifty years after we did. We don't have anything on us to track what year they came *from*."

"A very good, if disturbing, point," Agent Hessman admitted. "But that may not change much at this point. We know now that the Japanese have come back for Tojo. Ben, you said that it was Tojo who caused all that misery."

"He was the chief architect of everything that happened in the— that other war," Professor Stein replied, careful of his words with other ears around that shouldn't be hearing any of this. "The attack, the camps, all of it."

"So let's assume that we're in the first iteration of history," Agent Hessman continued. "Tojo did all the horrible things he did, which means now the Japanese team is here to change all that. They want to stop or even kill General Tojo before he becomes a general. The question is why? What do they gain out of it?"

"It could be any of several objectives," Professor Stein stated.

"They came out of that war pretty bad," Dr. Weiss suggested. "Maybe they want to stop their entry into it and avoid all that."

"But look what they grew into being in *our* day," Professor Stein countered. "Or maybe without Tojo, an even better general is allowed to come into play who could win them their part of the war before Germany loses theirs. We don't have enough data to really know."

"And even less for the Germans," Agent Hessman said. "But with them entering this mix, I can't help but suspect that both teams' motives lead back to the next Great War. Two of the three member nations of the old Axis back in this same time period? I'm not a believer of coincidence when it comes to this sort of stuff. If Italy had a machine, I'd expect to see them here next."

"Italy was more of a client state of Germany before the war was midway through," Professor Stein interjected. "But you're right. It's looking like that war is the focus we're looking for; we just don't yet know why."

Before their ponderings could get much further along, Claire finally managed to push her way forward and pry herself free of Harris's and Phelps's clamping hands long enough to launch a question in a more determined voice than before. "Now listen, I agreed to help you, but this is a *partnership*, and as such I demand to know what it is you people are into. First the Japanese, and now some Germans, and you still haven't told me what any of this is about. If you don't tell me something soon, then my next story is going to figure a few of *your* names rather prominently."

The men looked from one to another. Finally Captain Beck's gaze rested pointedly on Professor Stein, accompanied by a harsh whisper in his direction. "Ben, handle it before we're forced to find another way."

"Well, I must admit," he replied, "while I am starting to admire her tenacity, this is not the time for that." He moved around in his seat to face her, and Harris and Phelps scooted far enough away to give her a little freedom of movement while keeping an eye out on the road ahead. "Claire," Professor Stein began, "the parts we have to keep from you are a matter of national security."

"I get that part, but don't you think the secrecy is getting a *little* bit too melodramatic? I deserve to know *something*. I'll only write what it is you guys clear me for, but I deserve—no, I *need* to know."

He considered her words for a moment and replied with a nod, "You're right, but for reasons we cannot tell anyone, our secrecy must be maintained. Sue here? She's a lot more than you might suspect. Her orders are to see to the safety of this team under any circumstances. If she thought you were a threat, she would drop you in your tracks before you could take in another breath."

"What, her?" Claire said. "But she's just—"

"Watch it," Agent Harris cut in. "No version of that sentence will end up doing anything but displeasing me."

Claire glanced to the woman beside her, saw the challenging look in her eyes, and relented. "Okay, I apologize for that. But what manner of—"

"And Robert here," Professor Stein continued, "as far as *his* orders are concerned, every single member of this entire team is expendable as long as our mission is completed. So when I warn you that there are some things that we must keep from you, believe me."

She thought over his words for a few moments as the taxi turned a corner, then replied in a less harsh tone, "Okay, I get it. But what *can* you tell me about what's going on?"

"Well, all we know for certain is that a team from Japan is here on a mission that somehow involves one of their own countrymen and possibly the security of this nation. As far as the German we encountered, we know even less, but his presence means there's another team around here with a mission of their own. For reasons we cannot get into, we believe the two to be related, though in what way we honestly do not know. Is there something more that we're keeping from you? Yes, but as far as the pertinent facts, that's all of it. Will this satisfy you for a while?"

She coughed and after a moment, nodded. "I guess it will have to," she replied.

"Good."

Professor Stein was just turning around to face front again when the driver called out, "Central Park on the right. Just passing up the East Green with the menagerie coming up in a bit."

"Okay, driver, here would be fine," Agent Hessman told him. "And about our conversations—"

"You'd be surprised how many times I've been paid not to hear anything as much as I've been paid just to drive." The man grinned.

"Not a problem," Agent Hessman said as the vehicle pulled to a stop. "Will a twenty percent tip do?"

"Better make it thirty," the man replied. "There was some really odd-ball stuff that I didn't hear."

Agent Hessman pulled out a few bills, handed them to a rather pleased-looking cab driver, and exited the cab with everyone else. They were left walking down Fifth Avenue with Central Park on their right, and ahead of them the entrance to the Central Park Menagerie—what would one day be named the Central Park Zoo.

"Let's just hope it's not too late to catch them," Agent Hessman remarked as they walked.

"I'm thinking not," Agent Harris said, coming up alongside him. "Over there by the front gates. That's them."

A grand arch of brick and wrought iron spanned the flow of people coming and going beneath it, but amid that flow was a cluster of Japanese men milling about and seemingly making a point of not catching anyone's eye.

"I can't see their faces too well," Dr. Weiss stated. "How do you know it's them?"

"Can you think of any *other* group of five Japanese," Agent Harris replied, "comprised all of males who *aren't* a family that would be milling around in front of a zoo trying *that* hard to blend in and not get noticed?"

"She's right," Claire agreed. "Say, they probably don't know my face. Maybe if I just went up to them and—"

"Come *on*!" To her own command, Agent Harris waited for no one and started into a charge, followed nearly immediately by Lieutenant Phelps, who had quietly vowed not to let them get away this time.

"Just don't stand there," Agent Hessman told the rest. "There are no civilians on this mission. Before they spot us!"

They all took off as fast as they could run, before any of their targets might turn to see them.

16

CENTRAL PARK MENAGERIE

They were nearly to the front gates when one of the Japanese men turned and spotted the group of people running directly for his team. The men exchanged quick words and then bolted, heading straight through the gates and into the menagerie. Agent Harris led the charge after them, weaving around visitors and bolting through the main gate before she could be asked for any admission fee. After Harris came Phelps, who shoved the attendant aside, followed by Dr. Weiss with a quick "Very sorry," then Professor Stein and Claire, the latter making a point of pointing to the "Press" card sticking out of her hat while holding it to her head with her other hand. After them Agent Hessman went running past, shouting, "Important business!"

This left Captain Beck to bring up the rear and pause briefly at the gate as the admissions attendant was picking himself up. "Guess it's up to me. Well, uh, this should cover the bunch of us."

He pulled out a couple of bills, dropped them into the man's hands, then broke into a run while tossing a quick comment back over his shoulder to the confused attendant. "It's those tigers. We're all *really* eager to see them."

The chase brought them first to the sea lion pool and the people crowding around it, trying to get a glimpse of the creatures sunning themselves on their rock within the fence that surrounded the whole large pool. One of the Japanese knocked a lady's parasol out of her hands, another shoved a man in his way, while a third tipped over the cart of a passing vendor, spilling warmed peanuts across the ground. Anything to create some obstacles between themselves and their pursuers.

Agent Harris ran around the lady, retrieving her parasol, leaped over the fallen man, and didn't miss a step dashing through the strewn peanuts and the crowd of kids who had formed in eager retrieval of the vendor's stock of supplies from the ground. Behind her, Lieutenant Phelps paused to pick up the lady and her parasol, depositing them gently out of the way as the others ran past him.

"You're just making it harder on yourselves when I catch up with you," Agent Harris called out.

Around the perimeter of the large pond one of the five ran, passing a man carrying a large bucket of fish for the sea lions' feeding time. The worker gave a wide grin to the eager crowd, which quickly soured when one of the Japanese men reached in and threw a fish at Agent Harris, followed by two more before he continued running. Agent Harris batted the fish away, but dealing with that cost her a few precious seconds. Lieutenant Phelps and Dr. Weiss caught up to her just as she was starting up again.

"Where are the others?" she asked when she saw no one else with them.

"Going around the other side of the pond to cut them off," Dr. Weiss replied.

"Then let's *move* it."

As foretold, coming around from the other side to meet with the Japanese was Agent Hessman leading Professor Stein, Captain Beck, and Claire, who seemed to be enjoying everything about the chase except running in women's shoes. "Someone should . . . invent proper . . . shoes for running," she panted.

"You mean like something without heels?" Professor Stein ventured.

"Exactly!"

"Then maybe they'll call them sneakers," he added quietly with a slight grin she didn't catch.

Trapped between both ends, the opposing team headed straight toward the building behind them. Agent Harris saw them charge straight inside and pointed to signal the others as she ran after them.

"That's the bird house," Claire called up. "Nothing but bird cages, nowhere to escape to."

"It would seem so," Agent Hessman replied. "Hurry!"

Agent Harris was the first to make her way through, but as she reached the front doors, a charge of people made its way out, followed by a scattering of fluttering squawking birds.

"I have a bad feeling about this," Dr. Weiss remarked as he ran.

Agent Harris entered into bedlam. Ahead of her stretched the walkway that went past the various cages of birds large and small, several of which had been opened by the passing Japanese team, while yet another cage several yards down was being kicked open as well, followed by noises to encourage the flocks into chaotic flight. That got several people screaming and running, which in turn gave more of the birds reason to fly madly around.

"I don't know whether to start tossing people or birds out of the way," she remarked.

"You know how a cowcatcher on a train works?" Lieutenant Phelps told her. "That's me."

Not waiting for anyone's permission, Phelps brought his fists together, elbows sticking out to the sides, and proceeded to charge straight down the middle of the aisle, screaming at the top of his lungs. Be it person or bird, few had any taste for staying in the way of a human locomotive. The building filled with human cries, exploding with a storm of wings and protesting birds, but for a moment at least Phelps generated one clear path through the middle of it all, with the rest of his team following behind him.

At the other side of the enclosure, the Japanese team, thinking they might have finally made good their escape, took a glimpse back; but instead of seeing their pursuers caught in the midst of the mess, they saw what might have been an angry linebacker coming in for a tackle at the guy with the football—and they were the football. They exchanged quick words and used even quicker feet to head straight for the rear door, despite the presence of a sign saying, "Staff Only." They ran through and slammed the door behind them.

Lieutenant Phelps didn't bother using the doorknob to open the door but crashed right on through it. The team left flying feathers, angry birds, and confused attendees in their wake, and even more confused staff members. Ahead of them the path wound through another row of cages, branching out toward a small lake, a wooded area, an open field with a small herd of antelope from Africa, and other points of interest. The Japanese team was headed for the caged areas.

"If they open any of those cages the way they did for the birds . . . ," Claire began.

"Yeah, really bad news," Agent Hessman summed up. "Go for the slowest; if we capture one, we can question him."

Agent Harris saw one man lagging slightly behind the others and broke into a fresh run. The one she'd eyed was headed for a fenced-off brick enclosure, while his companions were each running for different caged areas.

"Not this again," Agent Harris swore under her breath. "I'm bringing at least *one* of them down!"

She increased her speed, but not without another remark under her breath. "Be a lot easier if I didn't have to run in these stupid boots."

One of the Japanese men went straight into the monkey cage, while another changed course and headed for the fenced-off grassy area where the African wildlife roamed free. The remaining two simply ran as fast along the path as they could.

"That brick building," Agent Hessman called back to Claire. "What is it?"

"The lion house," she said after a pant.

"You're out of breath," Professor Stein said as he came jogging up to Claire's side. "You should sit the rest of this one out."

"Not . . . on . . . your life . . . buster."

Harris and Phelps both headed for the lion house, while Captain Beck and Dr. Weiss ran for the man leaping the fence into the grasslands area.

"He's headed for those antelopes," Captain Beck stated.

"I think they're wildebeests," Dr. Weiss corrected.

"Same difference. Now *get* him."

The man they were after ran straight for the nearest creature, yelling and waving his hands at the complacent beast, until he ran up to the top of a convenient boulder, jumped . . . and landed right on the back of one of the creatures. This elicited two reactions, one each from man and creature. First the man howled in surprised pain, as one might expect the male of the species to do, coming down for a hard landing in such a way. Then the creature cried out and bucked, breaking into a run and trying to dislodge the interloper on its back.

Captain Beck and Dr. Weiss simply came to a stop and watched as the man rode the bucking creature across the field. "No," Dr. Weiss said, shaking his head, "not even gonna try. He can have this one."

"I'm with you there," Captain Beck agreed. "Come on, let's rejoin the others."

Harris and Phelps came crashing into the lion house to discover that their quarry had indeed tried opening the cage to create more chaos without first checking what was within it. Now he was backing fearfully away while the lion lazily wondered which of the screaming visitors before him to go after. A lion handler had just come on the scene, but that didn't seem to matter to the man as he backed away, shaking in fear, straight into two waiting pairs of hands.

"You got a choice," Agent Harris said into his left ear. "Come with us or we toss you to the lion."

"Take the lion," Lieutenant Phelps urged into the other ear. "It might leave you more intact if you struggle."

The man tried to spin around, but they had him in a firm grip between them, with Harris twisting one arm and Phelps simply squeezing his hand around the man's other arm until he feared he might hear something snap. The captured man spoke a few words in Japanese before he relented and spoke in English. "Okay, I come. Just get me away from that creature."

"That little pussy cat?" Agent Harris grinned.

Outside, Agent Hessman saw the two men running and the one going for the monkey cage and motioned Professor Stein and Claire back.

"Those other two can run faster than we can, and if the one going for the monkey cages has any success at letting those creatures loose, neither he nor we are going to come out the winners. Let's see what success Sue and David have had."

From the corner of his eye, he also saw Dr. Weiss and Captain Beck returning. Captain Beck simply shook his head.

"Got away," he said as they approached, "and there is no way we're going to catch him."

"Though I suspect he's not too happy about the mode of transportation that he chose," Dr. Weiss added with a grin.

A minute later, and much to everyone's pleasure, they saw Harris and Phelps coming out of the lion house with a single Japanese man gripped firmly between them.

"We got one at least," Lieutenant Phelps reported.

"Good, then we can question him and see what's going on," Agent Hessman said. "We need a nice quiet place."

"I suggest doing it outside of the menagerie," Claire told them. "If the local officials ever trace the chaos in the bird house to us—"

"Right," Agent Hessman agreed. "Which way?"

"The exit out into the park is that way," Claire pointed. "Plenty of peaceful open spaces."

"Then let's go."

With some guidance from Claire, Agent Hessman led the group swiftly through the zoo toward the exit into the interior of Central Park, ignoring for now what may have been the cry of some enraged monkeys as another member of the Japanese team tried to find his way out.

17

QUESTION TIME

They picked a spot under some trees around a park bench with nothing but a clear view of open lawn to satisfy Agent Harris's security considerations. Lieutenant Phelps had their prisoner in a discreet wristlock behind the man's back as he stood him before the bench where Agent Hessman and Dr. Weiss sat. Agent Harris took up position standing behind the bench, keeping her eyes peeled for possible trouble from all directions, while Professor Stein and Captain Beck stood with Claire several yards away.

"I can't hear a thing from here," the reporter protested.

"That is rather the idea, Miss Hill," Captain Beck replied. "Certain classified matters may come up during the questioning that I am afraid I cannot allow you to overhear."

"I thought this was a *team*," she protested, "with me as a part of it."

"You are, Claire," Professor Stein calmly told her. "And once we find out what he has to tell us, we'll fill you in."

"Filtered, of course," she pouted.

"It's as Robert said. There are certain matters that *no one* can be allowed to know about. More than that I cannot tell you."

"A fine partnership *this* turned out to be."

She folded her arms crossly and glared at Professor Stein, but if she expected him to back down or flinch, to her surprise he did not. He met her gaze, then likewise folded his arms as he turned to face her full-on. For a few moments the pair simply stood, exchanging determined glares, until Claire spoke first, though her stance never shifted. "I'd not have thought a man who hadn't seen combat action could be so stubborn."

"And I'd not have thought a woman of this age could be so . . . determined," Professor Stein shot back.

"Maybe I was born a few decades too early, but that doesn't change the fact that I *will* find out what's going on. You just watch."

"I will."

She coughed once before resuming her glaring contest.

At the bench, meanwhile, Agent Hessman was sitting calmly, looking up at their prisoner, who was short, of slender build, with black hair trimmed to his ears, and dressed much like most men in this city, with a suit, high white collar, and matching vest. While Lieutenant Phelps held the prisoner secure, Agent Hessman reached out and thoughtfully fingered the end of the man's jacket.

"A fine material . . . except, as I'm sure Ben might confirm, nylon was not invented until about a decade or more later. You have to watch slipups like that. What if one of you gets caught by the more *local* authorities?"

The man said nothing but met Agent Hessman's gaze in silent protest.

"I want to keep this friendly, but if it comes to it, David here can break your arm *and* paralyze your vocal cords at the same time so no one can hear you scream. Now, let's start with the basics. My name is Lou. What do I call you? And *please* don't reply with the old cliché of spitting in my face as an answer. This is not an old spy film; I just want to find out what's going on. So: Name?"

The man seemed to think on the matter for a moment, felt an increasing pressure on one shoulder from the lieutenant, and replied with a grunt before voicing an answer. "Eiji Sato."

"Very good. Okay, Eiji, I'll tell you what we know of things; then you can feel free to fill in the blanks, okay?"

Agent Hessman sat back, assuming a bit more relaxed position, but never once did his gaze leave the other man. Eiji's eyes darted around, pausing briefly on the glaring contest between Professor Stein and the reporter, then with a questioning look back to Agent Hessman.

"Oh, Miss Hill is not with our team. She's more of a local, so for both our sakes, if you could keep your answers to discreet tones, I would appreciate it."

Eiji nodded slightly. The next words he spoke were just loud enough to be heard by those at the bench and missed by the reporter several yards away.

"I do not know much," he began. "I am the weapons specialist. You killed our history expert."

"It was not our intent to kill, merely to discover what's going on," Dr. Weiss stated. "We recorded a TDW from this period, which necessitated an immediate investigation. When I searched his body, I found this." Agent Hessman pulled out the photo and held it briefly up for Eiji to see before repocketing it.

"General Tojo. Quite the notorious figure to be looking for, don't you think? Now, a few possibilities come to mind when I look at this picture. You could be thinking to offer him some advice on how to win a certain upcoming war, or at least when to stop pushing against the United States and simply hold on to what you've gained. Or maybe if you kill him, a better general might come along. So, which is it?"

Eiji said nothing at first, just looked around, but all he saw in the distance were groups of people enjoying the park, strolling, or sitting on the vast grassy lawn, a few clustering by a large fountain or recently added statue. Nothing, however, in the way of suggestive help.

"I doubt if your team's reassembled quite yet," Agent Hessman stated. "And I'm not waiting long enough for them to mount a rescue. We're on the clock here, so just tell us what you know."

The man paused briefly, considering his options, and finally he explained. "It is not as you think. Our involvement in the Second World War was a great dishonor upon the face of my nation. Before that, Japan was enjoying prosperity."

"Hold on a second," Agent Hessman cut in. "This sounds like something our own history expert needs to hear. Ben!"

Ben broke off from the glaring contest to see Agent Hessman signaling him, and gave a polite nod to the reporter. "I'm sorry, Claire, but my services seem to be required."

"And mine aren't? Why, I've half a mind to—"

Captain Beck laid a firm but gentle hand on her shoulder as Professor Stein walked quickly over to join the others by the bench. "You people are infuriating," she fumed, ending with another cough.

"And you should do something about that cough," the captain noted.

Professor Stein came over to stand before Agent Hessman and their prisoner.

"He was just telling us how Japan was enjoying a successful economy during this time period," Agent Hessman began.

"They were," Professor Stein replied. "It was quite the prosperous democracy until the military establishment decided to try things *their* way."

Agent Hessman then eyed Eiji, who picked up his explanation. "As I said, that war was a great dishonor for my country."

"But you rose to economic prominence afterward," Professor Stein pointed out.

"But we had it before," Eiji replied. "Between the war and the rebuilding, many years were wasted that we could have been enjoying the prosperity we had before."

"So you came here to kill Tojo?" Agent Hessman filled in.

"Yes," Eiji answered. "With General Tojo dead, we will not have entered the disaster that was the Second World War."

"Resulting in continued economic prosperity," Professor Stein added. "Economic victory without the war for which you would be reviled for many years thereafter. Not to mention that the atomic bomb doesn't get used."

"Exactly," Eiji said in terse syllables. "Japan enjoys far greater prosperity while erasing its dishonor."

Dr. Weiss now spoke up. "But Eiji, you must realize that time may not work out that way. There are many other variables involved that could still lead your country back into war or even worse results."

"It is not my position to debate such matters; I am just a soldier. If this is a chance for my country to maintain its post–World War I prosperity while avoiding the mess that was the Second World War, then it is my duty to see it through. I understand why you came back to check the TDE, but you should be wishing my team well. After all, no Pearl Harbor."

"Tempting, I'll admit," Agent Hessman admitted.

"But the flow of time may be self-correcting," Dr. Weiss pointed out.

"Or we might get a world without the atomic bomb," Professor Stein said. "Imagine that."

"But as you say," Agent Hessman stated, "we could also end up with something even worse. Eiji, what about the German team? What is your involvement with them? We know there must be a German team here also; we ran afoul of one of its members."

"We do not work with them," Eiji replied. "In fact, part of our goal is to discover what the German mission is. Much like yours is to discover *our* purpose."

"Hmm, another mystery," Agent Hessman pondered aloud. "The Japanese want to erase their involvement in World War II, while the Germans . . . what?"

He sat there for a moment, then nodded to Lieutenant Phelps, who pulled Eiji back far enough so Agent Hessman could stand up.

"What's our next move?" Dr. Weiss asked as he, too, stood up.

"We need more information on current events," Agent Hessman decided. "Gather everyone up. We need to find another newsstand."

At a motion from Agent Hessman, Captain Beck pulled Claire back into the group as they took off across the wide lawn of Central Park, though not without a few words from the reporter.

"What'd you find out?" she demanded. "Come on, you've got to tell me *something*."

But they did not, adding to the growing list of questions that Claire Hill had for her alleged partners.

18

REPORTER FACE-OFF

The team found another newsstand alongside the street outside Central Park, Captain Beck once again flipping out a coin for a paper while muttering something about not losing this one in a gunfight. Claire, meanwhile, was voicing her verbal objections to Agent Hessman, Professor Stein, and anyone else on the team who would listen.

"Listen, I know a *lot* about what's going on in this city."

"I imagine that comes with being a nosey reporter," Agent Hessman replied blandly.

"A *tenacious* one," she corrected. "And there's a lot that you could tell me, but you guys have *got* to talk to me. Tell me what's going on, or I don't talk."

"That hasn't seemed to have stopped you yet," Agent Hessman remarked as he leafed through the paper.

"What?" she gasped. "Why, I don't think I've ever—"

"Claire," Professor Stein cut in, "you have to understand that—"

"And what's more," she continued, "I suspect that you aren't federal agents at all. Now *that* would be a guaranteed story that I could take to the police. You guys get jail time, and I get a story about some rogue element or group of spies going on with their own secret mission. Sounds like a story that could *really* sell papers."

She planted her feet firmly on the ground and held her stance right there in front of them, the look on her face daring them to cross her. Agent Harris looked a question to Agent Hessman, who replied with a slight shake of his head, and returned Claire's determined gaze with a calm one of his own.

"I can keep this up *all* day," she said.

"She can," Professor Stein acknowledged. "She can glare with the best of them."

For a moment, Agent Hessman and Claire simply stared at one another, she with a focused fury, he with calm regard as he seemed to analyze her every nuance of expression. All the while, groups of pass-ersby came and went around them, ignorant of the import of what was transpiring within their very midst. Finally he broke the stalemate with a calmly voiced statement.

"You do a very good bluff, Miss Hill . . . Very well, we are not with any federal agency that you would know of."

"Ha! I *knew* it. So what are you, spies with some other faction? Anarchists?"

"However," he continued, "we *are* trying to protect the interests of the United States. That's all I can tell you for now, as you will not believe anything else."

"Try me," she said challengingly. "I'm quite the open-minded reporter."

"Claire." Professor Stein now intervened, reaching over to gently pull her around. "What Lou says is true. We haven't lied to you. *I* haven't lied to you."

"You just haven't told me the entire truth," she countered. "Okay then, look me in the face and tell me straight out. If you're lying, I'll see it immediately."

"A good trait for a reporter to have," he stated.

"It's come in handy," she admitted. "Now talk."

Professor Stein faced her directly, his eyes looking straight into hers, and spoke as simply and directly as he could. "What Lou says is correct. We are working for the benefit of this country but not with any federal agency you could ever know of. What we hold back from you is both for your own good and ours, and none of it is anything that you would believe. That is all there is to it. If there were more we could tell, we would."

For several seconds she stood staring into his eyes, looking for any trace of a lie, then broke off with a cough and a nod of admission. "You're telling the truth."

"I would never lie to you, Claire."

"I . . . believe you."

She stared into his eyes a moment longer, perhaps looking for something else, then broke away and faced Agent Hessman. "Okay, we're back to me helping you. What do you want to know?"

Agent Hessman turned another page of the newspaper, then folded it up and handed it to Captain Beck before replying. "We know that a meeting of some sort is involved. An important one that would involve high-level dignitaries. Perhaps you could start by listing any important events you may know of. Especially the kind that might not always make it into the popular press."

"There's a few that come to mind," she admitted. "Okay . . ."

Agent Harris guided them down the street, away from any overeager ears that might grow interested in what they were talking about as Claire listed events she knew about.

"Well, there's been that Fascist movement in Italy, and some anarchist bombings here that some believe are being led by an Italian named Luigi Galleani . . . The Paris Peace Conference was a few months back, and after the Treaty of Versailles, they started talking about forming some League of Nations. In fact, President Wilson is supposed to be arriving in town to give a talk to a few congressmen about the US joining in with this league."

Professor Stein suddenly broke in. "On his way to deliver the treaty to the Senate. He was supposed to do some campaigning about the

League of Nations, but I didn't know about a secret meeting with—Claire, do you know *which* congressmen will be at this meeting?"

"I'm not really sure." She shrugged. "It was all I could find out that this meeting is happening at all. It's really supersecret, with lots of security around it."

"Ben, exactly how important is it to know who'll be at this meeting?" Agent Hessman asked.

"It could mean everything," he said with a meaningful look. "Perhaps the single major opposition leader to the league was a congressman named Henry Cabot Lodge."

Here he pulled Agent Hessman a few paces away from Claire and continued in a more subdued tone. "He was the reason the United States never joined the league."

"Hmm," Agent Hessman mused. "So eliminate him and the US joins the League of Nations?"

"Well, it might take a bit more than that. History might be pretty resilient. Another opposition leader could rise up to take his place, for instance."

"But it's still a very good place to start. We're looking for an important high-level meeting, and this sounds about as important and high level as they get."

He motioned to the others and called out, "Come on, we've got a meeting to save."

"But to where?" Dr. Weiss asked.

"I said President Wilson was coming here for a meeting," Claire pointed out. "I didn't say where it would be. I wasn't able to find that out."

"Where else in this city would you hold a meeting involving the president and several key congressman?" Agent Hessman prompted. "City hall, of course. Now let's get moving."

They started down the street in search of the nearest sidewalk, Professor Stein walking next to Claire behind Agents Hessman and Harris, with Captain Beck and Dr. Weiss following them, and Lieutenant Phelps bringing up the rear with their Japanese prisoner still held securely in the discreet armlock. They had traversed no more than a few feet when their prisoner took advantage of a passing group of people and launched a kick to someone's shin.

As the pedestrian spun around, crying out in pain, Eiji pointed his free hand accusingly at the lieutenant, who then became the focus of the other man's rage. Before the lieutenant could do much to respond to the anger of the one with the sore shin, however, Eiji stomped his foot hard onto the lieutenant's foot, his other heel coming up hard between his legs. To a pained snarl from Lieutenant Phelps and a confused look from the stranger, Eiji quickly spun himself away until he was facing the lieutenant, who held him now by the hand, and brought his free elbow down hard onto the other's forearm with a sharp martial cry.

The lieutenant's grip released, and Eiji broke into a run, shoving his way rapidly through the crowd, all within a split second.

"He's going to warn his team what he heard us discuss," Agent Hessman said. "After him!"

An angry Lieutenant Phelps was the first one to break into a run.

19

SUBWAY TUNNEL CHASE

Agent Harris sprinted past Lieutenant Phelps only to be stalled by the passing crowd and a motor vehicle with an angry-sounding horn and an even angrier-sounding driver whose speech demonstrated a certain number of racial expletives. The others ran after them, but such a good-sized group of people trying to run through a crowded New York street was more of a guaranteed way of eliciting angry responses than of making any real progress.

Claire, however, saw the direction Eiji was running as the small man skillfully wove his way through the crowd. She tugged on Professor Stein's sleeve. "There's a subway entrance in that direction. He might be headed there."

"Lou," Professor Stein then relayed, pointing a hand in the indicated direction, "subway!"

To one man who took particular objection to a black woman and her "anarchist friends" trying to barge their way past him, Lieutenant Phelps took the direct approach. He bodily picked the man up and deposited him out of the way of the others as they ran past. "Behave yourself," he warned.

Before the man could snap himself out of his apoplectic shock, the large lieutenant was gone.

They raced across the street, weaving around horse-drawn taxis and Model Ts, and a policeman cautioning them with a sharp whistle, nearly colliding with another horse, then barging straight through a pack of pedestrians on the other side, in a race to the flight of stairs leading down to the subway below, where they saw their quarry leap down.

Agent Harris was in the lead but hampered now by others objecting to her presence, and Lieutenant Phelps could only manhandle so many out of the way, especially when it came to the ladies. Captain Beck and Agent Hessman ended up apologizing their way through.

They came to the bottom of the stairs in time to see Eiji leap over the turnstile, surprising the ticket man, and run for the train landing beyond.

"Stop him before he gets on a train," Agent Hessman called out as they wove through the crowd.

Agent Harris was the first to the turnstile, shoving her way past other customers, leaping over the gate and past the ticket man. "They're not going to hate me any more in this period than they already do," she muttered under her breath.

After her, the lieutenant barged his way past, but then came Claire with a quick smile for the man as she cut in front of some people. "Sorry, really important. But don't worry, the guy at the end is paying for us all." She pointed vaguely behind them, with a quick smile and wave for some undefined person far to their rear, then hurried on past.

After her followed Professor Stein. "Uh, the guy at the back," he said hurriedly.

Next came Agent Hessman, who had caught on to the game by now. "Guy at the back's paying."

Then Dr. Weiss hurried past with "Man at the back. Tweed coat. Can't miss him."

And finally Captain Beck. "Uh, man at the back's paying for me as well." He gestured in the general direction behind him and hurried past.

This left an actual customer stepping up to pay for himself and his girlfriend as the ticket man held out a hand waiting for a lot more money.

The landing was crowded with people waiting for the next train, but not crowded enough for a slender Japanese man no taller than five foot four to make his way quickly to the edge of the landing. But he wasn't about to wait for a train. When the team saw him leap down into the tunnel, a quick-thinking Claire called out with hand pointed, "Look! A Japanese anarchist with a bomb!"

Seeing the man leaping down into the tunnel seemed to be all the confirmation anyone needed. The crowd went from milling about to stampeding back toward the stairs, leaving Lieutenant Phelps to act as a water break against the oncoming tide of panicked humanity. But at least the way was clearing for them, enough that once they were past the initial wave of screaming subway riders, they broke into a dead run across the landing, and into the tunnel for Agent Harris.

One after another they leaped down, Eiji far ahead of them, running as fast as he could along one side of the tunnel. When it came to Professor Stein's turn to leap down, however, he was not without his objections. "We're chasing him through *there*? What if a train comes?"

"See what happens when you miss out on a war?" Claire countered. "You're afraid of one little train." She gave him a light shove to start him off, then followed immediately after.

With Agent Harris at the lead and Captain Beck bringing up the rear, they were a long line of people running down the tunnel, keeping as far over to one side as they could. The tunnel was dark, but from ahead they could make out the silhouette of their target when he became backlit by a single bright circular light, quickly nearing.

"Train!" Agent Harris shouted. "Flatten to the wall!"

They all did as advised, including Eiji ahead of them, putting their backs to the wall and pulling themselves as close against it as they could. Lieutenant Phelps had a slight problem doing so due to his bulk. As it was, the wall of the train shot past within an inch of his chest as the train's horn filled the tunnel with a deafening roar. Speeding cars raced by, filling the team with panicked adrenaline, save perhaps for Agent Harris, whose mind was on how best to resume the chase once the train passed.

The train was nearly past when, in those few seconds, Professor Stein realized his hand was on Claire's leg, while she found her arm flattened across his stomach. Neither dared to change the arrangement until the train had passed.

"Clear!" they all heard Agent Harris call out.

Professor Stein immediately jerked his hand away and began nervously stammering out an apology.

"Later," Claire snapped.

The chase continued down the tunnel, Agent Harris pouring on the speed until she was within a hand's breadth of the other. She was nearly there when Eiji turned his run into a spinning leap up, one foot swinging around directly for her head. Instinctively she brought up an arm to block, barely in time to deflect the worst of the blow but not without being thrown into the wall. She had no sooner hit than she pushed off with one foot to come at the man in a diving tackle for his waist.

She grabbed him round the knees, tumbling both of them to the center of the tunnel just as another blast from a train horn came echoing at them.

In the brief instant it took Agent Harris to note another bright light at the other end of the second set of tracks in this tunnel, Eiji snapped his legs apart with a sharp cry and rolled away. Agent Harris launched to her feet only to be jerked back by a strong hand to her shoulder. Lieutenant Phelps jerked her back an instant before the train coming down the opposing tracks raced by her nose. Eiji had made it to the other side of the track and was for a moment lost to view.

The others came running down the tunnel, catching up to the pair just as the train finished its passage. Once clear, they saw a set of running feet well down the tunnel, headed for a landing on the other side.

"That mouse is *not* getting away," Agent Harris vowed. She led the charge down the tunnel, leaping onto the landing in a single bound. Lieutenant Phelps stopped to help each of the others up, beginning with Claire. By the time the last of them was on the platform, the lieutenant now bringing up the rear, Agent Harris was well up the stairs to the surface in chase. She reached another wide walkway bordering a busy street and glanced around. She saw many people coming and going, cars and buses, and a multitude of visual obstacles, but her eyes were sharp and well trained. Just as the others came charging up the steps behind her, she spotted him. "There, in that alley across the street over there," she indicated.

"Get him before he gets away," Agent Hessman ordered. "Whatever it takes."

"I'll lead," Lieutenant Phelps said, pushing past her. "A black woman chasing someone in—"

"Okay, I get it," she snapped. "Just go."

With the lieutenant now in the lead, they bulldozed through the crowd, everyone else riding his wake. A passing bus and two taxis slowed them down, but they came as quickly as they could to the alley, where a lack of foot traffic allowed Agent Harris to break into a run past the lieutenant. She did not, however, have to run long. When she stopped abruptly before a large mound on the ground, Professor Stein held Claire back before remembering that she was probably better around bodies than he was.

Agent Hessman jogged up to join Agent Harris, while Lieutenant Phelps stayed at the rear to guard against anyone else coming into the alley. The rest gathered round to see what had stopped her, and though they already had their suspicions, there was still something to surprise them.

"*Two* bodies," Agent Hessman noted. "Who's the other one?"

Agent Harris bent down to turn over the first one. It was indeed Eiji, a hole in his forehead being all the autopsy that was needed. When she turned over the body next to him, she gave a startled look of recognition.

"The German? Lou, this is the same guy we tried to chase down before."

"And that brings up a very good question," Agent Hessman said. "Who would want to kill *both* teams?"

Two men with matching holes in their heads, one Japanese and the other German. A puzzle indeed.

20

ANOTHER BODY, ANOTHER PUZZLE

Captain Beck and Dr. Weiss stayed out of the way as Agent Hessman knelt down to examine the two bodies. Lieutenant Phelps stayed to his post at the entry into the alley, while the only reason Professor Stein was near the body was that he couldn't pull a curious Claire away from it. Agent Hessman pulled out a pocketknife and started digging for the bullets, an act that actually got Claire to flinch a bit.

"Okay, so maybe this part I don't need to see," she said. She averted her gaze while he went to work, operating first on Eiji's body then the German's.

"Okay, messy part's over with," he soon announced.

Claire went back to standing over the scene, her eyes absorbing every detail she could, while Professor Stein was ready to pull her away from anything she shouldn't be seeing.

"They both look like the same type of bullet," Agent Hessman noted. "Sue, what do you make of these?"

Agent Harris carefully took them both in hand and looked them over, mulling to herself some of the details. "Same type of ammo all right, and from the looks of it, same gun. The problem is . . ." She paused, looking back to Claire without saying a word.

"Okay, I know my cue," Claire said with a roll of her eyes. "Just let me know when there's something I'm allowed to hear." She turned away but grabbed hold of Professor Stein's hand in the process and jerked him along with her.

Agent Harris waited until they were far enough away before continuing. "The problem is that these bullets came from a forty-caliber Smith & Wesson."

"Which means what, exactly?" Agent Hessman asked.

"Smith & Wesson didn't start manufacturing this bullet until 1989. These two men were killed with a *modern* weapon."

"Hmm . . . so we have someone working against both the Japanese *and* the Germans that brought back with him a piece of modern weaponry. One wonders what other types of artillery this unknown assailant brought back."

"Sir," she said, "this complicates our problems considerably. For instance, if they're after President Wilson—"

"Then who needs to get near him when you can just use some plastic explosive or rocket rifle or something," he said, completing the thought. "But who would be working against both Japan *and* Germany?"

"And us, I might add. They haven't shot at us yet, but since no one's come forward announcing themselves as allies—"

"Then we have to assume the worst. But there are only three installations running: us, Japan, and Germany. There *is* no one left it could be."

"Well, it's gotta be someone."

Agent Hessman thought for a moment, then, taking the pair of bullets back from Agent Harris, carefully placed one on top of the exact center of each body's chest. "A message for our counterparts back in the present," he told her. "This should kick-start their own investigations on their ends. Now make sure that Miss Hill's back is turned while I search for their beacons."

Agent Harris jumped to her feet and quickly stepped over to where Professor Stein was keeping Claire busy by evading her small talk, which consisted mainly of trying to find out more about his personal history.

"Exactly what sort of a consultant *are* you, anyway?" she was asking. "What's your field?"

"History," he replied innocently. "I like studying the past."

"Interesting for a mission like this to have a history consultant on board. What period of history do you specialize in?"

For a moment he simply looked at her, catching a glint of cunning behind her pretty blue eyes. He'd not thought that the answer he gave could lead to such a suddenly uncomfortable position. "Uh . . . modern history," he ventured.

Fortunately, that was when Agent Harris came stepping over. She briskly grabbed Claire's shoulders to spin her around while talking in a level tone. "Why look, such an interesting pattern on this alley wall. What do you think it might be?"

"Oh, come on," Claire said. "There is nothing here to see. Now what is it you don't want me to see *this* time?"

"Just thought you'd want a good view of that wall there," Agent Harris stated flatly. "Now why don't you just keep looking at it for a bit longer."

"Claire, trust me," Professor Stein urged her. "For the security of this nation—for your own sanity—you do not want to look back."

"Yes, sir," Agent Harris said, with a firm hand still on Claire's shoulder. "Really interesting wall there. None better."

While Claire rolled her eyes at how she was being treated, Agent Harris kept an eye on Agent Hessman as he pulled out the beacons for each of the bodies, placed them on their respective chests, and activated them. Moments later the task was done.

"Okay, enough of that," Agent Harris said, pulling Claire back and releasing her. "It's only a wall."

As she spun around, Claire looked ready to voice any of several comments, but then saw where Agent Hessman was now standing and what he was *not* standing over. "The bodies—where'd they go? And if you say, 'What bodies?' I swear I'm going to go all unladylike on you. They were there a few seconds ago."

"And now they're not," Agent Hessman said simply as he walked over. "Sue, we need to track where this guy went. He can't be that far ahead of us."

"On it." She started by standing directly where the bodies had been found, then looked around, scanning the ground, the alley walls, and the rooftops above.

"Do you think she can actually do it?" Claire asked.

"This is the sort of thing she trained for," Agent Hessman replied.

"Even in a city this size?"

"I'm wondering that myself," Professor Stein added. "Our only leads just got murdered."

"Just wait for it," Agent Hessman assured them. "She's already realized that whoever it was didn't leave by way of our end of the alley or risk being seen by us, which leaves only one direction unless he was on a rooftop somewhere."

"He'd have to be a pretty good shot," Claire said, looking up the side of the left-hand building.

Neither man said a thing. Meanwhile, Agent Harris had decided to continue down the alley, at which point Agent Hessman motioned to Captain Beck and the others to join in following her. When she came to the far end of the alley, Agent Harris stopped. The alley came out into another busy street. She saw something down at one end that filled her with a new sense of confidence. When the rest joined her, she indicated the direction with a gesture of her arm. "He went that way."

"I'm curious as to how you arrived at that conclusion what with so many directions to choose from and all the traffic in the way," Dr. Weiss remarked. "Might I ask how you did so?"

She merely indicated a sign with an arrow pointing down the street. "I can't think of a better place where the killer would choose to hide," she replied.

"Good job," Agent Hessman told her. "Let's get going before he gets much farther ahead of us."

When the others saw the sign that Agent Harris had found, no dissenting voice questioned her judgment as to its being the perfect place for a runner to hide. For the sign read, "Coney Island."

21

CONEY ISLAND

Coney Island isn't all just one big amusement park and resort community, but it could seem that way, even in the year 1919, especially for the many families visiting its attractions every day. Or if you were trying to puzzle out where a criminal might hide. The fact that most of the crowd gathered in the amusement area acted like a beacon to Agent Harris as she led the way across the bridge and onto the island.

"Claire," she asked the reporter, "of all the places on Coney Island, which one receives the most visitors? Has the most attractions?"

"Oh, that's easy," Claire replied. "Steeplechase Park. But there's also the Coney Island beach, a couple of smaller parks based around some carousels, a couple of coasters . . . but Steeplechase would be the most crowded. There's the Pavilion of Fun, the parachute drop, the outdoor pool, the horse race—"

"I didn't know they had horses on Coney Island," Professor Stein interjected.

"Silly." Claire smiled back. "Wooden horses on metal tracks. You ride them, kind of like a coaster. At any rate, there'd be any number of places that one could hide. Too many to count."

"Then that's where we head to," Agent Harris decided.

"Agreed," Agent Hessman stated. "Miss Hill, you're far more familiar with this territory than any of us; lead on."

Through the surging crowd she led them, Agent Harris a step behind to make sure Claire didn't get too far ahead of anyone else, though the reporter seemed willing to keep to whatever pace Professor Stein decided to set. This earned a look between Agents Hessman and Harris but nothing more said. They saw the rides in the nearing distance, joyful crowds pushing along from one attraction to another, and any number of visual treats to greet them as they entered the park with the flow of bodies.

"I'll admit," Dr. Weiss said aside to Lieutenant Phelps, "even in 1919 this place is pretty spectacular."

"I just keep my mind on business," the lieutenant replied. "You should do the same."

"Oh, of course, but that's no reason why we can't—what's that over there?"

While Dr. Weiss scurried over to investigate a nearby booth, Agents Harris and Hessman conversed in low tones. "Just wish we could do some sort of facial-recognition scan through these crowds," Agent Hessman said. "I have pictures of all potential Japanese and German team members."

"I've seen the list," Agent Harris replied. "And made a point of memorizing the pictures just in case . . . Over there, eleven o'clock. The guy in the blue fedora. I need a confirmation."

Discreetly Agent Hessman pulled out his small pocket computer, Harris using her body to shield it from view as he scrolled through the stored pictures for a visual comparison. In only a few moments he gave a confirmation. "One of the Germans," he stated. "Let's keep this discreet. He may not have spotted us yet."

They quickened their pace, and when the rest saw them do so, they likewise walked a bit faster. Seeing everyone starting to move off, Dr. Weiss jogged back over to rejoin them, a half-eaten hotdog in one hand. He came up to the other side of Professor Stein with a big grin on his face. "I just got a hotdog." He beamed.

"Not into them much myself," Professor Stein shrugged.

"A *Nathan's* hotdog," Dr. Weiss continued.

"I still don't—"

"From *Nathan.*"

Professor Stein was about to verbally brush him off again, but then caught the meaning of what Weiss had said. He shot a glance over to the booth from where his friend had just come, and returned a wide-eyed look to Dr. Weiss. Dr. Weiss simply nodded and smiled in response, and took another bite of his hotdog.

"I don't understand what the fuss is," Claire remarked.

"You'd have to be there," Professor Stein answered. "Which I guess we are."

Harris and Hessman led them through tightly packed crowds, moving more rapidly across an open patch to catch up with the German. Suddenly Agent Harris led them into an abrupt change of course, cursing under her breath.

"What is it?" Agent Hessman asked as he, too, increased his pace.

"The guy spotted us. And he's only one person making his way through this mess, while we're seven."

Seeing what Agent Harris was doing, Lieutenant Phelps ushered the others along more rapidly, sometimes with a look and other times with a hard palm to the shoulder if necessary. First Agent Harris led them through thickening crowds, struggling to keep the German within sight. But the task was not easy, considering the crowd and the general bedlam of the area. Twice they almost got caught in a line for one of the Ferris wheels, once nearly pushed in the direction of the Steeplechase horse ride, and were nearly to the beach itself when Agent Hessman pulled them all aside.

"All eyes alert," he said to the rest. "Sue, where'd he go?"

Agent Harris gave another look around and admitted defeat. "Lost him. Too many faces around here."

"What we need is a better vantage point," Agent Hessman decided. He scanned his surroundings, and as his gaze alighted on one of the rides, he grinned. "Sue, think a Ferris wheel would do the trick?"

Agent Harris looked over to where he was indicating then answered with a nod. "That should do the trick, all right."

"Then it's you and Ben topside on that thing while the rest of us stay down here. David, on perimeter; Sam and Robert, stay close; Claire—"

"First, that's the *Wonder* Wheel," she explained, "and second, I'm going up there too. If Mister University Professor can go up in that thing, then I can too. Besides, I know the layout of this place better than you guys do. I might be able to spot something."

"Okay, no time for argument," Agent Hessman decided. "Sue, Ben, and Claire, get up on that thing. The rest of us will wait around the base."

"If we spot anything, we'll wave our arms or something," Professor Stein said.

"No, that might alert the other guys," Agent Hessman replied. "We'll keep an eye on you, just nothing too overt. Sue, just pay for the tickets like anyone else; nothing to attract attention."

"Barging up a Ferris wheel gets tricky anyway," she replied.

"You know this from personal experience?" Claire asked.

Agent Harris said nothing, just motioned to the pair. "Okay, come on you two."

While they got into the ticket line, Lieutenant Phelps kept an eye on their perimeter as the others stayed to one section of the observation railing, pretending to ooh and ahh along with the other spectators. When it came their turn, Agent Harris stuffed a couple of coins into the attendant's hand, then, in response to the puzzled look he gave her and the other two passengers, spat out a quick explanation. "Takes his maid with him *everywhere*."

Then, stepping in after her, Professor Stein added, "Hard to find good help, you know."

The three were waved on while a confused attendant promptly shook his head and continued on about his job.

"Well," Claire said once they were secured and slowly rotated up one position, "nice of you to take on the position of maid for the mission."

"Who says I was talking about me?" Agent Harris replied. "I was referring to *you*. Not my fault the guy didn't inquire any further."

"*Me* as the maid? But that would mean that you and Ben have the roles of—how would that even work? No one would believe that—no, there's just something not quite right about that."

Agent Harris grinned.

"I think you broke her," Professor Stein remarked.

"No, you just caught me by surprise," Claire replied. "I'd never considered—are you?"

As the ride lifted up another position, Agent Harris couldn't help but chuckle.

"She's just joking, Claire," Professor Stein told her. "It's as I said before: I don't have anyone. No matter what her race."

"Yes, I . . . sorry, I thought I was open-minded and liberated, but you caught me short with that one."

"Simply typical of the time period," Professor Stein said with an eye to Agent Harris.

"Enough fun and games," Agent Harris said after a moment. "Keep your eyes peeled. We were after a German, but that doesn't mean the Japanese aren't someplace around here as well."

By degrees their bench made it to the top as the ride filled in, pausing long enough for a good look around, but also long enough for a recovered Claire to corner Professor Stein with a few more questions. "Since you can't run out on me now, how about you tell me *which* university you teach out of. I might have some contacts there I could check up on you through. Unless of course you're afraid I might discover something unusual."

"You don't believe I'm a professor?"

"Oh, you are. But I've noted that you've avoided stating *which* university you're from, which in itself is a little unusual. Most people take a certain amount of pompous pride in stating which prestigious university they're out of; in fact, you can't shut them up about it. But you've said nothing, which as I said I find . . . curious. Or maybe you'd care to tell me where you grew up? Give me some good hometown stories for background on the article I'll write."

"Well I . . . it's a little town I'm sure you're never heard of."

"Try me."

"And as far as which university . . . for the same reason why we, uh, don't use last names—you know, for security and all—that is, we—"

"There," Agent Harris suddenly cut in.

"Oh, thank God," Professor Stein breathed out.

"One of the Germans," Agent Harris said. "Or at least he's a close enough match to one of the dossiers. The one in the brown fedora trying painfully hard to look normal."

"You're right," Claire agreed when she caught sight of the one Agent Harris was pointing at. "Who wears a hat standing in line for a ride like *this*? But what's he doing?"

The ride started into full motion as the three peered closely, bringing them down from the aerial view just as the German was pushing his way through the crowd in the direction of the same Wonder Wheel they rode upon. When they passed by ground level on their first rotation, Agent Harris shouted out to Agent Hessman and the others, "Spotted one of the Germans!"

Agent Hessman's response was lost to the winds as the wheel brought them around and back up into the sky, soon hovering briefly above it all once again.

"There." Claire was the first to see. "But he's stopped and taking something small out of his pocket. I can't see what it is."

"I don't need to," Agent Harris suddenly realized. "Anyone else in his line of sight?"

"Just . . . our people," Professor Stein said.

After a brief exchange of looks, three voices shouted as the wheel brought them down through another rotation.

"Lou," Professor Stein shouted, "the man has a gun."

"He's coming for you!" Claire exclaimed.

Agent Harris kept it more basic. She made a motion with her right hand as if working a pistol, while using her other hand to gesture desperately off into the crowd behind them. "*Enemy!*" she screamed.

The giant wheel was again passing by ground level when at least one of the others caught enough of what the riders were saying to act.

Lieutenant Phelps spun around, eyes searching the crowd, then spotted the man holding up both hands tight around something small and gun-like. He performed a flying tackle, arms spread wide to include both Agent Hessman and Dr. Weiss, as a sharp snap of thunder sounded out.

The giant wheel once again brought the three back up into the air, away from the scene of sudden shouting and screaming. Up to the height for a new view, this time they saw one man running away from the scene while Lieutenant Phelps lay unmoving atop Hessman and Weiss.

"David!" Agent Harris shouted.

"Oh my God, I think he was shot," Professor Stein said.

"I don't know what type of gun that guy used, but it looks like the entire back half of David's head just got blown off." Claire's voice wavered as she made the declaration.

Below them the surrounding people were screaming and working themselves up into a good stampede, while those on the Wonder Wheel were demanding to be let off before the shooter might take aim at their own helpless positions. The giant wheel stopped its stately turning and resumed its slow staccato rhythm as passengers disembarked one bench at a time.

By the time the three finally hit the ground running, it was all over but for the prayers. They were greeted by a hand each from Agent Hessman to Harris and Stein and some quiet words.

"Phelps is dead. Sue, did you see—"

"This way, and I got first dibs!" She ran off into the crowd, not waiting to see who was following. Agent Hessman was the first behind her, while Dr. Weiss stood over the fallen man and said a quick prayer. A stunned Professor Stein walked over to see for himself, then simply stood there looking. Captain Beck was squatting beside the body, searching for something in the man's jacket.

"He saved me and Lou," Dr. Weiss quietly stated.

"We . . . saw," Professor Stein stammered. "I never thought that—"

With a hand still in the lieutenant's jacket, Captain Beck looked up to address them. "You guys go on and get him. I'll finish up here."

"If . . . if I turn around," Claire began, "you're going to make him disappear just like the others."

"This isn't your story, Miss Hill," Dr. Weiss gently told her, "save to say that a hero died protecting his charges and there was nothing that you or anyone else could do to change it at the time. Now I suggest we get moving before Lou and Sue lose us in the crowd."

"Uh, right," Professor Stein replied. "I saw where he ran to as well. I . . . Goodbye, David."

After a last look and a quick breath, he turned and ran off, Claire and Dr. Weiss fast on his heels. Captain Beck waited until the reporter was out of sight, and no one else looking, before he activated the beacon and backed away. He stayed only long enough to witness the body dissolve into an implosion of sparks, then joined in with the chase.

22

STEEPLECHASE

gent Harris didn't care anymore how many offended white people she pushed her way through, nor was Agent Hessman in a mood to correct her even if he could catch up to her. She paused only long enough to verify which way he was headed, and ran after him.

They ran past gaming booths, where the pursued man leapt into one booth where the object was to knock over a stack of metal bottles. He picked up an armload of them and hurled them along the ground in his wake. Now, besides dodging people, Agent Harris had to leap over rolling bottles as well. After that, he threw a handful of balls at her from another booth and ducked into an entrance to something else. She had nearly caught up to him when another shot whizzed past her ear, but this one without the report of thunder as before.

Silencer, she realized. *Definitely* not *period*.

She ducked behind the tall pillar of a ring-the-bell-with-the-hammer strength challenge and, using that as cover as someone slammed the hammer down, had a better look at where the shooter had ducked into. It was a place labeled "Pavilion of Fun." She witnessed him ducking around the corner of the ornate pavilion entry; then another man came up behind him to whisper in his ear just as Agent Hessman ran up to join her.

"Status?" he asked tersely.

"Looks like he's just joined up with his teammates. Using a silencer now."

"That's violating all *sorts* of rules. Where?"

"Pavilion of Fun," she indicated. "Know of it?"

"From the history books, maybe." Agent Hessman looked back over his shoulder to see Professor Stein and the others quickly making their way through the crowd to join them.

Meanwhile, Agent Harris had something else in mind. The barker for the strength challenge was holding up the large sledgehammer for the next contestant when she bolted straight at him, yanking the hammer out of his hand while shoving him away and continuing on with it in a dead run. Both arms gripping it, she swung it around and around, screaming at the top of her lungs while doing so. Seeing a crazy black lady running around loose with a large sledgehammer in her hands was enough to quickly clear the crowd, leaving a nice open avenue between her and her targets.

The one who had shot Lieutenant Phelps was taking aim at her when she released the hammer to send it flying straight for him. With wide eyes, the man dove out of the way as the hammer came crashing past the edge of the entry wall and into the shin of the one who had been whispering in the man's ear.

Unfortunately, that was apparently not the only member of the German's team to have joined him. When she saw a third man raising a pistol as a fourth tended to the one hit by the sledgehammer, Agent Harris dove for the ground. The bullet sped over her head and ricocheted off the ground behind her. By the next shot, Agent Hessman and Captain Beck had joined her on the ground, while Claire and Professor Stein had taken cover behind one of the other gaming booths, along with Dr. Weiss.

"As soon as they move, we charge them," Agent Hessman decided. "Let's see if we can try for a German prisoner this time and get their side of things."

"Love to," Sue replied, "as soon as the one with the artillery stops shooting."

"From the looks of it, they *all* brought hardware with them," Captain Beck noted. "Is *anybody* obeying the rules?"

One more shot came, then nothing, and the three ventured to glance up. The Germans were gone from the entrance.

"They ducked into the Pavilion of Fun," Agent Harris said.

"That's an enclosed space," Captain Beck told them. "We can catch them there."

Up to their feet and into a run, Beck and Harris were quickly joined by Claire, and the other two men by the time they got there.

"We saw them go inside that place," Dr. Weiss called out as they now all ran together. "Looks like a little arcade or something."

"The Palace of Fun is anything but little," Claire countered. "They'll lose us in there for sure."

The Palace of Fun turned out to be the most immense indoor attraction that anyone from that time period had seen. Game machines, smaller indoor roller coasters, a carousel, side shows aplenty, a sunken garden by the vast entry, and even attached ballrooms—all were encircled by the Steeplechase Horse Race ride. In short, the fun palace was a nearly three-acre enclosure of steel and glass that bragged a life-size decorative elephant to top things off. And all of it was quite crowded.

"You've *got* to be kidding," Professor Stein remarked as he took in the breadth and grandeur of the place. "I've never seen anything like this place."

"Never?" Claire questioned. "Exactly how far out of town are you from?"

Through the surging masses, the barkers called out any of a hundred different games or a dozen different rides, including one who directed his attention at Professor Stein as he was passing by. "Perhaps you, my young man. Show your girlfriend here a good time on the ride of her life."

"My gir—no," he said after a glance back to Claire. "We're just—long story." He then grabbed Claire's hand to pull her along, more so as not to lose track of her than anything else, but the sight got the barker grinning before he went on to the next passerby.

The Americans almost completely missed the German team's next shot. Between the use of silencers and the noise of the crowd and attractions, a German was able to aim unseen at Agent Hessman, who missed getting hit only by a chance ducking behind the elephant. Immediately everyone took cover, Harris with Hessman, Beck with Weiss behind a large gong placed as a set decoration for some coming attraction, and Stein and Claire behind a small stage sporting a group of girls performing a dance number supposedly from the court of Queen Cleopatra.

Two more shots rang out, this time attracting some attention when one of them hit the gong behind which a now-deaf Weiss and Beck hid. "Ouch! There went my hearing," Dr. Weiss remarked.

"What?" Captain Beck replied.

"I said—never mind."

"So they got guns and we got nothing," Agent Hessman said to Agent Harris. "Besides Beck's little one-shot derringer—do you mean to tell me that you didn't violate the rules like everyone else seems to be doing?"

"Not that I'd care to reveal just yet," she replied.

"Okay, got it. But that still means we need—"

Another shot rang out, but this time a cry in German was followed by a man tumbling out from behind one of the gaming machine and into the open, holding a freshly wounded arm.

"Now where did *that* shot come from?" Agent Harris pondered aloud.

The wounded German lifted his good arm, staggered in the direction of the large elephant statue Agents Hessman and Harris were hiding behind, then let off a shot. The bullet, however, went wide of hitting either of them. Then a moment later a body dropped from atop the elephant above them, landing not more than a yard in front of them. The body was a Japanese-looking man.

"Answer your question?" Agent Hessman asked. "Looks like the Japanese team's here as well."

Two other men dressed similarly as the wounded German ducked behind one of the roller coasters, while Captain Beck dashed out from behind the gong, heading someplace else. A group that looked like Japanese tourists casually making their way through the crowd, or Japanese team members, tried to close in.

Behind the stage, Professor Stein and Claire were trying to differentiate between possible enemies and fun-seekers.

"Two over there," Claire pointed.

"No, they're Chinese."

"How can you tell? Oh, they all look alike to me."

"German over there." The professor now pointed.

"Not unless he's suddenly taken up speaking Italian as his native language."

"Then what's he doing skulking around behind that Human Wheel exhibit?"

"Probably a Fascist looking to make trouble," Claire replied. "Either way, that's someone else's problem."

Another man with a European appearance suddenly came running out into the open, making a mad dash for his wounded comrade. A Japanese man also leapt out, seemingly from nowhere, screaming at the top of his lungs. He went airborne for a moment as he dove off the top of the passing roller-coaster car he'd been on to tackle the running man amid a mixture of screams of terror and cries of delight, depending on who thought it was part of some show or not. The pair wrestled there briefly, while the wounded man continued nursing his arm and backed up nearly into the carousel.

"Hey, One-Arm!"

The man spun around in time to see Captain Beck standing on the carousel, one hand holding on to the pole of one of the wooden horses while the other held his derringer. He only had time for a single shot before the ride carried him away, but when you're only four feet away, a single shot is all you need. The German fell to the ground, never to move again.

The pair wrestling on the ground paused, facing each other, for a moment. People screamed, in the distance local police sirens closed in, and two bodies lay out in the open. "Hey, you two, first things first." They glanced over to see Agent Harris now holding the pistol the Japanese man who'd been shot from the elephant had been holding, while Agent Hessman squatted beside the body, holding the man's beacon over his chest and looking significantly at the man's teammate.

The Japanese man replied with a single nod to the German he now faced, and placed fist into palm for a short bow, which the German replied to with a slight nod. Agent Hessman slapped the beacon down onto the chest before him. The German ran for the one that Captain Beck had just shot, fished around in his jacket, and produced a similar-looking beacon.

At that moment, Professor Stein took Claire out from behind their stage cover by way of the Human Niagara exhibition booth to block anything she might see of what would come next.

Dr. Weiss joined Agent Harris, Captain Beck still huffing from his run off the carousel, just as the Japanese body before them was imploding upon itself. By the time it was finished, so was the German with his own teammate, while the other Japanese man had already run off. Professor Stein made sure not to rejoin them with Claire until after all lights had stopped flashing and sparkling.

"For a second it looked like everyone was going to kill everyone else," Claire remarked. "What happened?"

"We're in a shadow war, Miss Hill," Agent Hessman replied. "Whatever anyone's motives, none of us can afford to get caught by the local police, or pretty much anyone else around here. That's the one rule that none of us dares violate, even if it means covering the others' rears while trying to kill them. Now, what's our weapon count?"

"That was my last spare bullet," Captain Beck reported.

"I got the Japanese guy's gun," Agent Harris said, tucking it away before Claire could get a good look at it. "Looks like about three shots left."

"And I hear the police coming," Claire added. "We need to take your shadow war somewhere else."

"Recommendations?" Agent Hessman asked.

"Ever been to the boardwalk?"

"Only on a certain board game," Dr. Weiss remarked, then quickly amended, "which I guess hasn't come out quite yet."

"Lead on," Agent Hessman ordered. "And the boardwalk you're referring to is in Atlantic City, not here," he whispered to Dr. Weiss.

As the police were coming in through one entrance, Claire was leading the team out through another. By the time the American team made it out of Steeplechase Park and onto the boardwalk, all sign of both the German and Japanese teams had been lost. Of course, the same could be said of them versus either of the other teams looking for them.

Even more puzzled were the police, who could find nothing of the reported bodies people had sworn they'd seen shot during a firefight.

23

CITY HALL

After losing themselves from view along the boardwalk, another half hour passed before they could make their way discreetly back onto the main streets again without being spotted by either the police now swarming Steeplechase Park or any potential witnesses to the fight. Then they had to spend another twenty minutes traveling by taxi before they were anywhere near their original destination.

New York City Hall loomed across the town square before them. Wide stone steps led up to the ornate, symmetrical two-story structure with a clock tower rising high from the middle front. The grand structure that looked part palace presided proudly over the city. The 1919 version of the building had 3D window shades that jutted out from several windows, shades that were missing from the modern version of the structure.

The team gathered underneath the overhang of a building across the street, at first doing little more than watching the crowds milling about the square and coming from and going into city hall, Harris and Hessman keeping an eagle eye out for any faces in the surging crowd that might spark some interest.

"About twenty cops that I can see," Agent Hessman reported after a few minutes, "but that's to be expected. Sue, what do you see?"

Agent Harris lifted up the front brim of her large floppy hat that she had pulled partially down over her eyes, her gaze fixing on clumps of men here and there who were hovering around the grand building before them. She reported, "Two groups of three men each to either side of the top steps who haven't moved in about the last ten minutes, a few scattered around the square who have been reading the same page in their newspapers for at least as long, a doorman next to the entry with a gun-shaped bulge in his pants, and a few others that stick out for how hard they're trying to be a part of the background . . . I'd say about thirty plainclothes."

"It looks like you may be right, Lou," Captain Beck remarked quietly. "That's a lot of security for normal day-to-day operations."

"The meeting's here, all right." Agent Hessman nodded. "And since it doesn't look like the dignitaries have arrived yet, we may be able to lay a trap for our competitors."

Claire glanced over City Hall Square, saw only the crowded masses of people coming and going, and shook her head. "Assuming those are federal agents out there that Sue's looking at," she stated, "and if this thing is as serious as you make it out to be, then why not just identify yourselves to the other agents for some backup? If you're right about the president coming here, I'm sure they'd be glad to cooperate."

Before Agent Hessman could reply, Professor Stein whispered a quick answer. "Not possible, Claire, and don't ask us to explain."

"Yeah, it's a shadow war," she scoffed. "And even the shadows don't know what's going on."

Partially ignoring what the reporter had to say, Agent Hessman began plotting with Agent Harris and Captain Beck, while Dr. Weiss pulled his bowler hat a little lower over his face as he hugged back to the shadows.

"Getting inside shouldn't be a problem," Agent Hessman was saying. "Front door like everyone else, then we just look for wherever the general public is not being admitted and pick out some good spots to wait them out."

"Who do you think we'll be seeing?" Captain Beck asked. "The German team or the Japanese?"

"German, I'd say," Agent Harris said. She gave a slight tip of her hat to signal about something across the square. "In that I think that's one of them over there, if I remember the dossiers correctly."

"Gimme a minute to confirm," Agent Hessman told her.

She stepped in front of him while he discreetly pulled out his portable computer. After a quick scan through the list of faces of possible German team members accompanied by a couple of glances toward the man she had pointed out, he tucked the device back into his coat pocket.

"Make that three," he reported. "Sue's and two more I've identified. Ernst Fischer, Klaus Weber, and Otto Wagner."

"I see them," Agent Harris said after a moment, "but who are those other people they're talking to?"

The three Germans in question were slowly making their way across the square toward the large stone steps, while other men in suits and bowler hats who had been discussing something with them spread out.

"Could be local help," Agent Hessman reasoned. He then stepped toward where Claire and Professor Stein were standing, caught their eyes, and gave a slight nod in the direction of the Germans. "Our German friends seem to have picked up a few friends. Anyone someone recognizes?"

The professor studied the ones Agent Hessman had indicated and was trying to figure out how he could consult his pocket history computer without Claire seeing anything, when Claire spoke up. "I recognize a few of them from the local crime gangs. Fifth Street Brawlers, I think. They'll do anything for money."

"That sounds about right," Professor Stein agreed. "From what I know of the subject, there are a lot of small gangs in the city competing with one another."

"So the Germans paid them off," Agent Hessman picked up, "and these Brawlers are only too eager for the extra cash and anything else that'll get them ahead of their competitors."

"That's extra manpower we'll be up against," Captain Beck said. "Could turn into quite the shooting war."

"Not if we take out the Germans first," Agent Harris countered. "With no one to pay them, the gang members would have no reason to stick around."

"Then let's get them before anything else happens," Agent Hessman ordered, "but remember to keep it very discreet. You just have to knock them out, and then"—he paused to give a look to Claire, who let out an exasperated sigh as she rolled her eyes skyward, then brought up her hands to cover both ears tightly—"send them back with their own beacons. No need to kill if we don't have to."

"And whichever way it turns out, don't get caught doing anything," Agent Harris completed. "Got it."

Professor Stein elbowed Claire as a signal that she could now uncover her ears.

"Okay, no rushing, just keep it steady and no direct charging," Agent Hessman instructed. "Sue, if you spot anyone else from those dossiers, handle them. We'll take down the ones we've already spotted."

"Why does this sound like I'm about to be at the epicenter of a small gang war?" Claire remarked.

They were just stepping out into the square when Dr. Weiss pulled suddenly at Agent Hessman's jacket. "Lou, look."

Driving into the square, accompanied by a scattering of more police on motorcycles of the era, came a line of cars. With white-walled tires, dignified lines, high-roofed cabins, and black paint jobs, the Cadillacs drove up to the steps of city hall as the crowd parted before them. Agent Hessman held back as they waited to see who would come out of the vehicles.

"Looks like the dignitaries arriving," Agent Hessman reasoned. "Ben, who's who?"

The first to step out was blocked from view by both the vehicle and the hat he wore as he exited from the far side of the car with his attendants.

"Can't see him," Professor Stein reported.

The man was ushered up the steps by a couple of plainclothesmen as the car drove away. As the next car in line pulled up, Agent Harris directed everyone through the crowd to get a better vantage point, just as she could see the German team was likewise doing. By the time the dignitary from the second car was exiting, Professor Stein had a good enough view of his face. He was a distinguished-looking man with a neatly trimmed if bushy beard and mustache.

"That's him," he reported excitedly, for a moment forgetting the re-porter was within hearing range. "I recognize him from some old photos. That's Congressman Lodge."

"If he's here, then this is *definitely* the place where President Wilson's coming," Agent Hessman stated. "Good work, Ben. So the Germans want to take out the congressman so that the United States enters the league? No, that doesn't sound right."

"Maybe they're here to kill the president as revenge for the war," Claire suggested.

"That almost makes more sense than killing the congressman," Agent Hessman muttered. "No, there's something else."

They started advancing through the crowd once again, while ahead of them the three Germans and some of their gang allies did likewise in an effort to get to the front steps. Agent Harris wove more quickly through the crowd in an effort to sneak up on the Germans before she could be spotted. As the second car left, a third car driving up paused long enough for her to push her way through to one of the gang mem-bers in the bowler hats and grab the back of his neck. "Klaus, old friend," she said in a congenial tone. "Why, did you know that I can snap your neck before any of your friends here can react? Now why don't you tell us what brings you to town?"

The others with him looked ready to pile into her, but they paused when the German raised a hand to them. He didn't even turn to look at her but merely stood still as she held his neck. "You don't know what's going on, Agent—"

"First names only, please. You know why."

"Very well; Sue, then. Yes, we know of you. I assume this is all about to get rather messy then?"

"That's all up to you, Klaus."

One of the men Claire had identified as a gang member spoke up. "Listen, boss, I'm not about to let some ni—"

"Normal for the times or not, but finish that word and I drop the both of you where you stand," she immediately shot back.

He looked about to say something more but froze. The others there turned to see a man now standing behind him holding something to his back: Captain Beck with his derringer. The fact that he was out of ammunition did not seem worth the captain's time to bring up.

Another car was now letting out its passenger as the others in the team worked their way around the encounter. From another Cadillac emerged a Japanese delegation centering on a man in an important-looking uniform that several there immediately recognized.

"The man from the photo," Agent Harris stated.

"That's Tojo himself," Captain Beck confirmed.

"That means," Agent Hessman said from beside Captain Beck as he walked up with the others, "that the Japanese team has got to be—"

The shot rang out, catching Captain Beck in the arm; the silent shot did not match the sound a firearm from this era should have made. The captain dropped his derringer, and the German who'd had the gun in his back swung around to give Captain Beck a shove, while the distraction was enough for the man to elbow Agent Harris and push away himself. Agent Hessman shot a glance at the shooter. He recognized him as one of the Japanese team members they'd encountered back at Steeplechase. The Japanese man's gun discharged, and he cursed to himself in Japanese, then dove into the crowd. From there, events exploded into chaos.

24

CLANDESTINE SHOOTOUT

D r. Weiss rushed to Captain Beck, carefully helping the man to the ground. "Where'd he get you? Are you all right?"

"Right shoulder, and it hurts like a mother—"

Agent Harris started jogging through the crowd to catch up to her German quarry, then found three of the men in bowler hats blocking her way with grins and fists. "Really?" she told them. "Only three of you?"

Agent Hessman, meanwhile, gave chase to the Japanese man who'd made the shot, while bystanders puzzled at the strangely muffled gunshot, then gasped as the pair of men ran through their ranks. The Japanese team member seemed to be trying to get around the crowd, with furtive glances in the direction of the dignitaries assembling at the top steps of city hall. That's when Agent Hessman realized the gunman hadn't been aiming for Robert. He pushed past a couple trying to get a good view of the dignitaries. *It was Tojo; Robert must have been in the way!*

Professor Stein dashed over to the fallen captain whom Dr. Weiss was tending to.

"He's got a bullet in the shoulder," Dr. Weiss reported.

"That'll have to come out," Claire said. "Do you need a knife?"

"What?" the doctor gasped. "But I'm not a—"

"She's right," Captain Beck gasped. "You'll have to play field medic. There's a pocketknife in my upper vest pocket. Ben, if the Germans are after the congressman—"

"On it."

While Dr. Weiss worked hesitantly on the removal of the bullet, a nearby shocked spectator offered his clean handkerchief.

Meanwhile, Professor Stein charged through the crowd in the general direction of the city hall steps. As yet another car pulled up, the throng of curious bystanders grew as people realized that something important was about to happen. "I've got to get to Congressman Lodge. If they kill him—"

A sudden punch to the face cut off the rest of his words, and he fell back into Claire. It was one of the men in bowler hats. Claire caught Ben as he fell back and glared angrily at their assailant.

"Ben, are you all right?"

Ben stepped a foot back to steady himself, worked his jaw with a hand, then replied, "I'm not exactly built for fistfights, but everything seems to be in place."

The assailant took a step forward, Claire pushing in front of the professor to face the other man with a determined glare.

"Don't worry, missy," the man said, grinning. "I never hit a lady. Your boyfriend, though, is quite another story. Now get out of the way."

He placed a hand to her shoulder to move her out of the way and was rewarded with a boot striking hard into his left shin. The man dropped with a scream of pain.

"A pity I don't have the same restriction on hitting a man," she stated. Her next kick landed in his face and sent him sprawling on his back.

"Claire," the professor gasped as he stepped up beside her, "how did you—"

"Just save the congressman, and leave the details of how my father really wanted a boy for later."

He replied with a quick nod, then broke into a run, out into a clearing in the crowd, and straight for the steps as the last of the line of cars was pulling away.

"Congressman Lodge," he shouted, "duck!"

Another disruption was occurring not too far across the square, one that had the crowd parting and trying to get out of the way.

"It's a mad negress," someone shouted. "Straight from the jungle, from the way she fights!"

"Someone call the police!"

"It's terrible!"

Two of the three already lay at her feet, and the third was greeted by Agent Harris's wide-brimmed, floppy hat pulled suddenly down over his head, a knee ramming its way hard between his legs. "Something to tell your children about, if you can still have any," she remarked. "You got beat up by a black woman."

Her opponents mobilized, she spent a moment quickly surveying the situation. Pockets of people were starting to depart as they realized something was amiss, and the police and plainclothesmen were scurrying around as well. Agent Hessman had a clear line on the Japanese man he was chasing and saw the latter raising his gun once again. But he was not, from the looks of it, aiming for the American team's leader.

"Tojo!" Agent Harris realized. "Great, between that and who the Germans might be going after, this place is about to be a shooting gallery."

Agent Hessman tried a flying tackle for his quarry just as the other was pulling off his shot. The shot went wild, hitting instead the edge of one of the stone pillars to the side of the main steps. That got *everyone's* attention, especially the ones in charge of guarding the milling dignitaries.

Claire had watched Professor Stein run off for the front steps, shouting as he went, and for a moment looked after him, biting her lip. After a cough, she chanced to glance upon another man moving quickly through the crowd on an intercept course for the professor. She recognized this man as being one of the Germans that Sue had pointed out earlier. "That guy must have thirty pounds on Ben. He'll never know what hit him. Ben!" She burst into a run, shoving people out of the way, not caring how offended their dignities might be. Ben was oblivious as he burst through a line of policemen, screaming at the top of his lungs, "Congressman!"

The German pulled out a small gun, aiming it not at Professor Stein but at one of the men at the top of the steps. That's when the shot rang out that glanced off the pillar, but Claire heard another sharp noise that sounded like the nearly silent gunshots she had heard back at Steeplechase Park. A second shot was accompanied by the German dropping to the ground with a large hole in the back of his head.

Elsewhere in the crowd, Agent Harris snapped her head around, searching the crowd for the shooter. She had heard the double shot and now saw the German drop just as Professor Stein burst into the open before the steps. "Now where did *that* shot come from?"

The crowds were screaming and running; policemen tried to restore some order, while the plainclothesmen formed a line with their bodies ringing the base of the steps and the top landing where the dignitaries were assembled. While someone was ushering the dignitaries inside to safety, several of the local police converged on the one obvious target charging threateningly for the group at the top.

Three policemen tackled Professor Stein, one giving him a hard rap with his baton on the back of his leg. Claire gasped as she saw him drop. "Ben!" She ran up to the edge of the police line only to be pushed politely back.

Professor Stein struggled, screaming, "No, you don't understand. I'm here to *warn* the congressman. Someone's out to get him."

Agent Hessman was struggling with his Japanese opponent when he saw the professor get tackled. "Now what part of *clandestine* does no one understand?" he muttered.

One more muffled cry was lost to the events, but that came from Captain Beck as Dr. Weiss finally cut the bullet out of his shoulder.

25

SNIPER

Agent Harris could see no one in the crowd who might be responsible, other than the obvious targets, all of which were accounted for. Then she remembered the modern weaponry she'd seen in evidence on some of their opponents and cast her gaze upward. Following a quick survey of one rooftop after another, she saw a glint of sunlight reflecting off metal that brought her attention to a long gun barrel poking out from the edge of the rooftop of the building directly across from city hall—the same building, as it turned out, they had originally been hiding beneath while originally surveying the site.

Another muffled shot rang out as Agent Hessman was pulling his opponent to his feet. Before he could get a question out, though, the back of the Japanese man's head exploded, dropping him to the ground. Agent Hessman ran for cover, which turned out to be behind a parked Model T with a couple of policemen standing in front of it.

"Where the *heck* did that shot come from?" one of the policemen was saying as Agent Hessman dove in behind him.

"Does it matter?" Agent Hessman remarked. "There's still a shooter out there."

Agent Harris glanced discreetly around, then when she was sure that no one was looking, particularly her teammates, she pulled something out from beneath her dress, something roughly gun shaped. Not the one she had taken from the Japanese victim back at Steeplechase, but another. Then from her velvet belt she produced a length of barrel, which she quickly screwed onto the end of the normal one on the gun. In seconds she was holding a pistol very much not of the year 1919, one with sleek modern curves and a scope.

She brought the pistol up in both hands, aiming for the top of the roof with the glint of reflected light, and peered through the barrel. Beneath the noise of confusion now about City Hall Square, her shot rang out, flipping the rifle out of the hands of whoever was holding it.

Immediately she ran for the side of the building. "Got to be one around here somewhere," she muttered to herself. "Ah!" Spotting a fire escape, she headed straight for it, leaping up to pull the extension ladder down, and started into a mad dash up the metal stairs. One flight after another, taking some of the steps two at a time, she came out onto the uppermost landing next to a window on the upper floor. She still had a climb to the roof above that, though.

Sheathing her gun into her sash, she wasted no time and grabbed on to some brickwork on the side of the window and started climbing. She grabbed on to a couple of precarious handholds and braced a foot against the inside edge of the window, followed by the other foot against the other side. Inch by inch she scooted herself up, hands reaching for the next available handhold.

Then the window shade snapped up and a curious face glanced out. A woman inside saw the midsection and legs of what appeared to be a young black woman passing up her window. The woman screamed, and Agent Harris immediately grabbed tight on to whatever protrusion was available. "If you don't mind, I'm in a rather delicate situation!"

The woman screamed again, quickly brought down the shutters, and could now be heard babbling to someone else about some "jungle lady climbing the side of the building."

"I hate this century. Well, at least she didn't open the window."

Sue's feet were just reaching the top of the window, one hand barely making it to the edge of the roof overhang. Her other hand flailed out and found purchase, and with a deep intake of breath, she pushed off with both feet as her arms lifted. That's when the shutters snapped up again and the window opened, this time with an angry-looking man emerging to shout at her. "Just what are you doing up there scaring my wife like that, you black demon!"

"Chin-ups," was all she had the breath to reply.

Her feet flailed but found something else to continue pushing against; then by degrees she raised herself above the roof until she was able to bend forward at the waist, then kick a leg up and over. A few seconds later she was on her back, panting for a moment before she heard shoes running along gravel.

She was on her feet in an instant, gun already aimed. The approaching man had short blond hair, was well built, and had a freshly bandaged hand. He bolted across the roof. She pulled off a shot just as he swerved to the side, falling into a tuck and roll, then was up to his feet in a single smooth motion.

"No, can't kill him; Lou will want to question him."

She started running after him, sheathing her gun once again so she could devote both arms to pumping herself into greater speed. Across the roof he ran, not even slowing for the edge he was quickly approaching. From her angle she couldn't see much of his face but could easily tell that he was European, not Japanese.

He hit the edge of the roof and made the long jump across to the roof of the neighboring building, landing in another tuck and roll, then got to his feet once again. In that moment, Agent Harris got a better look at his face. She didn't slow down either, but increased her speed and also leaped, clearing the gap almost as well as the other. She made it back up to her feet just as skillfully, but by that time the man was already nearly across this second roof. She had to think quickly. At this rate, she could pace him but not catch up to him. So, taking out her gun, she leveled it and took aim.

"A wounded foot's as good as an arm, and we can still question him," she muttered as she peered through the scope.

The man leaped again and she fired. His legs snapped wide into a midair split, allowing the bullet to pass cleanly beneath him before he came down to land in a brief handstand and roll on the next roof over. Now with an entire building between them, he was still running.

"Damn! Missed."

She could only watch as he ran out of sight, doing her best to burn what she had seen of his face into her memory. "Definitely one of the Germans. But why was he shooting at his own people?"

After a last look, she sheathed her gun, turned away, and assessed her surroundings.

"Lou's gonna want to hear every detail of this. But first I need to find a way down from here."

26

PROFESSOR PRISONER

Professor Stein struggled as the men dragged him to his feet before one of the plainclothesmen, a man with the look of authority in his eyes.

"Well, what do we have here?"

"Some sort of anarchist, would be my guess," one uniformed officer replied. "He was running up the steps, screaming about the congressman."

"No, you don't understand," the professor replied. "I was trying to save Congressman Lodge from getting shot. There's a shooter out there."

"And an anarchist right here," the plainclothesman said. "Okay, get him over to a holding cell until—"

"Let me pass! Reporter coming through."

A determined-looking woman with long black hair beneath a large floppy white hat came barging through the line of cops, flashing her press pass as only a few women of this era seemed capable of doing.

"Miss, I'm afraid you'll have to—"

"Claire Hill, freelance reporter," she said as she brushed briskly past a pair of policemen. "And I saw the real shooter running off *that* way." She pointed off across the square, then, before anyone could say anything, continued, "I didn't get a good look at him, since I was interviewing this gentleman here at the time."

"The anarchist?" the plainclothesman asked.

"I am *not* an anarchist!"

One of the cops holding him gave Professor Stein a sharp rap on the back to quiet him while the plainclothesman continued talking with Claire.

"I'm afraid he's right," Claire told them. "I'm working on a story covering the history of City Hall and decided to interview one of the bystanders for his perspective on the matter when I saw another man pull a gun."

"So it wasn't the anarchist here?"

"For the last time, I am not—"

To one cop's glare, Professor Stein dropped into silence.

"It was someone else," Claire told them. "Tall, blond hair, I think. Muttered something under his breath that sounded German. Anyway, when the gentleman here saw him pull off his shot, I guess he saw the direction the man was aiming, because he immediately broke away to warn the congressman. That *is* Congressman Lodge up there, correct? Because any details for this story would be great. Well, the shooter looked like he was about to try for another shot, but when he saw this man bravely run out shouting for the congressman to duck, he turned tail and ran. I must say, diving into the way of possible gunfire like that was one of the bravest things I've seen anyone do since the war. Don't you think so, Officer . . . or is it *Agent*, since you seem to be lacking a uniform?"

Her words assaulted him like a torrent. He responded in a confusion of quickly spoken phrases, the flash of a press pass, and energetic mannerisms a dozen police might've been unable to handle. For a moment the man stood there confused, then shook himself back to alertness.

"Miss—"

"Hill. Claire Hill, freelance reporter. And you are . . . ?"

"Agent Becket. So, this anarchist here—"

"He is *not* an anarchist, Agent Becket," she replied in protest, "but rather a true *patriot*. He was willing to throw himself in front of

Congressman Lodge without thought for his own safety. That in itself is a story I think worthy of all the major papers. Though I wonder what sort of reaction a headline might get if it read, 'Hero Falsely Jailed as Anarchist.' Now that was Becket with *one t*? Because when this story hits, I just want to make sure that I get the details right."

The man sighed and waved the officers holding the professor away. "Let the man go."

"Thank you, Agent Becket," Professor Stein managed to say.

"Miss Hill," Agent Becket continued, "Which way did you say the shooter went?"

"That way," she said, making sure to point in the same direction as before.

"Get four men and see what you can find in that direction," Agent Becket told one of the policemen. "Then get some more up with—"

Another shot rang out, but this from no building. From somewhere in the crowd, someone else was trying to shoot at the dignitaries on the landing. Another person responded by firing in the general direction of the first shooter.

"Everyone down!" Agent Becket yelled.

"Sir," one of the officers called back as he pulled his gun, "I recognize some of those guys out there. Gang calling themselves the Fifth Street Brawlers."

"Is *that* who's behind this?" Agent Becket clarified. "Round them all up!"

As Professor Stein was limping away from the circle of cops, he glanced out to see snippets of what was going on. The bulk of the passersby had cleared away, leaving just the combatants and a mix of policemen and plainclothes officers. One gang member was making a run at one of the Japanese team members, who replied with a karate kick to his gut, while another pair was trying to get past some of the cops. Meanwhile, Agent Hessman found himself back to back with a local policeman behind the car they were both hiding behind, trying to duck the shots of a Japanese man from one direction and a German shooter from the other. Captain Beck and Dr. Weiss were simultaneously trying to find cover on the far side of the square, while another Japanese man found himself in a pitched battle against a pair of gang members on one side and a pair of cops on the other.

Claire grabbed hold of the professor's hand and used the confusion to lead him away to the side before breaking away from her reporter's face to one of far more concern. "Ben, are you all right? I saw them beat you."

"Only a couple of times. It's not like they did a Rodney King on me."

"A what?"

"Oh," he said, realizing his slip, "uh, I'm fine. Hurts a little but fine otherwise. Thanks for helping me out there."

"Well, I had to after you were crazy enough to go diving through a line of cops like you had a bomb or something. What did you think you were going to do, shield him with your body or something?"

"If I had to," he said after a moment's thought, "yes."

The response caught Claire short. She looked at him in surprise for a moment, then shook her head. "You keep surprising me, Ben. You've never been in a war, yet you would do something like that."

"It's . . . very important," he replied.

"Well, did it ever occur to you that there are fifty cops between the shooter and everyone at the top of the steps, every one of whom would have dived in front of that bullet? You could have gotten killed."

"It wouldn't have mattered," he replied. "I've got no one to miss me."

"You're wrong on *that* one, my friend," she half muttered.

"Though I do see your point," he continued. "Next time I'll just shout."

"You do that. Now let's find a place out of the way. It's a war zone out here."

"I wouldn't know," he shrugged. "Never been in one—as has been pointed out to me at least once before."

"That doesn't make you any less of a man. I can see that now."

She caught his eye with a direct gaze and a warm smile, then pulled him away from the steps and off to some safer cover.

27

THREE-WAY

A group of three Germans held position at the corner of the building opposite city hall; a couple of the bowler-wearing gang members waited at the other side of that same building, as well as a team east across the square inside a small deli. Farther up the eastern side, one of the Japanese team had commandeered a taxi to hide within, taking the occasional shot while trying to start the engine.

Agent Hessman was at the western end of the square, and south of him, the German was shooting with a not-quite-period pistol, while another Japanese man hid behind a corner of the city hall building. He was alternating shots with Hessman and the German behind him, then in another direction as some cops tried running across from the steps to get to him.

The police had formed a nearly solid line around the steps, with a ring of plainclothesmen on the top landing before the dignitaries, who seemed to be having some trouble getting inside the safety of the building. Agent Hessman could hear shots ringing out within the building behind them, leaving the dignitaries pinned.

Looks like that gang got inside city hall in advance, he realized.

The dignitaries had spread themselves across the landing to avoid being a single easy target. Toward the left-hand side was the first dignitary they had seen exit from the line of cars, with the Japanese contingent roughly center, and Congressman Lodge along with a few other men and his own private security off to the far right. Everyone with a gun was taking a shot at someone, while the dignitaries crouched low to keep out of harm's way.

From what Agent Hessman could see, the Japanese team was alternating shooting at both the Germans and the Japanese delegation, while the Germans seemed to be concentrating on Congressman Lodge, as well as the Japanese team. He could see Captain Beck and Dr. Weiss behind their cover, and saw Claire and Professor Stein heading for cover behind a large marble pillar behind the base of the steps.

"What about that derringer of yours?" Dr. Weiss asked the captain.

"Out of ammo," the captain replied. "When I stuck it into that guy's back, I was bluffing. Not to mention I dropped it somewhere. Besides, it doesn't have the range for this sort of gunfight. Strictly a holdout weapon. That's why I only brought two shots with me. What about yourself?"

"We weren't supposed to bring any weapons with us. This was supposed to be a covert mission so we don't muck up the timeline."

"Well," the captain began, "as long as no one from the past gets killed, we're still okay."

At the next gunshot, one of the policemen in the front ring fell dead. Dr. Weiss shot the captain a hard glare.

"It looked like he was shot by one of the gang members, so that should still be okay, right?"

From behind the car, the policeman with Agent Hessman was leveling his pistol at the Japanese man against the city hall wall.

"Just one good shot," the officer said as he took aim. "That's all I—"

A shot splintered the air, but it did not come from the officer in question. It came instead from the German behind them, and the officer now dropped dead. With shooters on either side of the car now, Agent Hessman was left with few choices.

"Bonsai!" The cry was accompanied by the roar of a car engine as the taxi came charging across the square directly for the steps. A Japanese man drove it with one hand, while with his other he took shots at the Germans and gang members, then at the line of cops between him and his target. His goal was easy enough to determine, as he made a straight line to the Japanese delegation at the center of the landing, where several of his team were shielding General Tojo with their bodies.

Professor Stein saw the car coming and realized their opportunity. Grabbing Claire's hand, he pulled her into a run along the western length of the building, just in time to hear a storm of gunfire erupting behind him. Twenty police and a dozen plainclothesmen opened fire on the taxi and its driver as he was drawing a bead with his own gun on Tojo. The car was riddled with nearly as many holes as the man within it was, and the vehicle spun off and crashed to the side of the steps.

"That was insane," Claire remarked as they scurried away.

"He probably vastly underestimated how much armor your average car can provide—currently."

He glanced back to see the limp, dying form of the taxi's driver weakly reaching into his shirt to activate something and begin his process of imploding into a point of light before his last breath. That glance, though, nearly cost him dearly.

Before Claire's warning cry came, Professor Stein bumped into the Japanese man who had been hiding behind the front wall. For a moment they stood facing one another before the Japanese man remembered to bring up his gun threateningly in their direction. Professor Stein threw his hands in the air as Claire connected a foot to the man's shin.

The Japanese man cried out, his finger reflexively pulling the trigger. Much to Ben's shocked surprise, however, nothing fired off.

Out of ammo! Ben realized, and he voiced his thought aloud with a grin, "You're out of ammo."

The other cursed in Japanese, turned, and ran off in the other direction. This left Professor Stein free to assess his surroundings.

"There." Claire pointed. "Behind that car. It's Lou."

"But it looks like he's got someone else pinning him," Professor Stein noted. "One of the Germans, I think."

"Not to mention the firefight in the middle of the square itself," she pointed out.

"Germans look to hold the east and south ends," he summed up.

"Where's Sue? She should be able to mop up half of them all by herself."

"No idea and no time to wonder. Come on, we'll make a run for Lou."

With the taxi now overturned and burning off to one side, a small group of cops ran toward the fallen vehicle to use it as a shelter while they attacked some of the people shooting at them. Because the Japanese man had left his post, Agent Hessman was able to scurry over to that side of the car and gain some protection from the German still firing at him as well as from the general fight that had broken out across the square. He now had a better vantage point to observe what else was going on.

He could see Ben and Claire, and now Robert and Sam as well. The latter remained in the deli across the street to stay clear of the shootout. Captain Beck was just poking his head out from behind a wall when a bullet shattered the glass window in the deli front. One of the gang members tumbled out of the doorway facedown onto the concrete. Captain Beck motioned to Dr. Weiss to take a circuitous route around the square.

Ben and Claire dashed over to join Agent Hessman when the German behind him sent another bullet whizzing by his ear. But Lou noticed that the bullet chipped a section of wall behind where the delegation on the left-hand side of the landing was taking cover. Curious as to the different teams' motives, Agent Hessman ducked low and waited for the next shot to come.

He was not disappointed. This time a shot cleared his head but drew an even closer bead on that first delegate. *He's not shooting at me*, Agent Hessman realized. He took a fresh analysis of the dynamics of the shootout. The ones hiding behind the corner of the building across from city hall seemed to mostly be aiming their shots for Congressman Lodge and the Japanese, while the remaining Japanese seemed intent on getting to Tojo and the Germans. A few of the Germans' shots, however, were also landing close enough to that first delegate to be less than mere chance.

They're after that first delegate and *Congressman Lodge*, he realized. *But then, who is he?*

The police opened up a solid mass of gunfire against the gang members hiding behind the building across the square, dropping half of them on the spot, as well as one of the Germans. The remaining gang members responded with a few shots of their own as they shouted their retreat, while the ones remaining in the deli had apparently found the back door. Some fighting still took place in the corridors of city hall, but that, too, was starting to turn in the direction of the defenders.

"Okay," Professor Stein said to Claire, "no better opportunity. *Now!*"

They made a mad dash over to Agent Hessman's position, while at the other side of the square, Captain Beck and Dr. Weiss saw the gang retreating and realized their own opportunity for escape.

"Lou," the professor said once they had joined him, "what's our situation?"

"Changing by the minute," came the reply. "That delegate on the left side: Can you identify him? The Germans seem as interested in him as they are in the congressman."

"Didn't see his face before," Professor Stein replied.

"The markings on his bodyguards' uniforms look German," Claire said. "But I wouldn't think any German delegates would be over here after the war."

Gunshots still rang out, but the captain and Dr. Weiss made their way across the square, pausing when the army of police made a final charge for the remaining gunmen. Within city hall itself, the fighting was nearly finished, and the delegates were ready to withdraw. There was little time left for subtleties.

Professor Stein took out his pocket computer, aimed it in the direction of the one in question, zoomed in for a good image, and snapped a picture.

"Running a search now," he said as he tapped the virtual keys.

When Claire glanced back at him, her eyes went wide at what she saw Ben holding, and wider still as the pictures flashed across the small window on the device. She was speechless until a cough finally escaped her throat. The device settled upon a name and accompanying dossier.

"Gustav Noske," Professor Stein reported. "Founder of the German—holy cow, I think we hit the jackpot with this guy. This is the guy responsible for the rise of Adolf Hitler himself! Lou, take a look at this."

He leaned in closer to show Agent Hessman what he'd found, the revelation immediately catching the latter's attention. But beyond that information, the device they'd used to retrieve it held Claire's bug-eyed attention. She remained speechless in her incomprehension.

28

ANOTHER PIECE OF
THE PUZZLE

Gustav Noske," Professor Stein explained. "Founder of the German Freikorps and the guy who led them in a series of bloody attacks against Communist uprisings after the First World War. Lou, the Freikorps is the precursor to the Nazi movement, and Noske here is the one who paved the way for Hitler's rise later on. This one man is probably the single biggest living turning point anywhere at this point in history."

The gunfire from behind them ceased, while across the square the police rounded up all other attackers. The inner corridors of city hall had apparently been cleared because the dignitaries on the steps were being hustled inside. This pair's attention, however, was fixed on the little screen between them.

"Hitler becomes his protégé," Professor Stein continued, "and the nationalistic Freikorps get a broken nation primed to accept the Nazi viewpoint as a viable way out of the economic ruin their country was left in. As far as the Germans would be concerned, this guy is their TDE."

"Which changes the entire purpose of what their meeting is about as well as the goal of the German team," Agent Hessman said. "He wouldn't be attending a meeting to hear Wilson speaking in support of the League of Nations."

"With Congressman Lodge out there, he'd more likely be here in a secret meeting of *opponents* of the league," Professor Stein said in agreement.

"So then, why would the German team be shooting at *this* guy? Lodge *and* Noske?"

At the sound of a throat clearing behind them, they turned to face a man looming over them. The German who had been keeping Agent Hessman pinned down was not looking too happy.

The throat clearing, however, had not come from the German but rather from the one standing behind him: a young black woman who had lost the large hat covering her short-cropped hair. She had a pistol to the man's back, the one with the scope that she had used before. Claire caught sight of the weapon and her eyes widened in wonder.

"What the heck happened here? I thought this thing was supposed to be covert," said Agent Harris.

Professor Stein saw the type of gun she was now holding against the man's back—a different model than either the Germans or Japanese had used—and shook his head. "Does *anyone* pay attention to mission rules? We were absolutely *not* supposed to bring any modern weapons with us."

"And if I hadn't," she countered, "you guys would all be dead and this mission over with."

"Okay, save the chastising for later," Agent Hessman told them. "Sue, what'd you find?"

At that moment, Captain Beck and Dr. Weiss arrived from the south edge of the square, unseen under cover of nightfall and the chaos of cops chasing down gunmen. Dr. Weiss carried a body while Captain Beck's good arm dragged another along the ground, his remaining arm in a quick and dirty sling made from the ends of his own coat. They deposited the bodies to the ground behind the car with evident relief.

"Had to take the long way around," Captain Beck said as he caught his breath. "Particularly with one wing in a sling."

Dr. Weiss appeared ready to say something but was so out of breath that he simply waved his hand vaguely.

"He means these guys are heavy and that he's out of shape," the captain translated. "I almost had to drag both of them myself with my one good arm. You academics need to exercise more. Anyway, this is the pair that first bought the farm when things exploded. I think the other teams already spirited away their own dead from the fight."

"About that," Agent Harris reported. "A sniper was shooting at both the Japanese *and* the German teams, including these guys we have lying at our feet. I wasn't able to catch him, but I did get a good look at him."

"Describe him." Now Agent Hessman pulled out his own miracle device, punching in the information as Agent Harris dictated it.

"Short blond hair, well built, obviously athletic. About forty-five would be my guess, but in really good shape for that age."

A couple more taps on his screen and Agent Hessman turned the display in her direction.

"Was it this guy?"

"Definitely," she said after a glance.

He took back the device and read off the basic information. "Major Günter Gabriel Greber, career German military."

"And armed with a very modern sniper rifle," Agent Harris added. "Way beyond what the locals currently have."

"You hear that, Fritz?" Agent Hessman stood up as he addressed the German, meeting his gaze eye to eye. "One of your own people was taking potshots at the Japanese as well as your own team. So, what's it going to be?"

For a moment the German looked with disbelief at the image still displayed on Agent Hessman's small screen, then the body of his dead comrade on the ground behind the Japanese man, and decided to talk.

"My name is Ernst Fischer, combat specialist. Major Greber is our military rep. I have no idea why he would be shooting at his own team, but . . . I will cooperate and answer anything you want to ask."

"Good, because I have a lot of questions," Agent Hessman began.

"Not as many as *I* do."

Claire had finally found her voice, and on hearing it everyone froze, reacting much like the kid caught with his hand in the cookie jar. Professor Stein had his pocket computer in hand, Agent Hessman his own similar device, and Agent Harris a pistol that could not be mistaken for anything other than out of this world by the standards of the year 1919. She glared at them all, stepping past Professor Stein and gesturing to both Ben's device and the weapon in Agent Harris's hand.

"You guys are *way* beyond feds, so what in all creation is going on here?"

The team exchanged looks but were silent for a long moment.

29

THE GERMAN'S STORY

A gent Hessman broke the uncomfortable moment with a more practical observation. "Not out here. Sue, secure the hardware; Ben, put the device away. We owe Claire an explanation, but right here and now is not the time nor place." He pocketed his own device while the other two did the same with the computer and gun.

"Exactly what kind of device *is* that?" Claire asked Professor Stein. "And, Sue, I've *never* seen a gun like that."

Then she noticed something about the German. "You . . . you're not on their team, and yet you aren't any more shocked by these devices than they are. You're enemies and yet both in on the same conspiracy."

"No," Ernst said, "not enemies. That is not the intent at all, I assure you."

"Someplace less out in the open first," Agent Hessman repeated. "Ernst, you can carry your teammate there; Sam, the Japanese guy."

A look of momentary horror crossed the sweaty physicist's face, an objection forming then quickly dismissed as Agent Hessman continued. "The dignitaries are all securely inside city hall so no one's getting to them for a while. Night's coming soon, so first good alley we can find.

Until then, no one says a word—no matter how much Miss Hill screams. And, Sue, make sure she doesn't go running off."

"Are you kidding?" Claire said. "I'm staying around for every last detail of *this* story."

In silence they made their way away from City Hall Square with the two bodies before the chaos of the search for more shooters might die down enough for someone to notice them. They navigated down a darkening street and thence into an even darker alley, until a nod from Agent Harris confirmed their location was about as good as they were going to get. They carefully lowered the bodies to the ground while Agent Hessman made some quick introductions.

"I'm Lou, team leader. That's Ben, Sam, Robert, and Sue. And that's Claire Hill, local reporter."

Ernst responded with a brief nod, then faced Agent Harris. "Are you sure that was Major Greber you saw shooting at *both* teams?" he asked.

"Absolutely," she replied. "Your man went rogue. So what's going on?"

"We came back here because of a TDW we picked up," Agent Hessman explained, "and best we can make out, that's part of the reason why the Japanese came back as well—to stop you guys from whatever you're up to. That means that *you* people are the original cause of the TDW, and the rest of us are along for the ride. So, what's the story?"

For a moment Ernst said nothing, just looked at his dead companion with a sigh as he organized his thoughts. Claire, though, was very attentive. She wasn't sure what she would hear, but she was not about to miss a single word.

"Yes," he began in his accented English, "our mission is to kill Congressman Henry Cabot Lodge and Gustav Noske. It is for everyone's good, however. We hope with these deaths to stop the Second World War and the Holocaust."

"Wait," Claire interjected, "what's this about a *second World War*?"

"Claire," Ben whispered into her ear, "not now. I'll explain later."

"Then you better get Jules Verne to help you guys out, because this is sounding more and more like something he'd dream up."

Ben laid a hand to her shoulder to lightly restrain her, then nodded to the German to continue.

"When our machine came through final testing, we saw this as an opportunity, a way to avoid the coming horrors as well as to put Germany in a more favorable position without harm to anyone else. Think of it: no Second World War, no Holocaust. All that gets avoided."

"And all it cost were the lives of a couple of scientists at the symposium," Agent Hessman ventured to say. "Or am I wrong in that assumption?"

Ernst nodded. "Yes," he continued, "it was a German who killed the two scientists at the symposium, but that was to protect the mission, to silence the discovery of how to more accurately trace our efforts back in time. At least until the mission was completed and the new, better world had settled in. Two lives for the lives of six *million* lost in the Holocaust, not to mention their lost potential descendants."

"Wait, six million people?" Claire interjected. "What kind of—"

"Claire," Ben began.

"Claire," Agent Harris said, her tone and look far more direct, "if you aren't quiet, I'll drop you and you'll *never* know what's going on."

The reporter shut up with nary a sound more, just a brief glance to Ben for support and a cough.

"Anyway, that is the basis of our mission," Ernst finished. "Two targets in the hope of saving millions. Six million from the Holocaust and some eighty million from the war itself."

Hearing those numbers, Claire's eyes bugged out, but a look from Agent Harris kept her silent.

"Major Greber is a member of our team, yes, but he has the same orders as the rest of us. I can't understand why he would want this mission to fail, if that's what's going on. As I said, this is for the good of the world."

"Is it?"

This time it was Dr. Weiss who spoke up. Agent Hessman gave him his attention.

"You got something, Sam? Sam here is our physicist," he explained briefly to the German.

"Simply that time may be self-correcting. If not Hitler, then who else in his place?"

"He's right," Professor Stein agreed. "Even setting aside the ones that I know of who might be in a position to take Hitler's place, there may be others lost to the eye of history who would have been in the right position if not for Hitler. We might avoid the Holocaust as we know it but end up with something far worse than the thousand-year Reich."

"Or we could avoid all that and end up with a world in peace at last," Ernst countered.

"So many questions," Claire said to herself.

Agent Hessman put up a hand for quiet and paced slowly with lips pursed. Four paces out then four back, he then paused to eye the two bodies before speaking again. "Both very good points, and before I continue on this mission, I want to know *exactly* what I'm getting into."

"Lou," Captain Beck began, "the mission is to—"

"See what's going on, then by my best judgment take action," Agent Hessman finished for him. "I cannot make my best judgment if I do not know all the facts. So, as long as we have a nice comfortable alley here and some time to burn before we need to take action against any possible targets again, I want to hear all of it. Both sides, pro and con. Ben, why don't you lead off the discussion, and don't hold back on account of Miss Hill's presence anymore. I need this *thoroughly* hashed out before we take any more action."

The look on Claire's face brightened as she silently mouthed the words "At last."

Agent Hessman gave her a direct look. "Miss Hill, you may want to pay close attention. I've a hunch I may want to hear your input as well."

And so the discussion began, with Professor Stein speaking first and Claire paying particular attention to what she suspected the future of her world might depend upon.

30

DISCUSSION

A gent Hessman walked a few yards farther into the alley, then leaned his back against a wall, one foot braced against it.

"In the old movies I suppose this is where I'd light up a cigarette while some woman tries to convince me she's innocent," he remarked. "Well, I don't smoke, but now's the time to convince me one way or the other. Question: Is what the Germans or Japanese are trying to do back here really for the good of the world? Miss Hill, you're in a unique position to play jury here. Just put aside all the unbelievable things you're about to hear and give an honest appraisal of the facts."

"I . . . I'll try," she promised.

She wasn't sure why, but for perhaps the first time in her life she felt nervous and uncertain. Instinctively she reached out for the nearest hand to hold on to for support as she focused keenly on what was about to transpire. The hand happened to belong to Professor Stein.

Outside the alley, daytime crowds were beginning to transition to the evening crowd, and streetlights flickered on. Police whistles sounded in the distance as the officers rounded up the last of the street gang that had tried to attack city hall. The group in the nondescript alley in New York, however, was oblivious to all except the important discussion about to take place. Agent Harris pulled the two bodies deeper into the alley, laying them side by side for potential examination, then positioned herself in the shadows of the mouth of the alley, while the others formed a loose semicircle around Agent Hessman as the debate began.

"Begin by listing off what we know," Agent Hessman said. "Both the Germans and the Japanese have told us that what they're doing is for the good of the world."

"And it is," Ernst stated. "At least for our part; I don't know about the Japanese plans."

"They plan on killing off Tojo, while you guys are aiming for Congressman Lodge and old Gustav," Agent Hessman summarized tersely. "Ben, what might happen if a team is allowed to follow up on either of these events?"

The professor pursed his lips and paced as he thought; he got only a step, however, before he realized that he was towing Claire along beside him. Gently working his hand loose with a brief smile for the reporter, he tried again, leaving in his wake a *very* attentive reporter as he thought out loud.

"Congressman Lodge led the opposition against the League of Nations. The absence of US involvement in the league is the reason why it was too weak to stand and fell apart by World War II. It is possible, of course, if the US *had* entered the league, then it could have been strong enough to prevent the Second World War, the Holocaust, Hitler's Nazi Germany, and so forth. Without Congressman Lodge's voice leading the opposition, that is exactly what might have happened."

"Which is why we were trying to kill him," Ernst remarked. "Without Henry Cabot Lodge to protest, the United States might have joined the League of Nations and thus prevented what is to come."

Now Dr. Weiss joined in the discussion. "Or his assassination might have sparked conspiracy theories and further protests in his name, leading to the withdrawal of the US from the league *anyway*. As I have said before, history may be self-correcting, at least to a degree."

"Which is why we had our backup plan," Ernst continued. "Gustav Noske led the Freikorps and was the first stepping-stone to help Adolph

Hitler achieve power. Remove that stepping-stone, and Hitler fails to rise to power. No one will mourn Noske or protest in his honor if he is killed. Even without a strong league, his death is our insurance against the coming war."

Agent Hessman said nothing but simply observed. Professor Stein paced again as he ran the argument through his mind. That, and he also had an eye on Claire. As overwhelmed as she obviously was by the nature of what she was hearing, he could tell that her keen reporter's mind was still absorbing and processing every word.

"The war would still happen," Professor Stein said after a moment's thought. "The economy of Germany was in shatters; it was just a matter of time before someone would have realized that war was the only way out. Yes, if someone else besides Hitler were to come to power to lead that war, someone without his hatred of the Jewish people, then the Holocaust probably wouldn't have happened."

"A significant gain even with the war," Ernst suggested hopefully.

"But do you want to know *why* Germany lost the Second World War?" the professor continued. "It was in part because of Hitler's ego. Toward the end he listened less to his generals and more to his personal fortune tellers; he put mysticism before tactics. Put someone in his place without those limitations and their alliance with Russia might have held. Or lacking the atrocities and tyrannical rule he visited upon his own people, a more unified front within Germany would have backed their leader. The war could end with England defeated and the US capitulating to a Nazi-Communist world ruling bloc. Considering the atrocities we know from Communist rulership, even when countered by a strong United States, would that be much better than Hitler's Germany?"

He stopped his pacing and faced the others. He could see no sign of a reaction on Agent Hessman's face, just studied attention. He didn't have the nerve to glance over to see how Claire might be reacting.

"At the risk of playing devil's advocate," Captain Beck interjected, "our Japanese prisoner said that they had singled out General Tojo as the focal point of *their* involvement in the Second World War. Without him, Japan doesn't enter the war."

"Or maybe Japan enters," Professor Stein countered, "but minus the atrocities of Tojo. Maybe Japan doesn't attack Pearl Harbor, which keeps the United States out of the war, leaving Japan free to run across the Pacific until it's too late. And I should also add that Pearl Harbor, as terrible as that attack was, forced the US to build a whole new modern fleet to replace the aging one and to do so in record time. Without the Pearl Harbor attack, the United States *couldn't* have stopped Japan. Japan would have their own Pacific Island empire that would include major portions of China."

"And thus prevent a Communist-controlled China?" Captain Beck countered. "How bad would that be in the long run?"

"I dunno," Professor Stein said after a moment's pause. "There are too many variables at this point. But at the risk of giving fair balance to our German friend's point of view, Japan never would have gone to war without Germany as an ally. Eliminate Hitler, and the Axis might never have happened. Or maybe it would have, but it would have been stronger than before."

For a moment no one spoke as everyone struggled to process the multitude of possibilities. But then the reporter in their midst spoke up with an uncharacteristically timid-sounding voice.

"Uh, a question if I may?"

"Anytime, Miss Hill," Agent Hessman replied.

"Well . . ." She coughed once, wet her lips, then continued, "Putting aside for the moment how you guys can talk of some war that hasn't happened like it's already history, but . . . how many people die in this great war of yours? They say that the war we just finished was responsible for some fifteen million or so casualties."

All heads turned now to their history expert for the answer. Professor Stein thought for a moment before replying, but made a point of not looking directly at Claire as he did so.

"Between fifty and eighty million people dead. But, there is also the factor of millions dead between the two wars due to colonialism that caused a multitude of smaller conflicts. A strong League of Nations might have prevented those clashes. A strong league might save many more lives than just the ones lost to the Second World War."

"But would it really?" Dr. Weiss wondered. "We currently have a United Nations with the involvement and backing of the United States, but how many wars has it prevented? How much have special interests twisted the original mission statement? Would the same thing have happened to the League of Nations? And if not initially, then how soon until it would have become just as corrupted? We might only be delaying the war by ten to fifteen years. How will the world *really* change, and is it worth it? Speaking as a physicist, I'm not sure if we can really steer time to a particular result. There might be a certain amount of temporal inertia working against us."

"Or maybe we end up with a League of Nations strong enough to prevent war and able to help Germany back into postwar prosperity," Ernst countered. "Before special interests can get a hold into it."

The group was silent for a moment as they considered each side, and then Claire spoke up once again. "I don't know anything about this other war, but I *do* know that the one we just came out of was horrible beyond belief, and if what these German and Japanese teams are up to can prevent anything more like that, it sounds like they both have the world's interests in mind. As well as their own, of course, but everyone benefits."

"That," Professor Stein countered, "may actually be a more complicated answer than you realize. There is a theory that, even if a person could, you would not be able to change history in such significant ways. If not Hitler, then somebody else. If President Kennedy hadn't been assassinated on that day, then it would have been a different day, a different place. Or there would be unintended consequences. Our world is a mess, but it could get even worse."

He turned now to address Agent Hessman, while Claire resumed her role as observer. "How about this angle: Do you know how many medical advances came about as a result of having to care for wounded men in the field? Penicillin, burn treatments, malaria medicines, and a ton of surgical techniques. Or the advances in aviation? The development of computer technology was spurred along by the need for ever better code-breaking and encryption technology, as well as calculation of missile trajectories. Radar was developed for the war. The atomic bomb was a terrible weapon, but from that we gained nuclear power, and from there the road to the moon and beyond."

Claire was hearing all kinds of ideas that had her spellbound and in shock, but she realized also that she was being permitted to hear this discussion for a reason. So shaking herself out of her stupor, she tried her best to do as Lou had told her and focus on the facts set before her and not the wonders being suggested.

"So suppose we *could* prevent that war," Professor Stein continued. "At what cost would that victory come? We might lose the few good things we gained as a result. Ernst," he said, now addressing the German, "even if your plan succeeds in every way foreseeable, there is absolutely no guarantee that it would not result in something far worse. Give up the Holocaust in exchange for . . . what?"

"Better the devil we know than the one we don't," Captain Beck summed up.

For a long moment no one said a thing. Their silence was punctuated only by the distant intrusion of the passing evening crowd. Claire's world was spinning from all she had heard, enough for the need to brace herself with a hand to the brick wall. Finally the German spoke, his head nodding in supplication. "I am afraid that I must concede the point." He sighed. "We ran numerous computer simulations, but I am afraid that even the best of simulations cannot deal with the unknowable. I . . . will help you to stop the remainder of my team, as well as the rogue Major Greber."

"Lou, it's up to you now," Dr. Weiss added. "I think we're all pretty much agreed, but you're mission leader."

Agent Hessman maintained his stance for a moment or two longer, then stepped away from the wall to pace slowly over to the reporter in their midst. "I would like to first hear from Miss Hill on the matter. Claire, I know you must be overwhelmed by what you've been hearing, but I would value your input."

"Overwhelmed," she said after a moment. "That's a word and a half right now. You speak of things yet to come, of some horror that makes the Great War look like a scouting expedition. I would avoid all of that if I could, but you also speak of such amazing effects that could result from it. Lou mentioned medical advances, and I heard the *moon* is involved. So many incredible things that . . . it is not for me to pass judgment on what may or may not happen."

Lou replied with a nod and backed away to face the others.

"Nor is it for me," he decided. "The only thing we can do, the only thing we *should* do, is to stop the other two teams."

"Agreed," Captain Beck said.

"But something Ben said has me thinking," Agent Hessman said as he knelt down next to the Japanese man's body. "That if the death of a single congressman, or any single person, might not be enough to stop what was to come, then it would have to be a series of escalating events."

Agent Hessman searched the body, while Professor Stein replied in an uncertain tone, "Well, yes, I agree. But to try to change so many events, we would have detected a number of TDWs. What could any single team do back here that would cause such an expansive ripple effect?"

Agent Hessman said nothing but began pulling out small wrapped packages that he found tied around the Japanese man's waist. "Sue," he called out.

She jogged over from her position at the edge of the alley. Agent Hessman handed her the packages. After only a moment's examination, she determined what she was looking at. "Plastique," she stated.

"Well then," he said, "would a *bomb* killing a lot of people be enough to get history to change the way one given group might want?"

Professor Stein thought for only a moment before reluctantly giving his answer. "It might be, if it's the right people. For instance, say, a meeting of other congressional heads or even the death of a certain Japanese general. Maybe another random bomb blamed on communist anarchists or some other group. That would probably give President Wilson enough reason to get the US into the league and from there possibly into a fight against Communist Russia well before World War II and any preparations the Soviets might be able to make. From there I would not dare to make any predictions. The United States would be in the League of Nations, General Tojo would be dead, and Japan would continue with the prosperous democracy they had at the time, but after that . . . Japan could blame the US, get bogged down in a ground war against Russia, or any number of things."

"Lou," Captain Beck stated, "we've got to stop them all—the Germans, the Japanese, all of them—and *immediately*."

Agent Hessman took the bricks of explosives back from Agent Harris and piled them carefully on the chest of the Japanese body. He then started searching the body for something else, while Agent Harris took that as a cue to begin a similar search of the German corpse.

"Ernst," Agent Hessman asked as he bent to his work, "how many originally on your team?"

"Six," came the reply, "including myself and Major Greber."

"This is the second corpse from the German team," Agent Harris said, pulling a large pendant out from the jacket of the German body, "so unless someone was killed in that last firefight that we don't know about, there's you, Greber, and two others left."

Agent Hessman pulled out a pendant from the Japanese body similar to what they'd found once before, and laid it on top of the corpse's chest. Following a nod to Agent Harris, they each activated the respective beacons, then quickly backed away.

"Miss Hill," he advised, "don't blink."

If she had thought any of what she had heard thus far was a fantasy made up to lead her astray, all doubts were removed by what she now saw. Twin cocoons of light enveloped the bodies, while sparks like shooting fireflies swarmed around and through them until only man-shaped, glowing outlines remained. These remnants then pulled back in upon themselves until only the two beacons remained, and a moment later these, too, vanished from sight.

Claire's jaw hung open.

"And on that note," Agent Hessman said, "Sue, show me where on that roof our sniper was positioned. Time to look for more clues."

He led the way out of the alley. Claire couldn't even move without a light prodding from Professor Stein.

31

EXPLANATION

When they returned to the building where Agent Harris had climbed the fire escape, it was full night, and the square had resumed some semblance of normalcy, though still with the increased security. Agent Harris showed her team the fire escape she had taken and was directed to the building lobby by Agent Hessman. "We'll take the regular stairs up to the roof," he told them.

"Do we all have to go?" Dr. Weiss asked. "I'm probably not up to climbing all those stairs, and Robert here has his wounded arm."

"You *really* need to join a gym," the captain remarked.

"Only Sue and I need to go," Agent Hessman replied. "The rest of you—"

"The rest of you," Claire corrected, "are not going anywhere until I get some answers. What is it I just saw, what are those devices you have, and who *are* you people? Really, somehow I don't think—" Her words ended in a short fit of coughing, accompanied by a brief shudder running through her body.

"Claire," Ben asked, "are you okay?"

"I'm fine. Just a little chill. It's evening and I don't have a jacket on. Now, about those answers."

Agent Hessman caught the professor's eye, to which Ben removed his pocket computer and began tapping the controls.

"Like *that* for instance," Claire gestured. "I've never even *heard* of anything like it."

When he found what he was looking for, he sighed and replied to Agent Hessman with a single slow shake of his head. Agent Hessman responded with a tersely worded command before he and Agent Harris turned away. "Explain it to her."

Ben watched as the pair entered the lobby to head for the roof, then turned back to see a determined reporter glaring straight at him. He glanced over to the captain, Dr. Weiss, and the German, who all backed away, leaving him alone with Claire.

"Well?" she asked.

"Claire, what I've told you so far has been the absolute truth . . . just not all of it. Yes, we're federal agents and I am a history consultant . . . but from over a century from now. My specialty is the history of the early twentieth century, what you call the Great War and the decades thereafter. These devices you've seen, Sue's futuristic handgun, all of them are from the future. I was never in the war because my *grandmother* hasn't even been born yet."

She found herself once again speechless, though more for being unsure which of many questions to ask. "Why? How? I mean, I guess I believe you. I *have* to after seeing those bodies disappear like that. Is that how you got rid of the others? Just disintegrated them or something?"

"That's not quite what happened. Sam could give you a better explanation, but basically the time machine we use does not project back our actual bodies but rather duplicates of them, maintained by a sort of energy conduit back through the portal to our own time. A traveler's consciousness then hitches a ride back into such a projected body. Those devices we activated were their beacons that maintain the connection through the energy conduit. Shut them off and the connection terminates, dissolving the projection and drawing the consciousness back into the traveler's original body in the time machine chamber."

"But, does that mean they might still be alive?"

"We're not quite sure on that matter," he admitted. "This is our first trip back in time; their consciousnesses may have snapped back to their original bodies, or they may have gone to wherever they would go upon a normal death. We won't know until we return ourselves."

"Astounding! Then this important mission of yours—"

"We detected a TDW; that's a temporal displacement wave. It means that someone else traveled back in time and caused a major disruption to what we know of as history. In this case, it was the Germans followed by the Japanese. We didn't know the nature or extent of this disruption, just that it happened."

"So that's why you had to come back here," she said, "to find out what happened, then prevent it from happening. You said that you didn't know who had done what. This is why. Then this device in your hand—"

"A pocket computer. You have basic computing devices in this time. Well, this is something like that, only many orders of magnitude more advanced. This simple little device contains all we have on record of this time period. I use it to supplement my own knowledge of this time period. I could fit the contents of the Library of Congress in what you see me holding in my hand."

The word *dumbfounded* would fail to adequately describe Claire's expression, with her mouth moving but little coming out. He showed her the device and passed a finger across it to show her screens of information passing by before her. Miniature pictures of old newspaper articles, images from the World War I battlefield, photographs of New York City at the turn of the century. When he took it back to press another icon in private, she could only gasp and sputter for a second or two.

"Again, astounding. I don't know what else to say. But aren't you afraid I might tell someone? I'm a reporter, after all, and this is the biggest story that—well, *anyone* has ever come across."

"Even if someone were to believe you—which you'll have to admit is a far-fetched chance in itself—there is this."

He turned the device back around for her to see what was now displayed. It was an obituary with her picture on it . . . and a date not all that far in the future. For a moment she could only gape while he continued.

"That cough of yours, and now the chill. It doesn't look bad right now, but . . . Claire, like your hero Nellie Bly, you will die of pneumonia. Two full years before she does."

"Pneumonia," she gasped. "But it's just a cough. The chill night air."

"And the influenza outbreak of this period. Here in 1919, it's fatal."

"And . . . in your century?"

She looked up at him with pleading eyes, her whole demeanor thunderstruck. He felt for her, he really did, but he knew before he'd left for this mission that everyone back in this time period had already died.

"Curable if treated in time," he answered.

He shut off his pocket computer and put it away, not sure what else he could say. He wanted to comfort her, to offer some gleam of hope, but what? Before he could say a word, however, she reached her arms around him and buried her face in his shoulder.

32

THE NEXT STEP

Agents Harris and Hessman made it to the roof by way of more traditional methods than a fire escape climb and a jump from an adjoining building. Agent Harris showed Agent Hessman where she had seen the sniper, and Hessman bent down to examine the area. He found bullet casings, strips of cloth, and some blood splatter. "Powder burns along the wall and on the cloth, and the blood splatter . . . It looks like you got him, all right. By the time you made it up here, he was able to give himself some quick first aid before escaping."

"I could tell he was wounded," she admitted, "but that didn't stop him from running. I know my shot flipped the rifle out of his hands, but that's it."

"From the only angle you would have had from the ground, you could have gotten him in the hand or arm. Alternatively, you hit the gun itself and the impact caused the damage, which means that he could also have a sprained wrist." He pocketed the cloth and fingered the shell casings. "In this primitive age," he continued, "there's nothing to easily trace where others like these might be."

"Not to mention that was a modern sniper rifle he used," she pointed out. "We know exactly where it came from and that no one else in this period possesses one, but that doesn't do a thing to help us."

"Agreed." He passed the shell casings to Agent Harris, who pocketed them. He shook his head. "Besides, it's a bomb we need to trace now. Or at least the people holding it. Any ideas?"

"I'm just the muscle," she replied. "You'll want to bring this up to the rest of the team. I can tell you that if it's plastique, and assuming that one body wasn't the only guy with a sample of the stuff, then it's on their persons right now. If this was back in our time, we could break out a bomb sniffer to try to trace its location, but even that would be highly problematic in a city of millions."

"Agreed. Let's get back down."

After the long walk down the stairwell, as they rejoined Dr. Weiss and Captain Beck outside the building's lobby, they caught sight of Claire pulling away from Professor Stein to wander off in the general direction of city hall.

"He told her everything," the captain said to the other two. "Including that she's only got a few months to live."

Agent Hessman sighed. "It had to be done," he said. "But on the matter of more practical considerations, Sam, do you think that—"

"Should be no disruptions to our timeline," Dr. Weiss replied. "No one will believe such a fantastic story, and she'll be dead soon anyway. It sounds harsh, but . . ."

"I know," Agent Hessman said, "but all these people we've encountered are dead already, from our point of view."

Ben rejoined them, nodding to Agent Hessman as he neared. "Find anything?"

"Nothing useful," Agent Hessman replied. "How's your girlfriend?"

"Feeling a little lost," Ben said. "She says she just needs some time to take it all. And she's not my girlfriend."

"Are you sure *she* knows that?" Dr. Weiss asked with a grin.

"It doesn't matter anyway," Ben replied. "Mission aside, I'll have to leave her behind anyway. I'm not going to do anything that might interfere with history, even if it means—I mean, there's nothing between us."

"Uh-huh," Agent Hessman said evenly. "Ben, I'm the detective, remember? Sam?"

"She's had the hots for him since Steeplechase," Dr. Weiss replied.

"Earlier than that, I'd think," Captain Beck added.

"The BRT ride," Agent Harris stated. "She switched seats to be next to you."

"She was simply," Ben began, "expressing a reporter's normal curiosity about—"

"Interested," Agent Harris stated flatly.

"Now cut that out, all of you," Ben protested.

"Okay, enough of that," Agent Hessman told them. "Back to business. Our problem is to trace where the Japanese team may be placing a bomb. City hall is out; after the ruckus, local security will be all over that place. Even a team from the future wouldn't be able to get in."

"That doesn't mean that either team is going to stop, though," Captain Beck said.

"Agreed," Agent Hessman stated. "So where does that leave us? Where else might they try to plant a bomb?"

"Maybe we don't have to find where the other teams took off to," Ernst now suggested. "We know that Major Greber's own personal mission is to stop both my team and the Japanese team. Find him, and we find the others."

"An excellent suggestion, Ernst," Agent Hessman agreed. "So where would our rogue friend go hunting?"

They discussed the matter for several minutes, each person floating an idea about where the teams might be, or at least where Major Greber might be looking for them. The problem was that the city of New York, even in 1919, presented too many possibilities. They were still deep in discussion when a far more spritely Claire Hill came walking confidently back to join them.

"Well, come on," she cut in. "We've got a bombing to stop."

"Miss Hill?" Agent Hessman wasn't sure whether to question her statement or her abrupt change in attitude first. "I'm afraid that we—"

"A good reporter uses whatever is at her disposal to get her story," she quoted. "A *woman* reporter particularly so."

"Claire," Ben began, "I'm not sure that I—"

She grinned. "And if that includes using the fact that you're dying of pneumonia as a sob story to get a line on the best story of the century, then so be it."

"Miss Hill," Agent Hessman said with rapidly growing interest, "I've the strangest feeling that I'm going to want to hug you. What'd you find out?"

"Oh, not much," she said, shrugging. "Just that city hall isn't where the actual meeting is supposed to take place, just where the dignitaries are assembling before moving off to the *real* location. They'll be traveling by convoy—police, military vehicles, the works—to where President Wilson is going to speak with them."

"And where would *that* be?" Captain Beck asked.

"That part's super secret," she replied. "I couldn't get it, but I *can* tell you that the route crosses the Brooklyn Bridge."

She finished with a victorious smirk, to which Agent Hessman replied, with an agreeing nod, "Which would be a perfect place for a bomb. The site of such a high-level meeting would have far too much security for any sort of covert team to get through, but planting something beneath a bridge along the way would be the perfect solution."

"It appears," Ernst interjected with a grin, "that your recruitment of the local talent worked out a lot better than it did for my team and the street gang."

"A modern-day bomb is not something anyone from this era will be able to see or detect," Agent Harris added. "Speaking as an expert, they could mold that plastique to look like part of the girders or something. Nothing about it would stand out like a few sticks of dynamite would. They'll drive right over."

"Then no more bridge, no more dignitaries, no more world as we know it," Professor Stein said. "It would be catastrophic."

"Then we need to get there *now*," Agent Hessman stated. "Miss Hill, what is the fastest way there?"

"Really?" she said, her head slightly tilted. "Have any of you people been to New York in *any* time period? The pedestrian walkway's literally around the corner and down the block. If we jog real fast, we might be able to get there in a few minutes."

"Then lead the way," Agent Hessman told her. "Sue, stay extra alert."

Claire took a step back, then came back to grab hold of Ben's hand to pull him along with her as she led the way quickly down the street.

Dr. Weiss couldn't help but smirk at Ben's expense.

33

MAD DASH

m I ugly?" Claire asked Ben as she pulled him along ahead of the others, Agent Harris a step behind them keeping an eagle eye on their surrounds with the others in turn behind him. They managed a swift walk without running, since that might arouse the suspicions of an already-alert local police force.

"What? Claire, I'm not sure I get what—"

"Because I've been sending signals since that first train ride. Or don't you people from the future know how to read people anymore? No, it's gotta be the fact that you're an academic; no other explanation. Emotionally blind, the lot of them."

"Claire, are you s-saying that—"

"It's like you purposefully hold back from being more affectionate. Is that because of the importance of this mission of yours, or because you know you're just going to have to leave me behind? Of course, now that we both know I'm dying, that should change something. Does it change anything, Ben? At the least it means I'm running out of time."

"C-Claire, I'm not sure what to say."

"It's not what you're supposed to *say*," she replied.

They briskly rounded a corner, nearly bumping into a tipsy man coming out of a local bar as Ben stammered. The tipsy man took one look at the two of them and grinned. "Kiss her, you fool." The man then staggered away, leaving Ben for a moment confused before Claire once again pulled him along.

"I'm a reporter, and that means I have some skills at reading people. You've had more than a passing interest in me, but I couldn't understand why you wouldn't say anything. I assumed it was because you were trying to keep your mind on this important mission of yours, and that afterward I might have a chance to get to know you a lot better. But then I find out *when* you're really from, and that puts a new angle to the situation. You didn't want to get involved with someone who was a part of history. I get that; didn't want to mess up the timeline. But now we know that I'm not about to *be* a part of history because I have no future. So where's that put us now?"

They stopped for a moment, somewhere far behind them a huffing Dr. Weiss struggling to catch up. As Claire had led the one-sided discussion, the pace of not only her words but also her footsteps had increased until her walk had bordered on a fast jog. Agent Harris had managed to keep up with them, Ernst not too far behind her, but Captain Beck was helping along a fatigued Dr. Weiss with his one good arm, while Agent Hessman found himself uncomfortably alone midway between the two extremes. Now Professor Stein found himself on a street corner with Claire glaring at him.

What he wasn't sure of, and what made him most uncomfortable, was whether the person looking at him was the determined reporter or the pretty young woman. "Claire," he began, "you are . . . even for my century, you are a rare woman. A very outspoken and determined woman, particularly for—how old are you again?"

"Twenty-four."

"Only twenty-four?" He gasped. "And you're already—I think the standards of my century have definitely slipped a little."

For that he earned a brief smirk, Claire was back to her same determined mask.

"I'm not sure what to say."

"Not used to forward women in your century? I admit it's rare and considered unseemly in *this* century."

"No, it's not that. It's just that . . . I don't know."

For a moment they simply stared at one another. He saw the fire in her eyes, the passion waiting to boil. She saw the longing in his, held in check by restraint, duty, and uncertainty. She saw his intelligence, his pleasant features and good physical shape, but something else as well. "Oh my God," she said quietly. "You're a virgin."

Ben could do little more than stutter in reply. Then the moment was interrupted by the intrusion of another, several others in fact. Agent Hessman came up, leading the captain and Dr. Weiss, while Agent Harris and Ernst held the middle ground until the gap between them closed.

"I definitely wasn't expecting this much running for this mission," Dr. Weiss remarked as he joined the rest.

"Sue," Agent Hessman asked, "where are we?"

"Bridge and waterfront straight ahead," she replied. "We just have to get across the street."

They stood at a corner, ahead of them a wide stretch of pavement crossed by Model Ts and similar old-styled cars, the occasional horse-drawn taxi, a scattering of pedestrians going on about their evening's enjoyment, and a skyline that was already sporting the rise of several taller buildings. Beyond the highway, though, was a park, and beyond the park a stretch of water that ran almost as far across as it seemed to go from side to side. What loomed before them, however, held their interest.

The Brooklyn Bridge was fully lit up, its tall towers stabbing like Roman candles high into the sky, cables like gleaming webs for some giant mechanized spider. A bridge to the heavens, it seemed, or perhaps crossing into Asgard itself. Even in this bygone era, the bridge was a wonder to behold; more so when you considered how far advanced more modern construction methods might be than those available when it was built.

"Miss Hill, best way across?"

"Oh, uh, *that* way." She pointed across the highway to a walkway that began at another street corner and led away along the bridge onto a paved length parallel to the main highway crossing. "That's the pedestrian crossing, but the delegates will be in cars, which will mean the main road. Will your explosives be able to take one out from the other?"

"Depends how much they brought with them," Agent Harris answered. "If they go for the area underneath it, they'd just have to rig it for as far out as it would take for the whole caravan to be on the bridge. Say, about a hundred feet out over the water."

"We aim for that then," Agent Hessman decided. "I doubt if their entire team would be any more equipped for long-distance climbing than we are. But they have the jump on us and may have already started. Sue, take lead."

Agent Harris took a cautious look around before she led the way across the busy intersection using a designated crosswalk. Cars paused to let them pass, then rushed past before the pedestrians had barely moved on. A cacophony of honking horns, choking car fumes, and the occasional cussing voice woke up the night. They were midway across when a taxi leaped out from the line of pausing cars and stopped directly in front of them, straddling the crosswalk completely. Agent Harris didn't wait for anything else to happen. "Duck!"

She tackled Professor Stein and Claire to the ground, Agent Hessman slamming into Dr. Weiss on the way down. Ernst quickly flattened himself, while Captain Beck dropped as best as one arm would allow. From the window of the taxi emerged the barrel of a gun, and from it a rapid series of shots barely missed their heads.

Agent Harris rolled from her stomach to her back while whipping out her futuristic pistol. From her back, with arms outstretched past her head, head and neck arched back to see behind her, she pulled off a shot, kept rolling, then pulled off another one while returning to a prone position.

The first shot glanced off the side of the vehicle, while the second crashed through a window, narrowly missing the driver. She caught sight of a figure leaping out the far side of the car, leaving the vehicle parked in the way as an obstacle.

The surrounding crowd erupted in a furor. People screamed, cars rushed to get away, and a horse spooked by the sound of the gunshots bolted into a run, carrying a taxi along behind him. A police whistle was nearly drowned out by the rising ruckus, but that was only the start of it.

Agent Harris darted to the stalled taxi, sticking an arm through the broken window to fire a shot through to the other side. The gunshot shattered the opposing window, and from the resulting cry came evidence of at least a partial hit. That and the brief view of a mop of blond hair before it ducked away into the pedestrian walkway was all she needed to know.

"Germans," she shouted back.

"We're sitting ducks out here," Agent Hessman called out. "Everyone, run for it; Sue in the lead!"

As the others sprang into a crouching run, Agent Harris fired off a couple of shots into the crowd across the street. Her shots appeared random at first, designed to spook the people into fleeing, but when one seemingly random person in the crowd shot back, the crowd turned into an all-out stampede. Then, when two other different sets of guns fired from other unseen directions, the crowd turned into a confused mob. People abandoned their vehicles, trying to gain some element of presumed safety. Others raced their engines to get away, only to end in a pileup farther down the road. Soon the highway was little more than an obstacle course of abandoned cars and spraying bullets.

Agent Harris decided to make use of said obstacle course. She waited until the next gun fired off, then ran out from behind the taxi to another abandoned car away from the intersection to the right, pulling off another shot herself.

"One by the waterfront," she announced in as loud a voice as she could manage. "One on the bridge entry, and it looks like the third just found himself some cover. No sign of their gang-member friends."

Agent Hessman reached the taxi straddling the crosswalk, taking cover behind it while Professor Stein hurried up with Claire. Captain

Beck had found his way over to the side behind another abandoned car a couple of lanes behind where Agent Harris was, while Dr. Weiss dove behind one of the vehicles that had been waiting behind the crosswalk, inside of which a young couple hovered in fearful cover.

"Don't mind me," he apologized to them. "I'm just passing through."

Ernst, the German, snuck his way through the fleeing crowd to another vehicle abandoned in the middle of the intersection, the better from which to get another vantage point.

"They probably thought things were getting too messy for them," the professor remarked.

"It's getting too messy for *us*," Agent Hessman said. "There's no telling who in these crowds may be someone of historical importance. We've got to take the modern teams out fast."

"There may be another way," Professor Stein added. "We now know something that they don't—that their Major Greber's gone rogue. All we have to do is tell them that."

"Ben, the world doesn't work that way. They won't simply—"

"I've got to try," he insisted.

With that, he spied an opening in the dispersing crowd and made a run for it, Claire calling after him, "Ben, *no!*"

He ran as fast as he could, weaving between fleeing men and woman, leaping behind one stopped car then another, narrowly getting hit by a spooked horse and the equally spooked taxi passengers it was dragging along with it, then ending up crouched behind another car nearly at the other side of the street. He waited there until the bulk of the crowd had fled, the mob having become a roadblock for the police trying to get on-site.

With the crowd mostly gone, cowering behind a bridge pylon, or ducking deep into their vehicles, he had a better glimpse of where the opposition was located. He verified what Agent Harris had announced: one on his belly by the waterfront with a sniper's rifle in hand, another taking cover on the entry to the pedestrian bridge crossing, and another behind the wall of the main bridge roadway.

"I can't let this go on," he said to himself. "I just have to make them believe. We know the truth; now they will as well." Steeling himself, he slowly raised both arms high and rose from his crouched position. After taking a deep breath, he carefully slid out from behind the car.

"I just want to talk," he called out. "We found out something that you don't know. Your plan will not come out as you expect. This will not lead to a better world. What's more, your man Major Greber has gone rogue. He's already killed one of your teammates that we can confirm, possibly another who was chasing us earlier. He has plans of his own. Even your man Ernst Fischer knows this. Please, just put down the weapons and let us talk. There is great danger in what you do here."

He took one slow step at a time as he talked, coming farther out into the open, while a streetful of enraptured spectators a block away looked on, holding their breaths. He tried to catch the eye of each of the three German gunmen and saw what he hoped was doubt in two of them, but then he saw the one on his belly by the waterfront with the sniper's rifle. From that one he saw quite the opposite of mercy.

"Stop your man Greber and talk. History is not as easily manipulated as you think. There are too many—"

From the one on his belly came a cry in German; then the other two Germans stepped out just long enough to aim loaded firearms straight at him. By this point Professor Stein was a good twenty feet from any sort of cover. Three assassins pulled their triggers, and one woman's voice cried out, "*Ben!*"

Someone tackled Ben to the ground from behind just as the shots were fired. The bullets from two handguns and one sniper rifle all passed through the space where his head had been a split second earlier. He hit the pavement with one hand to brace him, barely avoiding getting his face scratched up, though the wind was certainly knocked out of him. At the same time, Agent Harris popped up from behind another car, both hands on her pistol from the future as she aimed true. With a single shot, the one by the walkway entry was slammed back against the concrete wall, along with most of his head. Two other shots now fired in her direction, but by that time she had ducked back out of the way.

The shots continued now as the remaining two shooters tried to target the lean black woman with the short hair as she dashed from behind one car to another.

Ben let out a moan and turned carefully onto his back.

"Ben, that has got to be the most insane stunt I have *ever* seen anyone do. Are you *sure* you've never been in a war before?"

Claire was lying on top of him, hugging close to him and the ground, while gunfire passed through the air above them.

"Claire, what? Did you just save my life?"

"Well, *someone* had to. You're cute, you're smart, but also about as naïve as they come."

"Claire, I don't . . . for a woman of this era, shouldn't this be a fairly compromising position?"

"I wasn't born in the right century, just leave it at that. Now, do you want to stay out here waiting for the guy with the weird rifle to hit us, or do you want to start crawling back to safety?"

"I'll take safety. Let's get going."

From her position, Agent Harris saw Claire slip off the professor. Ben rolled onto his stomach, and the two of them crawled their way back across the street. From a little deeper into the intersection but a couple of car lengths behind them, Ernst rolled out from under cover to fire a couple of shots at the one on the grass by the waterfront before rolling back under cover. Alternating with him, Agent Harris let off another shot, ducked as another set of bullets made short work of the front window of the car she hid behind, then dove toward another abandoned vehicle.

Meanwhile, Dr. Weiss had joined Agent Hessman behind another car midway between where the two had been hiding. Captain Beck was slowly making his way through the maze of abandoned and stalled vehicles while the focus remained on Agent Harris and the German Ernst.

"Ben, over here!" Agent Hessman shouted.

He dared not even look up for fear of getting his head blown off, but continued to quickly crawl in the direction from which he'd heard Agent Hessman's voice. Beside him Claire crawled as well, though it was no accident on his part that he found himself between her and possible targeting by enemy fire.

Captain Beck crouched low as he dashed over to the next car, ducking out of sight as another volley of gunfire passed through the air, then made another run. He was now one lane away from Agent Harris and a car length behind her.

"Sue! That gun you got from the Japanese in Steeplechase. Toss it to me."

She glanced back to see Captain Beck motioning to her from behind the other vehicle, so risking another shot to keep the Germans down, she ducked and pulled out the other gun while Ernst kept the other guys pinned. Captain Beck caught the gun she threw at him and resumed the attack-and-duck strategy.

"I'm assuming the guy on the grass with the rifle is Greber," she called back. "If we can outflank him—"

"Then the other guy will surrender," he finished. "Got it."

While Captain Beck scrambled to find a better position, Ben and Claire finally finished crawling their way over toward Agent Hessman's voice and got up into a squat to join him and Dr. Weiss.

"I know, foolish," the professor admitted before any more could be said, "but I had to try."

"Foolish only because we don't have the time to convince them, and Greber's a lost cause," Agent Hessman told him. "Even with Ernst to back us up, we have at most a couple of days to finish the mission, and maybe under an hour before that convoy passes across that bridge. We're out of time for talking."

"I know," Professor Stein said with a sigh, "but I had to try. All things considered, it was worth the risk."

That's when Claire made a realization, and a new look of admiration evolved across her face. "It's not getting killed that you're afraid of but the killing of others."

"A little of both, actually," he admitted. "But death is the one option you can never take back. It's permanent and irrevocable. Right now I have a grandmother who is soon to be born into an unimaginable world of hate and forced to raise herself without a mother because some maniac thought that killing six million Jews was a good solution. It wasn't; death never is."

For a long, pregnant moment she stared at him, and hugged herself close to his side as the shots once again rang out.

Captain Beck checked the chamber of the gun. "Two shots. Have to make them count." Readying himself, he waited until Ernst had shot his load. Then Agent Harris made a running dash across the remainder of the road for a car parked by the edge of the park, aiming the pistol for the guy with the sniper rifle. One shot was a clear miss, tossing up a small mound of grass in front of the man on his belly, but the other shot found its mark.

Unfortunately, the other shot was not Captain Beck's.

The remaining German by the bridge stepped out to pull off a shot directly at the captain, the bullet slamming into him and tossing him to the ground. In that same instant, both Ernst and Agent Harris sprang out and filled the other man's body with bullets. The German fell back onto the street, unmoving, and Ernst ducked back for cover before the sniper could get his next shot off.

"Robert!" Agent Harris dashed out, grabbing on to the captain's shoulder to drag him back under cover. A red stain grew rapidly around his midsection.

"No," he gasped. "The beacon."

"But you need medical attention; you're about to die."

"*This* body's about to die," he reminded her with a feeble grin, "but my original's waiting for me back home. Now activate it while I've time."

With no time to argue, she reached into his jacket and pulled out the round beacon, slapped it on his chest, and pressed the button before diving back for her cover. She watched as the captain dissolved away in a rainbow shower of sparks until nothing was left behind. "Here's hoping that actually works as expected," she said to herself.

Once he was gone, she took a quick survey of her surroundings. Only the man with the sniper rifle remained. He aimed one last shot in Ernst's direction, then ran straight for the underside of the famed bridge, lost to sight. She waited a second more to be sure he was gone and then ran back to where the rest were gathered, soon to be joined by Ernst as well.

"The captain?" Agent Hessman asked.

"I sent him back before he expired," she reported.

"Well, that's something," Agent Hessman remarked.

"I saw the big hole that guy blew in him," Claire objected. "Surely even in *your* time a wound like that is fatal."

"It doesn't matter," Dr. Weiss explained. "While he may have some residual mental trauma from the experience, as long as he was still alive when his recall button was activated, his mental essence should be jerked back into his still-healthy original body back in the temporal chamber. Remember, what you see of us right now is mere projection via a time-space wormhole. He should be okay. Now, if one of us were to die back in this time, then I'm afraid that *would* be a real death."

"Uh . . . yeah," she replied uncertainly. "I'll take your word for it."

"Same as the rest of us." Ben grinned. "Lou, Greber's still on the loose."

"As are the Japanese," he replied. "We have maybe minutes left to get over there and stop everyone before that convoy arrives. Sue, in the lead; Sam, try not to hold us up. Let's *move* it!"

No need or time for cover anymore, Sue led the charge across the open avenue straight for the park and the area beneath the bridge where Major Greber had run. Desperation now fueled them as they tore across the landscape, leaving behind a puzzled populace and some confused police who had finally arrived on the scene.

Claire Hill did not know what further dangers lay ahead of her, but she could not now be away from Ben's side for any reason. "Ben," she asked as she ran, "what's your last name?"

"Stein," he said after a moment's hesitation. "Why?"

"No reason."

She said nothing more as they ran beneath the first girders of the great bridge, but silently she mouthed something to herself: "Stein . . . Claire Stein."

34

BROOKLYN BRIDGE SHOWDOWN

The base of the bridge was a massive brick foundation, with the elevated highway of the bridge projecting out from its top some distance above their heads. The underside was a horizontal latticework of wide metal girders that fed into the brick foundation, stretching some fifty or more feet from where the highway first entered it up to where the span of the bridge left the foundation to reach across the waters. An old fence surrounded the immediate area around the side and back of the foundation, with one gate that still swung from having been roughly opened. Agent Harris led the charge through the gate.

It was full night now, and while the bridge was lit up to display its full glory, that was the *upper* side of the bridge. Underneath it things were blacker than the sky above. The team ran the length of the foundation until they came to where the superstructure reached out to span the river.

Agent Hessman stopped, waiting to see what Agent Harris would do. Her head snapped around as she sniffed the air, eyes alert and one hand gripping her gun tightly.

"Well?" Agent Hessman asked as he came up beside her.

"Too dark to track. He's got to be around here somewhere, but I can't tell where—"

Her sentence was cut off by a gunshot that narrowly missed her feet. Instinctively she raised her hand and pulled off a shot in the general direction of its source, while the rest flattened themselves to the ground.

"That came from above," Agent Hessman called out as he hit the ground.

"Underside of the bridge," Ernst called up.

"But that's fifty feet up!" Professor Stein exclaimed. "How'd anyone get up *there?*"

Agent Harris dropped to one knee, gun held out in both hands while she searched the dark recesses high above. Then a voice with a thick Japanese accent shouted down to them, "Tojo must die, but you don't have to. Let us finish this."

Agent Harris swung her gun in the direction of the voice but held her fire. Too many dark shadows along with the maze of metal made any shot nearly impossible.

"They have the advantage," she said quietly to Agent Hessman. "We've got to get up there."

"Love to know how," Agent Hessman said. "Must be an access door someplace in this thing. Has to be where Greber vanished off to as well."

Dr. Weiss came crawling up next to Professor Stein and Claire, while Ernst crawled up to join the two government agents. "I'd say they have us pinned," he remarked. "But what about Greber? Why didn't they shoot at him as well?"

"Probably didn't see him," Professor Stein replied. "He's one person and we're a whole crowd. And the Japanese team must have still been getting into position."

"How many of them do you figure are left?" Dr. Weiss asked.

"Well, I think that one said they had a team of six, so subtracting the dead bodies we've seen"—Professor Stein did some quick figuring before continuing—"should be just two . . . I think."

"Could just two men carry enough of that explosive to do any damage to the bridge?" Claire asked.

Ben turned to reply, then paused when he saw the look in her eyes. He saw the ever-curious and persistent reporter's face he had come to know in so short a time, but beneath it was something else as well. Her eyes shimmered hesitantly in the evening's light, as if searching for something to grab on to—some*one* to grab on to. While she spoke with the voice of a confident reporter, her eyes spoke of someone looking for a stable vessel in a storm-tossed sea.

Ben reached out a hand to hers and held it tight, his gaze catching her own as he replied, "Not if we get to them in time. We're going to save the bridge and everyone in that motorcade."

She held his eyes for a moment, then replied with a smile—the first real smile he had seen from her since they'd met, and this one directed at him alone.

"We have to find a way up there first," Dr. Weiss said, apparently oblivious to the silent exchange.

Claire drew in closer to Ben, her head sliding over to his shoulder when she suddenly stopped and returned to full alertness. "Access door," she said. "At the base just underneath where the main bridge sticks out from the foundation. I remember from an article I did a few years ago."

"Good girl," Ben replied with a grin.

"But that will put us in direct line of sight to the shooter," Dr. Weiss pointed out.

"We leave that little detail to Sue and Lou," Ben told him. "Come on, start crawling."

While the three crawled up to join the rest, Ernst was in a quick conference with Agent Hessman while Agent Harris continued to scan the girders for signs of movement. "Two men could not carry enough plastic explosives to bring down even a section of bridge," Ernst was saying.

"We killed one at the beginning of this over at the Japanese Society building," Agent Hessman told him. "They could have grabbed some explosive off his body before running."

"In that case, we may have a problem," Ernst admitted.

Agent Harris noticed the flicker of a shadow, like a darkly clothed phantom scurrying through a metal sky. "There." She pointed with her gun. "I think I saw one of them."

"Don't waste your bullets unless you have a firm shot," Agent Hessman told her. "And that's assuming we can't talk some sense into these guys."

"We have little time to complete this mission," Agent Harris told him. "You can try to talk them down, but the second I have a kill shot lined up, that's all the time I'm giving you."

"Good enough," he agreed.

"Lou." Agent Hessman saw Professor Stein crawling up to join them, Claire and Dr. Weiss alongside him. "Claire knows of an access door into that foundation, but it's at the base, directly below the bridge."

"We'll be in full view of the shooter," said Agent Hessman.

"You leave that part to me," Agent Harris told them. "If there's a door there, I'll get you to it. Just get them talking."

Agent Hessman replied with a nod, then rose into a squat, at least until a shot above his head paused his movements.

"We must complete our mission," came the call from above.

Agent Hessman replied as loudly as he could, calling up toward the dark workings of the bridge, "It won't come out as you figure. You can kill them all, but there are still too many unknowns."

While Agent Hessman was dialoguing, Agent Harris made a mad dash for the underside of the bridge, flattening herself against the brick wall once she made it there.

"We have a duty to complete this mission," came the call. "It benefits your people as well."

"This benefits no one," Agent Hessman replied. "Our history expert has confirmed it. At best, you'll just get the world into more of a mess." He received no response at first, so he tried rising up a little higher. Another gunshot woke up the night, but this one sounded no place near Agent Hessman or those with him. "Now where—" he began.

"That sounded like it was up in the bridgeworks," Dr. Weiss remarked.

"Someone else shooting at them?" Professor Stein pondered aloud.

"Greber," Agent Hessman realized. "Come on, we may just have our cover fire."

Without another thought, Agent Hessman bolted, accompanied by Ernst. Ben exchanged a look with Claire, then found himself trailing a pace behind her, while Dr. Weiss brought up the rear.

"I am definitely not," Dr. Weiss wheezed, "an athlete."

Two more shots rang out, each ringing off a thick metal girder somewhere overhead. By the time the last of them had made it to the underside of the bridge, Agent Harris was already edging her way toward a heavy metal door fixed into its base—a door with a lock but no knob to turn. Agent Hessman, meanwhile, used the echo of gunshots overhead to better locate the shooters involved in the hidden fight. Following another shot, his eyes zeroed in on the assailants.

Two men, dressed in dark clothing, clung to the underside girders. One of them stood behind a tall metal strut for cover while aiming his pistol as the other bent over a large rectangular package he was working on.

"I see them," Agent Hessman stated. "About a hundred feet out, up in the middle."

"I see them," Ernst said after a moment. "And that bomb they're working on looks big enough to take out a couple of lanes at least, depending on what else they have in it."

"I'm going to assume they came prepared," Agent Hessman remarked. "Enough to leave a good-sized gap in this bridge, or they wouldn't bother. Now where's Greber?"

Another gunshot rang out, this one coming from somewhere closer overhead and barely missing the Japanese shooter. The bullet deflected off the girder the man hid behind, then ricocheted off two more girders before it was spent. It was enough, however, for Agent Hessman to locate the second shooter.

Greber, fifty feet over their heads and a few yards out, was climbing through the network of metal beams and access walkways. "Stop shooting," Greber called out to the Japanese team. "I want that explosive to go off as much as you do. It's the Americans we need to stop. They don't want to see final peace in the world."

"Don't believe him," Agent Hessman called out. "There's more to it that—"

Another bullet ricocheted off the bricks above their heads, and everyone flattened against the wall.

"We're sitting ducks out here," Agent Hessman said. "Sue, about that access door?"

The sound of another gunshot came at them, but this one exceedingly close and directly behind them. The access door swung loosely open as Agent Harris stood before it with gun still in hand. "It's open," she announced.

"Quick," Agent Hessman ordered, "everyone in. Sue first; Ernst, guard our rear."

Agent Harris ran inside, followed by Agent Hessman, then Professor Stein urging Claire in ahead of him, while Ernst had his own gun out, taking aim at anything above them that moved. The Japanese man with the gun was about to level another shot at Major Greber when he saw the activity by the now-open metal door below. He quickly changed targets and pulled off two more shots.

The first one barely missed Professor Stein as he leaped in after Claire, while Ernst ducked just in time to avoid being hit by the second shot. But one team member had not ducked in time.

Dr. Weiss was ahead of the German and making his way through the door behind Professor Stein. When Ernst ducked, the less than athletically inclined Dr. Weiss caught the shot meant for the German. He fell facedown to the ground behind Professor Stein, a large hole in the back of his head.

"Sam!" Ben cried out.

"No," Claire gasped.

Ernst took another shot, aiming straight at the one who had briefly exposed himself from behind his steel cover. His shot winged the man in the shoulder before he ducked through the door himself. Professor Stein, meanwhile, was trying to pull Dr. Weiss fully in through the door before turning him over. The second he did so, Ernst slammed the door against any further gunshots.

Behind the door, a short tunnel ended at a set of metal stairs slanting up to a landing before slanting again in the opposite direction to the next landing, and so on twice more. A string of weak bulbs hung across the ceiling provided lighting after Agent Harris found the switch. She was already at the first landing, aiming her pistol ahead, when Dr. Weiss fell.

"Sam," Professor Stein said again as he shook his teammate. "Sam."

A tender hand lightly touched his shoulder, the breath of a consoling voice in his ear. "He's gone, Ben," said Claire. "But maybe he'll be back in that time chamber of yours."

"I . . . don't know," Ben said with a sad shake of his head. "He's the only one who knew how the physics of that might work out, and even *he* wasn't sure. If he's killed here, then . . . Oh, Sam."

Ben sat for a moment beside the body, a tear forming in one eye, while Claire wrapped her arms around him from behind in her display of support. The others there, however, were of more practical minds.

"Mourn later," Agent Hessman reminded them, "or there'll be a lot more to mourn if we fail here."

"He's right," Ernst agreed. "If you like, I can set his beacon."

"No," Ben said after a moment. "I can do it."

Ben reached into Dr. Weiss's coat and produced the amulet-like beacon, placed it on the body's chest, and hovered his hand over it for a moment. "Here's hoping you wake up back home, my friend."

He slapped a hand down on the beacon, then quickly leaped back with Claire. All watched as the body was surrounded with shooting lights, filling the body until it was an outline close to bursting. As with the other returning bodies, the brilliant shell fell in upon itself, imploding to a single point before it was gone completely.

A single tear left Ben's cheek at the sight, though Claire was still more than a little fascinated by the sight itself.

"That is utterly *amazing*," she remarked, still staring at the spot where the body had vanished.

"It is still a little shocking to us as well," Ernst said with a grin.

Agent Hessman gave him a second more before stepping over to pull the professor away. "If you can't complete the mission, I'll send you back myself right now," he warned.

"No, I'm . . . okay," Ben assured him. "Sam and I had just grown to be close colleagues on this mission."

"Sometimes," Claire interjected, "unusual circumstances can bring two people together who might otherwise have never even met."

Ben nodded in agreement, then turned away to join Agent Hessman and the others before he realized what Claire might have meant. He paused, glancing to Claire, who had not left his side, and offered a questioning look.

She replied with a quick smile and then pushed him on ahead of her. "Come on, you guys have got the future to save."

They ran up the steps, Agent Harris in the lead. She paused at the second landing to scan the shadows above while the rest caught up, then ran up to the next landing and repeated the same procedure. By the time they made it to the very top, Ben's mind was back on the mission.

The top landing came out onto a catwalk that ran parallel to the girders imbedded into the concrete and brick wall behind and above them. A metal walkway ran out into the latticework of steel girders outside and from there was lost to the night. Agent Harris stepped up to the edge to look past the brick floor to the drop beyond. The angle was one that few people ever got to see of the Brooklyn Bridge, though she had no time to enjoy it. "Careful how you move around here," she warned the others. "If you slip and fall, try to hit your recall button on the way down because, no matter how you land, you're not completing this mission."

She scanned the darkness ahead as Ernst and Agent Hessman caught up to her, leaving Ben and Claire alone now to bring up the rear. From where they all stood, they could hear the echoes of the night: distant traffic, a scattering of honking horns, a greeting bellow from a ship passing beneath the great bridge. Cool air massaged her face when she spotted her quarry.

"There," she indicated. "It looks like Greber's joined up with the Japanese."

"He was trying to kill them all off before," Ben remarked. "I don't think that partnership is going to last."

"It'll last long enough," Agent Hessman reminded him. "Now remember to hold on tight."

Agent Harris took a step to test the weight of the catwalk, then nearly sprinted ahead to take cover behind the first available girder. The sound of the catwalk clanging to the beat of boot-shod feet attracted the attention of another gunman, whose shot glanced off the large girder just as she reached it.

"Ernst, you're next," Agent Hessman said. "See if you can get enough separation from Sue to lay down a good crossfire to cover the rest of us."

"Right."

Crouching a little, the German dashed off down the catwalk, pausing when he got to Sue, and climbed over the catwalk onto one of the horizontal beams. From there he took one careful step at a time, both hands steadying himself against whatever other steel beams were within reach as he made his precarious way through the bridge's underworks.

The wounded Japanese man stuck out a gun, but before he could pull off a shot, Agent Harris took aim. Her bullet deflected off the beam directly above the man's head, but was effective in getting him to duck while Ernst finished his crossing. Agent Hessman waited until Ernst had crawled through another twenty feet of latticework before motioning to the professor.

"What am *I* supposed to do out there?" he objected. "Even if I had a gun—"

"We may need your knowledge," Agent Hessman told him, "in which case I want you near at hand. Miss Hill, you don't have to come with us."

"I'm dead already, remember?" she said with a cough.

"In which case, all of us in a line," Agent Hessman decided. "Ben behind me, Miss Hill last. Sue and Ernst will cover us."

"And what are we going to do once we catch up to those guys?" Ben asked.

"I have no idea," Agent Hessman admitted, "but I'll think of something."

As Agent Hessman led the way, Sue and Ernst kept a steady eye out for the opposition. The one Japanese was working on his explosive package while his wounded friend was looking for another opportunity to shoot his pistol. Major Greber, however, had broken out the rifle they had seen him use earlier, one that, despite the darkness, Agent Harris was able to get a better look at.

"He's got a scope on that thing," she called out to the others. "I'm betting a night scope."

"Night scope?" Claire asked from behind Ben.

"It means he can see in the dark with it," Ben replied, "which in turn means we just lost the cover of night."

"Boy, your century is just *full* of surprises."

Agent Harris saw the end of the rifle protruding from behind a distant beam and ducked behind another one. Following her lead, Agent Hessman crouched low, and Ben and Claire got the notice to duck as well. When the shot came, it took a visible chip out of the edge of the girder in front of Agent Harris.

Claire was astounded, and her eyes widened. "What kind of a rifle *is* that thing?"

"Guns aren't my specialty," Ben replied, "but that's not the worst thing from my century. Just what he could bring with him."

"If the Germans would have had a few guns like that," she remarked, "the war would have come out *very* different."

Ernst replied with another shot of his own, but the other side had too much cover. He could, however, see the one working on the explosive package.

"I could hit the explosive," he called back to Agent Hessman, "maybe get the detonation cap and take them all out."

"But if that sets off the plastique, then we do their job for them," Agent Hessman replied.

Everyone ducked in response to the next shot, and Agent Hessman made it the last few feet and swung around behind another girder next to Agent Harris; there he took out a gun of his own. This left Ben and Claire to take up position behind them, with Ben clinging desperately to a vertical girder and Claire clinging mostly to Ben.

"I never thought I was afraid of heights until now," she remarked nervously.

"Don't worry," he said to her. "Heights aren't really a problem."

"They're not? How can you say that? We're fifty feet up, perched on a steel beam with no railings."

"Still not technically a problem. The problem is the *stopping* if we ever fall."

It took Claire a second or two before she stopped her fearful shivering and glared straight at Ben. "Was that actually a *joke*? Up here?"

"I thought it worth a try," he admitted. "Take your mind off things a bit."

Another gunshot echoed off one of the girders—which one they couldn't tell, nor was it that important. The wounded man was shooting, and in that brief instant in which he exposed his location, Sue, Lou, and Ernst all fired their guns at once, hitting him enough so he stumbled even more into the open. Then, as his feet were slipping from their precarious hold on the girder, the next round of shots spilled his jerking body over the edge with a final cry.

Everyone watched as he fell the fifty feet to the ground below, but from the number of holes now in him, he was clearly dead before he hit the ground.

"Give it up," Agent Hessman called out. "We've got three guns to your two."

The gunfire stopped temporarily while the Japanese man and Major Greber discussed something; then the Japanese stepped partially into view. He didn't hold a gun, but something smaller in the palm of his hand, from which a pair of wires led to the explosive package at his feet. "I release this button and the explosive detonates," he announced. "Now go while you can; history is already rewritten for us all. You will see: it will come out far better."

225

From his position, Agent Hessman had a good enough view of the highway leading to the bridge entry behind them to see the flow of traffic. Cars that had paused from their previous firefight were being ushered out of the way by a group of local police riding motorcycles some distance behind them. The line of cars approached from a side street, the first car waving a tiny United States flag from the front hood ornament.

That's the motorcade, Agent Hessman realized. *We're outta time.* "Sue—"

"Working on it now." She was leveling her gun with both hands, taking careful aim as she shut one eye and squinted through the other. "Just keep him talking and out in the open."

Ernst, meanwhile, saw what Agent Harris was doing and lined up a shot of his own, leaving Agent Hessman to call out to the man with the trigger, "Don't do it. History will be worse off, and Major Greber there has other designs of his own. Or did he already tell you that *he* is the one who's been killing both your team members as well as his own?"

"You will say anything to keep me from my mission, but the stain of the past will at last be removed. Once that motorcade crosses over—"

"Got it," Agent Harris said under her breath.

She carefully squeezed the trigger, but she was not aiming at either the Japanese man or Major Greber. The wires leading from the trigger in the Japanese man's hand snapped free, dangling uselessly from his hand, no longer connected to anything vital.

The bomber looked confused for a moment before Ernst pulled off his own shot. He *had* been aiming for the man. The man tumbled to the water far below.

Major Greber did not wait for the other to finish his fall. The second he noticed the wires had been cut, he leaped for the bomb, abandoning his rifle in favor of the explosive package. He deftly rewired the package.

"Give it up, Greber," Agent Hessman now addressed him. "You're outgunned and outmanned."

"Am I?"

He stepped partially into view with a wide grin across his face. Held between his hands was the explosive package, only now with a trigger directly on it. Greber firmly held the button down. Agent Harris slipped back into the shadows, visually surveyed her options, and began climbing up into the higher levels of the latticed superstructure.

"No wires to shoot out," the man called out. "Just my finger on this trigger. A dead-man switch. Kill me and my hand releases, detonating this bomb, and I take you people with me. When the motorcade passes above, I leave behind a large gaping hole in this bridge."

"Günter," Ernst called out to him, "why? We had a mission, but this . . . it won't turn out as we thought. I have consulted with their history expert."

"Won't it?" Major Greber grinned. "Of course, you're assuming that *your* mission was the same as *mine*. Hitler was right. The German people are the chosen race; we *deserve* to be the rulers of the world. The current leadership would see us do it economically, but that is the coward's way out."

"You're a neo-Nazi," Ernst realized.

"I am a loyalist! I want to see Hitler win the coming war, a victory the German people were denied."

As the man talked, Harris crawled furtively through the latticework. Carefully she snaked along one horizontal beam above their heads, one eye on the streets and the motorcade now pulling onto the main highway that would lead to the bridge. There wasn't much time left, but one slip and it was all over for her and the mission.

"The president's motorcade will soon cross this bridge," Major Greber continued. "And when he does, I will complete the mission that *I* started on, even if I have to become a human bomb to do so. President Wilson will be killed and the League of Nations will never form, leaving Germany in a far more favorable position at the start of the Second World War. With my sacrifice I will give my Führer the world!"

He's rogue, Agent Hessman thought, *not state-sponsored. That's what I wanted to find out.*

Major Greber looked ready to launch into what some might term a typical villain's laugh at impending victory, when an unexpected voice called out.

"Uh, excuse me. Claire Hill, reporter, here."

She poked her head out from behind the girder she and Ben were clinging to, timidly holding up a hand for attention.

"What is this? I don't do interviews," Major Greber snapped.

"No, it's just I thought you might want to get the facts straight. I'm not from the future like you people, but I *do* know a few things. Like for instance that President Wilson's convoy will *not* be taking this bridge."

"Huh? What are you talking about?"

Agent Harris was nearly above him in the steel rafters, while the parade of dignitaries' cars was turning onto the ramp leading up to the bridge. She searched for something in particular while the others kept Major Greber distracted. Agent Hessman had one eye on Greber and one on the motorcade as he motioned Claire and Ben out to him. Major Greber no longer had his rifle in hand, so the pair stepped out into the open as the reporter continued to speak.

"It's just that—President Wilson will be taking another route," she explained. "I don't know which one; that's a secret."

"But the motorcade," Major Greber snapped. "I can see it from here!"

"That's the convoy of dignitaries that the president is going to speak to," Claire explained. "*They're* the ones about to cross this bridge on their way to meet with the president."

"Congressman Henry Cabot Lodge," Ben now called out, "leader of the opposition to the league in this country. General Tojo of Japan and chief engineer of Japan's involvement and strategies in the war. And your own Gustav Noske, the man who *made* Hitler. *They're* the ones in that convoy, not Wilson. Kill them and you might actually guarantee the league's formation."

"No," Major Greber said, shaking his head, "you lie!"

"Without the congressman, the US joins the league," Ben iterated. "Without Tojo, Japan never enters the war and Germany is deprived of a key ally. And without Noske, there is no one to mentor Hitler and he never rises to power in the first place. What happens instead, we have no way of knowing, but it won't be the Nazi dream world that you've envisioned."

"No . . . you lie."

"Why do you think the Japanese were trying to blow up the convoy?" Ben asked. "Their mission was to kill Tojo and *stop* the war, the same mission the rest of your team had. They certainly wouldn't be trying to blow up the president!"

For a moment Major Greber stood in confusion, his left hand wrapped around the package with his finger on the button, his right hand moving uncertainly to a bulge in his pocket. Then, in a single swift motion, he reached in with his right hand and pulled out a small handgun. The weapon was not as deadly as his abandoned rifle, but at these ranges, deadly enough. He leveled the revolver in Claire's direction. In that motion his coat opened enough for Agent Harris to spot what she was looking for; now she just needed the opportunity.

"Try to lie to me *now*, you American bitch!"

"No!"

Ben stepped in front of her. Then from another beam came a shout from Ernst: "Günter!"

Major Greber turned to see Ernst boldly presenting himself with his pistol in hand. He fired the shot intended for Claire at Ernst, hitting him full in the chest and knocking him off his girder to fall to his death, while the bullet he'd fired at Major Greber narrowly missed. The major hid again behind a tall girder.

Now the major was directly below where Agent Harris had been waiting. As the motorcade of dignitaries started its escorted journey up the bridge, she leaped down, one hand aiming for his coat as the rest of her body slammed straight into him. With a cry she tackled him straight off his perch, his hand releasing its hold on the dead-man switch precisely as hers found what she'd been looking for: his recall beacon.

They were caught in a midair fall as the explosion began, but in that instant, the familiar appearance of spinning lights surrounded them both as she activated his beacon. Major Greber and Agent Harris both lit up, as did the explosive and the bright flare now loose from the major's grip. Suspended in flight, a small star gave birth to itself in a storm of racing colors before the star collapsed in on itself, gone in a wink.

No explosion, no Major Greber, and no Agent Harris.

"Sue," Ben gasped.

Directly overhead, an important parade of official cars sped by, escorted by a combination of local police and military soldiers. Away to a meeting with history while the three beneath them let out a collective sigh of relief, then bowed their heads out of respect for another lost teammate and friend.

35

CLEANUP

For a moment they watched the lingering afterimage of the ball of light that used to be their friend fade away, while from overhead they could hear the official convoy rumble its way across the Brooklyn Bridge.

Claire was the first to break the silence. "Sue. Did she . . . ?"

"She activated Greber's beacon," Ben quietly replied, "and was taken away with him by the German time machine."

"Then she's back in the future?"

"Along with that explosion," Agent Hessman stated. "It would have detonated right in the middle of the German time chamber. No telling how much damage it did to the facility, but as for the major and Sue . . ."

He let his statement linger, nothing more needing to be said. Claire stared at the empty spot in space that was the last place she had seen Sue, while Ben reached an arm around her to hold her close. After a silent moment to give their respects, Agent Hessman made his way across the girders to where Major Greber had abandoned his rifle. It still lay on the wide beam waiting for him to retrieve it. He rejoined Ben and Claire a couple of minutes later with rifle in hand.

"Come on," he said quietly. "We have some bodies down below to send back. We must not leave behind any sign that we were ever here."

The team walked solemnly back along the catwalk, then down the steps and out into the night to retrieve the fallen. Ernst's body had landed on the other side of the fence enclosing the bridge's foundation, and the two Japanese somewhere over by the riverbank. They left through the open gate and reached the German first.

Ben finally spoke as they neared the body. "We never had a chance to get to know him all that well, but he seemed like a fairly honest and upstanding guy."

"A man of character," Agent Hessman agreed. "That's why he didn't hesitate to draw Greber's fire when a distraction was needed."

The three stood around Ernst's body, heads bowed, for a moment. Then Agent Hessman laid the rifle he had retrieved down the length of Ernst's body, bent down, and proceeded to search him for his beacon.

"When he died, do you think his mind snapped back to his original body, or . . . ?" Ben asked.

"Not for me to say, save for this," Agent Hessman replied. "He would have appeared in the same facility as the explosion that Greber took back with him. Same facility, in a pod right next to his. No matter if his mind made the trip back after this body died, there is no chance that he survived in the end."

Agent Hessman pulled what had been made to look like a large pendant out from the dead man's jacket, laid it on Ernst's chest, pressed the button, and stood back. In silence they watched as the body dissolved in upon itself, until nothing was left but a vague imprint in the dirt where he had landed.

Next they reached the river's bank and the first of the two Japanese bodies. As Agent Hessman bent down to retrieve and activate the first one's beacon, Ben said a few words. "They were trying to save the world from suffering through a very ugly piece of history. I have nothing but respect for the attempt and the courage it took such a man to stand behind his honor to the very end."

Once again they watched in silence as the flare of speeding photons lit up the night, too quickly gone from sight.

"I'm getting kind of worried," Claire remarked once it was done. "I'm starting to get used to seeing that."

Then last they repeated the procedure with the second Japanese body. They located the beacon, lowered their eyes as it was activated, and watched as the body proceeded to sizzle away.

"Do you think they might try this again?" Claire asked as they left the empty riverbank. "I mean, how many time travelers do we have to worry about?"

"I don't think they will," Ben assured her, "at least not back to this same time and place. I am sure that Sam, were he here, would say something about risking too many causation loops or some such. History will go about the way it was meant to go—for good and bad."

They returned to the park and for a moment simply looked out across the river. The Brooklyn Bridge sparkled with light while a smattering of wheeled and foot traffic crossed its length, and beyond that the view of the nascent New York skyline completed the perfect evening. Claire even dared to lean her head against Ben's shoulder, his arm finding its way around her waist.

"Will it still be here in a hundred years?" she finally asked.

"The bridge?" Ben asked.

"All of it. The bridge, the city."

"All of it and far more," Ben assured her with a smile. "It suffers through some losses, but there remains no finer bridge on the entire East Coast."

"Just the East Coast?"

"There's a little something that gets built over in San Francisco a few odd years from now. But let's not worry about that right now. In the years to come, the New York skyline will evolve to something that no other city on this planet can boast of."

"I'm glad . . . It's just a pity I won't be here to see it."

Agent Hessman let them stand together for a few minutes undisturbed while he silently reviewed all the team's movements and anything they might have left behind. He briefly combed the area beneath the bridge for any pistols that had fallen out of the grips of the dead and pocketed what he found. Beyond that, however, he found nothing.

He finally went back over and gently tapped Ben on the shoulder. "It's time to go. Our mission is at an end, and the future awaits us."

"Yeah . . . I know." Ben sighed. "But Lou, there's one little detail that I've been thinking over."

"Something we missed?" Agent Hessman asked. "We've stopped both other teams, and the secret meeting will go off as it once did."

"No, nothing about that, it's just that . . . when Sue activated Greber's beacon, the German time machine looked like it took the both of them away at once."

"Agreed."

"Then . . . once she was back in her proper time, did Sue really end up in the German time machine or back in her body in our own?"

"Hmm . . . well, reasoning logically," Agent Hessman began, "her projection would have appeared in the German facility along with Greber; then, once the bomb destroyed that and her beacon, she would have been snapped back into her original body in *our* facility. But if you're looking for a chance that she might have somehow survived—"

"No, that's not it." Ben remained motionless, his gaze distant as he held on to Claire. "The point is that Greber was able to being someone back with him."

It took Agent Hessman only a moment to realize what the professor was getting to. "Ben, no. We can't alter history in the slightest."

As Ben turned to face Agent Hessman, a puzzled Claire looked at them both briefly, wondering what they were talking about.

"We won't be altering a thing," Ben said. "Claire has all the signs of influenza and will not survive through 1920. I've checked, and there is nothing that a Claire Hill contributes to history."

"Well, I like *that*," Claire pouted. "I know I haven't made it yet. But . . . wait, what?"

"Ben—"

"What she has will kill her in her century, but in *ours* she can be saved. Quite easily, in fact."

"Ben, we don't even know if that would work."

"It did for Sue; we *saw* the two of them whisked away."

"You could end up a pile of tangled limbs bleeding together for all we know."

"It'd be just like anything else on us. The clothes we wear, the tools we have on us. Lou, I could bring Claire back with my beacon; then we get a med team to fix her up. History would not be altered in the least. The machine will dump my consciousness back into my original body and create a projection for Claire from the energy of her body, which will then become her new permanent body once the machine shuts down."

Claire followed about half of that, shook her head, and gave up.

"She'll be out of her time," Agent Hessman countered.

"I already am," Claire snapped, and then more gently to Ben, "You would do this just to save me?"

"It would be a one-way trip," he told her. "We could get you fixed up, but there would be no coming back for you because history—"

"History records me as dead and gone in a year. Yeah, I get that. I get to live, but forever in another time."

"That's about the size of it. That is, if Lou here says it's okay."

"Give me one good reason why I should allow this," Agent Hessman said.

Ben said nothing but reached out his hand for Claire to slip hers into.

"Yeah, it always comes down to that." Agent Hessman sighed. "Very well; I leave it up to Miss Hill."

"Claire," Ben said, "you'll be encountering all sorts of new things and strange sights, but if you're willing, you can join me in my time."

"It sounds a little scary," she said after a moment's pause. "Heck, it sounds a *lot* scary . . . Do they have women reporters in your century?"

"Are you kidding?" Ben grinned. "Your hero Nellie Bly was just the first in a small army of them marching through history."

"And *you're* going to be there?"

"Well, of course. And I'll always . . . that is, I'll . . . be there for you."

She saw the sudden shy look, grinned, and spun around to face Agent Hessman. "Then let's do this."

"Very well, but not here," Agent Hessman said. "Someplace less out in the open. Quickly."

He led them in a swift march back beneath the bridge, where the three of them stood near the shore of the river. First Agent Hessman took out his beacon, then Ben his while Claire clung close to him. They stood for a moment looking out across the water as Claire held close and nuzzled into Ben's shoulder and chest.

"You two first," Agent Hessman told them. "That way I can confirm the disposition of the last of my team."

"Okay then," Ben said. "Hold on tight, Claire."

She wrapped both arms around his waist, her chest pressing up against his and head tilted up to regard him with a look of longing. Ben held up uncertainly, his beacon ready in his left hand while the woman in his arms looked . . . expectant. When he failed to do anything but stammer and look uncertain, Claire rolled her eyes.

"Oh, for the love of God, are *all* men in your century this afraid of kissing a woman?"

Because the year 1919 was during a comparatively conservative time period regarding relationships, Ben was caught by surprise when Claire reached up and planted a kiss right on his lips. His eyes bugged out wide as they held the pose. Then, with lips still locked, Claire reached down and pressed her hand into Ben's, specifically the one holding the beacon.

Lights exploded from within them both, that look of shock frozen on Ben's face as he and Claire melted away into the night. A new star grew beneath the bridge and was gone in a wink.

"Well," said Agent Hessman once they had both fully vanished, "about time one of them did that. I thought they'd *never* kiss."

With that, he pressed the button on his own beacon, and soon he, too, was lost to a flare of twisting lights, no longer to be seen in this place and time.

36

LOVE FINDS A WAY
. . . FINALLY

nbound travelers. Looks like our last two returning."

General Karlson came rushing up to the control booth as the announcement was made. The chamber before him and the team in 2019 had a ceiling resembling a small star, and through its central pupil some returning specks lit up the room, accompanied by a thunderous roar. Already all but two pods had been opened and emptied, and now the technicians were ready to scurry in yet again once the remaining two travelers returned to their bodies. First came a flicker of starlight lashing out from the eye down one of the cables, awakening the status monitor of one of the pods below.

"Special Agent Hessman's vitals coming to life," one technician reported from his monitor to the general. "All signs look alive and well."

"That's a good sign," General Karlson said with a breath of relief. "What about Professor Stein?"

"He's coming in slower than he should, but it looks like . . . Wait a second. We have a mass imbalance."

"A *what?*" the general said. "Explain."

"I can't," the technician replied, frantically working his controls. "We have something else coming through that wormhole. Attention, all techs," his voice rang out through the chamber below. "The instant Professor Stein wakes up, get him out of that pod *immediately*. We have a biomass signature coming through. Repeat: Stein's carrying a passenger, and there's not enough room in that pod for the both of them!"

From the rear of the control booth, General Karlson heard but still shook his head in disbelief. "But how can that be possible? I thought only their consciousnesses were sent back.

"And a new body formed for them at the other end, yes," a second technician quickly explained as he worked his own part of the board. "But it might be possible, if he was holding on to someone at the other end, for the energy umbilical to dissolve that person into an energy stream that he draws back with him the same way he would anything he was holding. If theory holds, a new body forms here around the consciousness of that other person."

"Wait, a *person?*"

"Yes, General; I'm getting a second set of brain waves."

Another spark lit up on its way down to the one remaining pod. A pair of technicians was helping Agent Hessman out of his pod when Professor Stein's pod popped open. No time to let him rouse on his own, the instant the instruments showed brainwave activity, another pair rudely yanked him out and slammed the lid behind him. They were thus barely in time to witness the unexpected.

Directly from the eye of the wormhole itself, a second pulse of energy shot down Professor Stein's cable and passed harmlessly through the pod's lid to meet with the interior workings and fill the pod's interior with a blinding blaze of white light. Professor Stein was barely on his feet as the brightness enveloped the pod, a concerned look crossing his features, while off to the other side Agent Hessman managed a tired grin.

A final flare nearly blinded all within the chamber and then was gone as suddenly as it had come. All was normal save for the reading on a screen in the control booth.

"We have biosigns within Professor Stein's pod. Repeat, we have additional biosigns. Medics and quarantine team to the chamber immediately."

That voice was followed by another bellowing out from the control booth, one that needed little in the way of amplification to be heard.

"This is General Karlson. Shut down the wormhole. Shut it all down. Then someone tell me what the heck is going on out there!"

Ben didn't wait for anyone to help but burst past the techs helping him and sprang open the lid. She lay there, dressed as she had been a moment before, eyes fluttering open to behold Ben standing over her, backlit by the light from the star behind him as the spinning blades gradually slowed.

"Now *that* was a kiss." She smiled. "Not bad for a first effort."

"Claire," Ben said, reaching down a hand, "how do you feel?"

He pulled her up; then one leg at a time she climbed out of the chamber, her eyes never leaving his own.

"Pretty spry for a one-hundred-twenty-four-year-old lady," she quipped.

As her eyes adjusted to the dimming glare of the apparatus overhead, she found herself panning from one miracle to another. She saw wondrous devices she had no names for, as well as materials of a workmanship unknown in her era. She glanced up to see the blades and giant ball they were attached to now coming into focus as they spun ever slower, enough now to see the walls of wire wrapped around the hundred-foot bubble above them. Then she looked over and saw in the control booth the somewhat displeased look of a man with three stars on his shoulders.

"I'll handle the general," Agent Hessman said to the pair, "but first someone get me a computer pad."

One tech rushed out to one of the devices at the far end of the chamber to retrieve the requested item, while General Karlson left the control booth and entered the chamber as another team marked with red crosses on their shoulders came in through the main entrance.

"Over here," Ben signaled to the medics.

Ben led Claire to the center of the elevated circle of pods, Agent Hessman following them, though more to interpose himself between them and General Karlson as the latter came storming over, an obvious question the first thing from his lips.

"Who, in all creation, is *that?*"

"In a minute," Agent Hessman replied, holding up a hand. "First have to check and see what's what. Ben, I'll need to synch with your hand computer as a cross-check."

"Immediately, Lou."

As one tech brought up a computer pad to Agent Hessman, Ben took his portable computer from a pocket and walked over to stand next to him. Seconds later, both devices were synched.

"Doing a quick comparison on history of the period," Ben muttered. "Should have the results in a moment."

Frustrated by the lack of anyone willing to face his wrath, the general turned to Claire, who replied with a bright smile and an offered hand. "Claire Hill, reporter. Late of the year 1919. I think I may have some catching up to do."

"Miss Hill," General Karlson replied, not taking the hand but managing to reign in his anger with a polite smile. "Now, if someone would kindly explain—"

"Results coming in," Agent Hessman suddenly called out.

For a moment all fell into silence. No one spoke, even the general holding his tongue, and the sound of the blades above quickly disappeared completely as they drifted to a stop. The only thing that mattered at this point was if the mission had been a success or not.

"World War II . . . ," Agent Hessman read off, "check. All parameters match up. The Holocaust . . . sadly, that too lines up. From the looks of it . . ."

Agent Hessman spent another moment to confirm, reading through the screen's display comparing the data from the main computer versus what had been stored in Professor Stein's computer upon his departure.

"Everything checks out. General Karlson, we have complete mission success."

A scattered cheer went up from the milling techs, even General Karlson letting out a sigh of relief. A moment later an announcement came from the booth: "Mission confirmed. We are no longer reading a TDW. Repeat: we're clear."

"Good," General Karlson said with a tired nod. "Now, Special Agent, if you would kindly explain a couple of things."

"All will be detailed in the briefing," Agent Hessman replied, "but first Miss Hill here has an old-fashioned case of influenza that needs looking after."

"Medics"—Ben signaled to the ones who were waiting by the sidelines—"the lady here needs some looking after."

Two medics stepped forward, but Claire clung all the closer to Ben as they came.

"It's okay, Claire," he assured her. "They handle this sort of stuff all the time."

"I'm still not leaving your side."

"It's okay," the first medic said with a smile. "We can give you a quick antibiotic, then examine you more thoroughly later."

"An anti-what?"

While the medic was fishing out a pill for Claire to swallow, the general was back to glaring at Agent Hessman.

"First off, what about the others?" Agent Hessman asked.

"Lieutenant Phelps and Dr. Weiss are currently in comas," the general told him. "I don't know what happened out there, but their consciousnesses returned and they haven't woken up."

"And Agent Harris?"

The general hesitated for a moment before replying, "Phelps and Weiss might come out of it, but Agent Harris . . . her readings completely flatlined at one point. We took her out of her pod immediately and have her on life support, but no one knows what to make of it. Now, what happened, and who is this young lady?"

"What about Captain Beck?"

"What about me?"

Agent Hessman spun around to see Captain Beck walking up to the platform with a tired grin on his face. Claire had just finished swallowing a couple of pills and something blue and fluid when she saw him and brightened. "Robert! You're alive!"

She leaped over to greet him with a big hug and a quick kiss on his cheek.

"I awoke in a very much alive and well body, though a bit mentally frazzled," Captain Beck replied. "Still am, actually. Just something about going from near death to perfect health in the blink of an eye that gets a bit confusing. But what about yourself? How is it that you are here?"

"Ben took a chance." She shrugged.

"Then may I be the first to say welcome to our century, Miss Hill."

"You may indeed."

"If that's all finished with," the general interjected, "can we try this once again?"

"General," Ben said, stepping up beside Agent Hessman in support of his friend, "there's a lot we have to tell you in the briefing, but may I now simply say this. At one point we had a discussion on if all our modern benefits are worth what we went through to get them. Of the people on the two different teams we found back there like ourselves, the bulk of them were trying to get a better Present for everyone, but we finally decided that the present we know and have dealt with is better that any unknown alternate possibility. It may in fact be that World War II and the Holocaust were inevitable. That maybe the larger events are beyond anyone's ability to change when it comes to time travel."

"A nice sentiment that I shall include in the report," the general began, "but if I may—"

"But, as I think we have just proven," Ben continued, with a smile to Claire, who slipped over to his side, "there may be times when we can at least change the *little* things."

"I see," General Karlson said, his tone a bit more subdued, "and I might even approve save for one question." He stepped over to look at them both, his gaze settling on Claire as he spoke. "I gather they swept you up from the past."

"Direct from the year 1919," she said with a smile.

"Are you anyone that history will miss? I hate to sound harsh, but before you leave this chamber and see anything else, I must know, or you're going straight back to when you came from."

They held gazes for a moment, and the general soon discovered that Claire was someone who could stand up to his practiced glare. Ben was quick to rise to her support, his arm wrapping itself around her waist.

"From everything that I can tell," he said, "she is no one of any historical consequence . . . except that I think I love her."

"About time you said that out loud," Claire began. "Now do I have to get forward again, or are you going to—"

Ben quieted her with a kiss, one long and deep, for the first time in his life taking the initiative. An act which neither Claire, nor anyone in the chamber grinning at the sight, seemed to mind.

"Good enough for now, I suppose," the general said, turning away.

He was about to question Agent Hessman further on some matters, but the other had stepped away from the techs and soldiers to a relatively quiet spot in the chamber. While the medics came in to escort Claire and Ben away for a more complete examination, General Karlson joined the team leader.

"Lou, you're worried about something, and that worries *me*. What have we missed?"

"About the mission? Nothing," Agent Hessman answered. "But this whole thing just got me to thinking. If one group traveled back to change history—"

"Then someone else might try to do so again?" the general finished for him. "And next time not be as nice."

"Three time machines, three chances at messing up history," Agent Hessman stated. "And that's not even counting the possibility of something like a terrorist group getting control of one for their own purposes."

"An unsettling possibility, I'll admit. What would you recommend?"

For a few moments Agent Hessman paced; then he stopped and looked the general straight in the eye. The answer he gave was one the general expected, indeed had seen coming since before the start of the mission, but now Agent Hessman at last gave voice to it.

"We need to set something up to monitor time travel before history outruns us."

CPSIA information can be obtained
at www.ICGtesting.com
Printed in the USA
FSHW011103300720
72064FS